Off the Grid

John Hunt

Black Rose Writing | Texas

ISBN: 978-1-68433-333-2
PUBLISHED BY BLACK ROSE WRITING
www.blackrosewriting.com

Printed in the United States of America
Suggested Retail Price (SRP) $18.95

Off the Grid is printed in Calluna

PRAISE for author JOHN HUNT

Doll House

"Olivia. She's a brilliant character, broken, but trying to survive on her terms." – *Ginger Nuts of Horror*

"The female lead, Olivia, is a great character. She reminded me of Jamie Lee Curtis." – *Cedar Hollow Horror Reviews*

"It is certainly shocking and gruesome, but John Hunt manages it quite impressively." – *The Novel Pursuit*

"I was engaged from the very first to the very end." – *Strong Book Reviews*

"Doll House is a deeply felt and admirably realized tale of an unending real-life nightmare." – *Mallory Heart Reviews*

"My head is spinning... I was clenching my hands and biting my nails the WHOLE time." – *After the Pages*

"I absolutely loved this book." – *Bolton Library*

"If you want a 'scare your pants off' type horror thriller, then look no further." – *Clues and Reviews*

"Doll House was one heck of a psychological thrill ride!" – *Butterfly's Booknerdia Blog*

"...the author has created a masterpiece thriller." – *Gothic Moms*

"Superb book in a gruesome way." – *Love Books 'n' Family*

"A book of the year!" – *Buried in a Book*

The Tracker

"John Hunt is the author to watch in the horror and suspense genre." – *The Novel Pursuit*

"...another one of John Hunt's amazing terror stories." – *The Savvy Traveller*

"A dark thriller that draws the reader in." – *Morning Bulletin*

"It is pure horror." – *Kat Loves Books Blog*

"I never want to hear mention of bolt-cutters, a live rat and a bucket in the same sentence again. EVER." – *Ginger Nuts of Horror*

"...a fast-paced, gruesome tale." – *Thoughts from Irene*

"Plenty of action and horror." – *Diane Capri Crew*

"A good story that kept me guessing." – *Red Lace Reviews*

This book is dedicated to my wife, Louise.

And a special thanks to my sister, Alana, who spent hours and hours of her free time to read and suggest ways in which to make the book better. And her suggestions almost always make my work better. So, thanks.

And of course, another special thanks to Ethan, the boy, for reading and tweaking my work as well.

In general, thanks to all of my family for their encouragement and support.

Thanks also must be given to my friend, Kyle Grant, a great beta reader, who tells me where I messed up and where to fix it.

Off the Grid

Prologue

Graham, Meghan and Evan walked around an outlet mall, the sun high overhead and warm on their shoulders. They navigated their way around and through other families vying for sidewalk space on the crowded Sunday afternoon. Their boredom drew them to the outlet mall. Evan had been playing the Fortnite video game all morning and got snippy at Meghan when he was told he had been playing enough and maybe, just maybe, he'd benefit from some exposure to the sun and playing with his friends outside. Evan argued he was already playing with his friends. He was playing with them online and on the TV, the sun shone pretty bright and a bonus was that the TV sun didn't cause skin cancer. Is that what she wanted? Evan asked with headphones covering one ear and the glowing controller sweaty in his hands. For him to get skin cancer? Would that make her happy? Meghan walked over to the TV and turned it off. Evan wanted to yell, wanted to scream, but Meghan's face was able to convince the self-preservation part of his brain to keep his mouth shut. He turned off the console. His face was red and his eyes were shiny. They ate lunch together at the kitchen table. Meghan and Graham talked about how to fill the afternoon without video games and when Graham was scraping his plate into the green bin, he saw a flyer lying on top a folded down Corn Pops cereal box in the blue, recycle box. The flyer was a glossy, colour photo of a smiling family standing under the sign for the newest outlet mall. He plucked the flyer out of the bin and opened the folded advertisement. Everything they didn't know they wanted, but needed, was at this outlet mall. Graham noticed the name of running shoe stores which he liked, an H&M store, a Forever 21 store which he knew Meghan liked and yup, a few video game stores which Evan liked. He showed Meghan the flyer and after cleaning up, they loaded into the minivan and drove to the mall.

Eight different running shoe stores later, with all of them promising in giant letters that they had the best sale, the best deal going, or the best prices for all your running needs, he was shoe-stored out. Besides, Graham didn't think the deals were better. He'd seen a better deal at a specialty running store for a pair of Newton runners minutes from their home. The flyers delivered were a way to draw you in, getting you to walk around and going into stores for things you didn't know you wanted until you saw them and buying them for no other reason than that you could. They had been walking to the food court for an afternoon snack. Evan had gotten over what he thought of as an injustice done to him this morning and was actually smiling. Graham could smell the cinnamon buns before he saw the sign for them. Evan wanted a blue slushie. Graham had thought of getting a coffee and a tea biscuit, but that cinnamon bun scent was changing his mind. His mouth fairly salivated at the thought of the sweet icing on the warm bun. Meghan hadn't decided what she wanted but it would probably be something obnoxiously healthy.

Meghan said, "Is there a Booster Juice here? I could really go for that vegetable smoothie. What's it called again? And is it weird that I'm craving one, you think?"

Graham said, "Yes. Yes, it is. The one you like is called Tropi-Kale, I think. It's gross and it has Kale in it."

Graham stepped behind a concrete pillar to let a heavyset man, laden with shopping bags, grunt pass with a sweat dotted forehead. The man nodded at Graham in acknowledgement of the courtesy. Graham returned a corner-of-the-mouth smile and a red hole appeared in the man's head spraying Graham with a dark, red liquid before the man dropped to the ground, spilling a Lego Star Wars set from one of his many bags. Graham flinched and froze. He frowned. A loud bang made him twitch. A piece of the concrete pillar by his head burst. The powder and grit puffed into his eyes. He felt a sharp pain above his right eyebrow. Warm blood leaked down his face. Graham blinked. Tears flooded his eyes, a biological reflex to flush out the concrete grit. He opened his eyes, trying to focus on the scene around him. Mouths of people stretched open, an orchestra of undulating screams pierced his ears. He stood straight while people around him were dropping to the ground either because they had been shot or because they sought cover. Graham didn't know. He didn't know anything except it had been a beautiful day with his family, window shopping for things they didn't need and now what? Gunshots? They were thunderclap loud. Graham had been aware guns were not quiet, because, well everyone was aware of that, but this, he had no idea they could be this loud. Not in the way that experience teaches you.

"Graham! Get down!"

He knew that voice. He spun to see his wife, Meghan, crouched low like everyone else. She was holding Evan in her arms, her long dark hair fanning out over Evan's pinched and shiny face. Evan had the look of a child in some war-torn country, like those terrible pictures Graham had seen on a TIME magazine cover wanting to expose child soldiers in some far off place on the other side of the world. Everything became real then. The blood on his face, the screaming crowd and the dead man at his feet. His body joined the present. Adrenaline palsied his hands. Graham ducked low, putting his body in front of his family, and spotting an open doorway he yelled, "That way! Let's go!"

Screams rent the air. Bullets kicked up bits of sidewalk and whined past like angry wasps. To the left of Graham, a woman's face exploded into a red mist. Warm liquid covered his face and his hands. He tasted her on his tongue.

"Go!"

They got into the doorway and Graham saw brightly packaged candy lining the shelves, a fridge filled with sodas and a slushy machine spinning red, blue and green.

"Behind the counter!"

They crawled behind the counter and crouched beside an elderly man in an apron holding his hands over his ears. His eyes were giant shiny plates behind the lenses of his glasses. The elderly man flinched with every gunshot. The frequency of the shots merged into an endless angry popping. And then the firing stopped. Graham's ears were ringing. Meghan's eyes leaked tears, Evan's hands were clamped firmly to the sides of his head and his eyes were squeezed shut. He reached out to touch Meghan, just to feel her and before his hand touched the T-shirt on her shoulder, he heard something hard, something metallic, hit the ground nearby. The silence after the constant shooting and the metal sound striking the ground made Graham think, *rifle magazine, he had dropped the empty magazine and the man was reloading.* He didn't know if the person shooting was a man except he'd never heard of a woman spree killer. The calm part of his brain wondered if he was being sexist. Faintly, so light he considered he might be imagining it, he thought he heard the sound of sirens approaching. He glanced at Evan. Snot glistened on his upper lip. His body trembled in Meghan's arms. He was quiet. Graham's heart jerked in his chest thinking about how brave Evan and Meghan were. He had frozen. They hadn't. They woke him from his stunned immobility when the insanity started. If

Meghan hadn't yelled, well, he might be dead right now.

Outside he heard a man wailing, "Yusuf! You wake up now! We have to go! You have guitar lessons and we're going to be late!"

A flat, deep voice said, "He's dead." A gunshot made Graham flinch. The same voice said, "And so are you." How close was this man now? He wasn't in the store. Not yet and with luck, he might walk right on by.

Footsteps crunched over broken glass. Other cries and moans and Rick Astley's voice singing, *Never going to give you up, never going to let you down*, playing through the outlet mall outdoor speakers competed with the noise of approaching sirens. More shots followed. More moans and cries were silenced. The heavy footsteps moved closer, sounding as though the man had stopped right outside their hiding spot. Graham glanced at Meghan. Her liquid eyes quivered. A dribble of blood spilled from her lip and Graham knew she had been biting it. She did that when she was stressed but only a little bite, an endearing nibble on the bottom lip. She had never bitten herself to the point of bleeding.

The steps came closer.

Graham waved at Meghan to get behind him. Quiet as could be, she patted Evan's hair down and quietly crawled behind Graham. She hugged Evan to her chest. Footsteps thumped towards them. The old man covered his ears and closed his eyes. He turned his back to them.

Graham saw the top of the man's head first. Wearing what looked like something a tactical officer would wear before going into a house like he'd seen on those stupid reality TV shows. A black shell, like the black carapace of a beetle or large insect and for a second, Graham was convinced that's what he would see, a giant bug with multitudinous eyes studying him. The arrogance of revenge, the narcissism of murder.

Graham shook, his jaw clenching. The helmet came into view above the counter and under the black shell was a man. A regular man. Glasses foggy, jowls heavy with sweat. Someone you'd see in a Staples store wearing a pocket protector and asking you if you needed help setting up your home network. A harmless yet helpful salesman. The comparison was shattered when the barrel of the rifle cleared the counter and Graham found himself staring into the end of it. The indifferent eyes were anything but harmless.

Graham squared up in front of the man hoping to block the man's view of his family behind him. Graham's hands were up and his head was bowed, a posture of submission. He kept his gaze on the man through the hair of his eyebrows. Graham said, "Wait, wait, wait. Whatever you think it is I've done to you, I haven't. None of us, we ha-haven't done a thing to you," Graham said.

The man sighed and said, "I'm tired." Graham heard the sadness in the voice. The man's gaze went above Graham's head while keeping the rifle pointed at Graham. The man blinked a few times and then his body shook as though a sudden chill ran down the back of his neck.

The man said, "None of this is real." The man's face crumpled. He whispered, "What am I doing?"

The man canted his head to the right side until his neck produced a cracking sound. He straightened his head and inhaled a gulp of air. He exhaled it. The man's breath fluttered the hair on Graham's head and Graham caught a scent of coffee. With one hand, the man wiped away the sweat under his glasses. He placed both hands back on the rifle and lifted it so Graham could see the man's one eye staring at him from the back of the rifle sight. The man shot Graham in the face.

PART ONE: WINTER

Nadine worked behind the counter at the Giant Tiger, which in her opinion, was a crustier, smaller version of Wal-Mart. That big store's shadow hadn't made its way to their town yet and she hoped it never would. She did shop at the Wal-Mart in Guelph, about half an hour away, and liked to shop there, sure she did, because there was so much more stuff. Aisles and aisles of stuff. From toys to nail care to tools to car repair to movies to games to phones to, well, everything. Having all that stuff in one place was damn convenient. Even still, Nadine didn't want one in Erin. Wal-Mart was a big store, a chain store. She knew the big stores tended to close down the little ones and she liked the little ones. She enjoyed walking down Erin's main street in the summer with an ice cream cone in her hand, staring in the windows containing handmade furniture or summer dresses designed and stitched by a neighbour. She knew the people in town and they knew her and even though the store paid her barely more than minimum wage, she got benefits and all in all, was treated fairly. It wasn't her dream job but with her education, what else could she hope for? Not much, that's what. She sighed, popped the bubblegum in her mouth and took in the empty store. Not for the first time she wished she had done better in high school. She could be away right now, at university or college, smiling at boys who didn't know a thing about John Deere tractors or argue about whether or not Ford trucks were superior to all others.

Instead, here she was, wasting her time and if she didn't lay off the chips and candy bars, wasting her figure. Her mother told her she would end up following in her footsteps if she didn't take her studies seriously. Like all teenagers, she thought she knew better. Nadine had a home, someone to buy her food and clothes and enough of her own money to buy some weed and booze now and again for an impromptu field party where she'd get a little buzz and let one of the jocks feel her up a little even though, truthfully, she didn't particularly like men. It was just the thing to do in a small town. Nadine liked women because, in general, they had less hair, smelled better and for the most part, didn't give a crap about pick-up trucks.

In high school, she had liked Hannah. A pretty blonde with subtle freckles across her nose and dimples in her cheeks that when she smiled, made Nadine go all tingly. Except Hannah left town a long time ago. She went off to university and never looked back. Nadine had heard Hannah was starting veternarian school. Damn. Hannah was pretty and smart. She snapped the bubblegum again, sighed and thought some girls had all the luck. Nadine worried she'd die in this town with a house full of cats. Nadine never understood why she always pictured cats around her in her solitude. She didn't even like cats and didn't think loneliness would change that. Still, she pictured herself wandering around her little home in a housecoat and slippers with cats meowing at her feet and the heavy scent of dirty kitty litter wrinkling her nose. She woke up at night from the fear of it.

The sound of the sliding doors whooshing open drew her to the present. Cold wind, the kind that bites the skin and freezes nose hairs, traveled up her arms until the doors whooshed closed. She zipped up her sweater and hugged her arms to her body. A man walked in, the hood up on his thick coat and he disappeared down an aisle. Nadine glanced at her watch and frowned. Seven hours to go. Time may fly when you're having fun but at work, it almost seemed to move backward with how slow it progressed. Does something progress if it moves backward? She should have paid more attention in school. Then maybe she'd have an answer for such stupid questions.

The man dropped items in front of her. She flinched. She hadn't heard him approach.

She ran the products across the scanner, beeped, and placed them in a bag. Rope, duct tape, a padlock, and chain. Incongruously, a book of poetry by Emily Dickinson.

"That'll be $24.75, please."

He took money out of his pocket and drew his hood back to count it. A gasp escaped her and her face flushed red. She knew it was rude and her mother, bless her kindness, had taught her better than that but she couldn't help it. The man's face drew the reaction from her. He was a tall man and with his head tilted down she could see the shape of his face. It didn't look right. His bearded jaw bulged on one side and a jagged scar ran across the high part of his face, across his cheeks, over the bridge of his nose. The man seemed not to notice her gasp or if he did, he didn't pay it any attention as his manners were apparently better than Nadine's. Most likely though, he had gotten used to such a reaction.

He handed her the money as he lifted his head to draw the hood up. One eye socket was empty. A sunken lid the only suggestion of what had been there. With the hood up and his face in shadow, Nadine exhaled a breath she hadn't known she'd been holding. Nadine handed the man his change. He left the store without a word.

•   •   •   •   •

The next day on the local news, Nadine learned a little girl had been taken from her bedroom in the middle of the night. A massive search was being conducted and the police were looking for volunteers. Normally, Nadine avoided any volunteer work. Paid work was bad enough in her opinion. Thinking of the little girl taken in the night, she thought maybe she could spare some time if something better didn't come along, that was. Then Nadine remembered the man in the store and more importantly, the strange items he purchased.

-2-

Terry and Bernice tucked Francine into bed at eight in the evening every night. They lived in a three-story home on a cul-de-sac and were considered well-to-do by Terry's mother who couldn't help but comment on the size of their house and ask them why would they need so much room for such a small group? Despite the unsolicited comments and questions, they didn't think they were wealthy. They thought they were doing okay and lucked out when buying their house at the time that they did. Years ago, before kids but knowing they would have them, they bought their home for two hundred thousand, which at the time, caused Terry to wake up in the middle of the night in a panic at least once a month for two years. But, if they sold their house now, judging by what other houses in their area were going for, they could probably net seven hundred thousand. Terry secretly dreamed of selling their home and retiring sooner rather than later. He would love to spend his retirement on golf courses. Canadian ones in the summer and American ones, preferably Arizona, in the winters. It was a dream he didn't think he could realistically pursue anytime soon. Francine was still in elementary school and their oldest kid, Harold, would soon have his hand out for the piles of money it would take to pay for his university. Terry's retirement dream would have to remain a dream a while longer. But that was okay. Terry always knew that family comes first.

On school nights, the goal was to have Francine in bed by eight o'clock. On weekends, she could stay up until nine, sometimes nine-thirty which always amazed Francine when she noticed the numbers on her bedside clock. Nine-thirty seemed so late and mysterious to her, as though all the exciting things happened after nine o'clock. Terry and Bernice rotated reading duties every night.

On the night she was taken, Terry had read her Dr. Seuss' The Fox in Socks, a tongue twister that made Francine laugh every time he read it to her because he struggled with the prose...a lot. Terry would read her the book, talk to her and joke with her while she brushed her teeth and after she climbed into her bed, he would pull her My Little Pony comforter up to her chin. She was six years old and from what Terry could tell, she had a hell of a personality developing inside. She understood his jokes and even rolled her eyes at him at the bad ones. And dad's were notorious for telling bad jokes. At least that was the rumour Terry had heard from his kids and the memes Harold sent him sometimes through text. Terry wondered at what moment did his jokes become bad? As soon as he became a father? Is that something that happened as soon as your child left the womb? Bad-joke-itis? Terry kissed Francine on the head. He turned out the light. The clock read 8:00pm. Terry remembered thinking, *right on time,* and he also remembered congratulating himself on his parenting.

Terry made himself a coffee and Bernice a tea. He joined Bernice on the couch, handing her the tea while she was reading a book. The book had a white, drooping flower on the cover. It looked like a sad book. The kind of book she preferred to read which would more often than not, leave her crying. Terry didn't bother asking what it was about. He clicked on the TV, settled into his chair with a groan, and fell asleep within ten minutes. It was their routine and Terry liked it. There was comfort in routine.

Bernice woke him at nine-thirty and he poured out the remaining contents of his coffee cup into the sink. He placed his and Bernice's cup in the dishwasher and turned it on. He waited until the hum and splash of water started before walking up the stairs. He waited for the sounds of the dishwasher working because sometimes, the stupid machine didn't start and he'd have to hand-wash the dishes like some savage. Maybe savage was too harsh, but he definitely hated hand washing dishes while the dishwasher sat there doing nothing. Halfway up the stairs behind his wife he stopped. Terry sighed and walked back down the stairs. He locked the front door and then the back door. Even though they lived in a small town he always locked the doors. He watched the news after all. Not only was it his habit to always lock the doors, Terry specifically remembered locking the doors that night. He mostly remembered being annoyed at having to walk back down the stairs to do it.

When their son Harold, returned home from work at ten-thirty, he unlocked the door with his key. Harold couldn't remember if he locked it again after getting inside. He was in high school and after being in school all day and then hustling his ass to work at the Tim Horton's, he was tired and didn't think much of anything except for getting into bed to sleep so he could wake up and do the same crap all over again the next day. Harold hadn't locked the front door and a part of him knew that he hadn't. He didn't want to think it was his fault his little sister had been snatched from her bed and so he said he couldn't remember. After examining the doors and windows, the police came to the conclusion that Harold hadn't locked the front door when he returned home from work.

In the morning, Terry awoke at five, had a shower, drank a coffee and ran out the door with his lunch bag in his hand. He had an hour commute to work every day and for some reason, every morning he felt rushed even though he always made it to work on time. No, he hadn't checked on Francine and no, he didn't remember if the door had been unlocked when he hurried out. Terry did know he had locked the front before hopping into his car. He always did that. Because he watched the news. From the timeline provided by the terrified family, the police believed that sometime between ten-thirty at night and five in the morning, a man walked into their home, took Francine from her bed and left without waking anyone else in the house.

Most mornings, Bernice would wake up, have a shower and with a towel wrapped around her head and one around her torso, she would wake Francine and Harold before blow drying her hair and getting dressed. And that is what she did that morning. She came out of the bathroom trailing steam with a towel wrapped tightly around her and walked straight to Francine's room. The cold air drew bumps on her skin and she was thinking about getting back to the bathroom and the warmth therein when she opened the door to Francine's room. The police asked her if she had been sure she opened the door or could it have been already opened? Bernice shook her head, saying no, the door had been closed. It was always closed. She would have noticed right away if it was standing open. What did grab her attention was the empty bed. Odd, but not crazy odd. Francine had left the bed before and had been found eating cereal or watching Netflix on the family iPad oblivious to the world beyond the flickering images before her eyes.

Bernice stood at the top of the stairs and yelled in the way only mother's can, "Francine? If you're down there can you wake Harold?"

No answer. Once again, odd, but Bernice wasn't thinking someone had taken her child in the middle of the night. She thought maybe Francine had headphones on her ears while watching Netflix or for some reason, decided to use the washroom in the basement outside Harold's room and couldn't hear Bernice calling to her. The idea that Francine had been kidnapped didn't occur to her.

Annoyed and cold, Bernice fast-walked all through the house, her bare feet soft on the carpeted stairs until they slapped against the cold, tiled floor of the kitchen. Francine wasn't at the table. And she wasn't in the living room. Although she couldn't think of a reason why Francine would be in Harold's room, she opened the door to check and nope, not there. She closed the door and with her thumb and forefinger pulling at her bottom lip, she considered. Was Francine in her bed? No. Was Francine watching Netflix somewhere? No. Was Francine in Harold's room? No. Conclusion? Francine wasn't in the house. She blinked and shook her head. Before panic could crouch on her heart, she called Terry. Bernice was hoping Francine went to work with him, and maybe there was a take-your-kid-to-work day she hadn't seen on the calendar and had forgotten. Talking to Terry though, she learned Terry hadn't taken her to work. Back in Francine's room, the phone crushed against her ear as Terry was asking her questions she didn't hear and couldn't answer, she saw that the comforter, the thick My Little Pony comforter Francine loved, was gone. Why hadn't she seen that before? Icicles of fear branched out along her veins. She hung up on Terry and with shaking hands, struggled to dial 911. The dispatcher answered, saying, "Police, Fire, Ambulance. What is your emergency."

Bernice screamed.

Jodie Reyes slapped the alarm clock, wanting it to shut up and when it didn't, she opened an eye and considered beating the damn thing with a hammer. Her phone was vibrating on the bedside table and she understood why assaulting her alarm clock had not stopped the racket. She answered her phone and twenty minutes later with her hair still wet from the shower, got into her car and sped for the home of the missing child.

She arrived in forty-seven minutes and not the hour her boss thought it would take her to drive there. Jodie had a heavy foot and applied it when it mattered. In abducted children investigations, a speedy response always mattered. All the major case police courses she passed and conferences she participated in taught her the bleak statistical fact that eighty-eight percent of abducted children were killed within the first twenty-four hours. Knowing that, she knew she didn't have a lot of time. She stepped out of her car, patted the gun on her hip and picked up her backpack with her notebook, cell phone and all other investigative essentials inside from the seat beside her. She slammed the car door and walked to a big RV parked outside of the missing child's home with Ontario Provincial Police Command Vehicle printed on the side. Antenna's, like metallic fingers, pointed at the sky from the roof.

Officers in uniform stood outside the RV arranging people into search parties. TV vans with talking heads standing in front of cameras spoke into microphones while gesturing towards the house behind them. Jodie didn't mind the media. They could be self-serving, insensitive, egotistical jerks, but she used them as much they used her. And she would use them today.

She stepped up to the trailer, reaching for the handle when from behind her she heard, "Hey! What do you think you're doing?"

She turned to see a young officer, swimming in his uniform, jutting his chin out and stepping towards her with his hand out to grab her. The type of officer who lacked the confidence to be polite. The kind who preferred to bark fearing if they didn't, they wouldn't get the respect they craved. Jodie disliked him immediately. Before he could touch her, she said, "You touch me and you'll be directing traffic in the smallest town in this province."

He pulled his hand back as though he'd dunked it in hot water and Jodie thought she might have been too harsh. Softening her tone, she said, "I'm Detective Reyes. I was called to come here. Who's the supervisor on scene?"

He sniffed, scowled and said, "You the detective, huh? Took you long enough to get here."

She wasn't sure if the guy had a problem with her being a woman a higher rank than him or being a black woman in a higher rank than him. Maybe she hadn't been too harsh. Seems like her initial instinct about his level of jerk-ness was accurate. She ignored his statement. She learned long ago to respond rudely usually tended to reinforce a biased person's view. She heard it described as confirmation bias. Besides, being polite always seemed to piss them off. She shouldn't take pleasure in that, but she did. Jodie asked again, "Who is the supervisor?"

"Staff Sergeant Marks."

Turning her back on him, she said, "Thank you."

She opened the door and stepped into the RV. Staff Sergeant Marks, Reggie to his friends, smiled when Jodie stepped up and said, "Am I glad to see you."

"I bet you are, Staff. How are things? How's Brenda and the three brats?"

Reggie was the proud, but tired, father of triplet daughters. He and Brenda went the in-vitro fertilization route after years of natural attempts at conception resulted in years of disappointment. They ended up with three kids. All at once. Reggie complained about them, but anyone listening to him talk understood he adored them.

"Staff huh? C'mon now, Jodie. To you, I'm Reggie. The kids? Brats are right. Coming to work gave me a break from their constant crying, but after this I think I'd rather be at home with them."

"That bad?"

"Yeah. Yeah, it seems to be looking like it might be."

•   •   •

Police attended for missing children reports routinely. Almost all of the time, the child would be found somewhere close to home. They'd be at a friend's house or the park and like just about anybody, young or old, the time would get away from them. Sometimes the missing child never even left the house. They'd fall asleep in the closet or under the bed, for reasons only a kid would know. Because of that, the first thing any officer did when they went to a missing child call was to thoroughly check the house. If the child wasn't in the home, that's when they would reach out to friends and visit local parks or places the kid would be known to visit.

In this case, the house had been checked and the friends had been called. Every available officer in a patrol car drove down the streets near Francine's home and cruised past all the parks even though no one expected to find her in a park playing. For one reason, it was winter and it was cold. The second reason, the more concerning one, was that all of her winter clothing was hanging in the front closet and Francine's boots were still on the mat by the front door. The whole situation had an ominous feel to it and it was reflected in the serious countenances of all the officers searching. Still, the police followed the established routine and Staff Marks, directing it all, made the call to bring in Detective Reyes sooner rather than later because of the ominous feel. This didn't seem like a runaway or a misplaced child. This felt more and more like an abduction. He got the media involved early too for the same reason. Staff Marks explained to Jodie all that had been done so far and nodding, she said, "Good call on the media. If this is an abduction, and I'm operating as though it is, we gotta keep pressure on this guy."

"How do you know it wasn't a woman?"

Raising her eyebrows, she said, "It's always a guy. Well, almost always. Anyway, you have a media officer handy? I'd like them to hold an impromptu press conference. I want to get video of all the volunteers working to show that the whole community is out looking for Francine. Hopefully, that will make the bad guy keep his head down and thinking about how worse all of this could be if he kills her. Like going to jail for life kind of worse."

"Yeah, I have already called in our media guy. She can deal with the vultures circling out there."

"Who is that officer out there? Skinny guy? Always hitching up his gun belt?"

"Paul? What about him?"

"He's going to be a problem."

"Yeah? How so?"

"He likes the authority. He's either going to hurt someone who doesn't listen to him or get hurt by someone who doesn't care he's in a uniform. And I think he has some prejudices he's not hiding too well."

Reggie had known Jodie for a long time. He knew her to be a smart cop with good instincts. When she said he was going to have a problem with an officer, he believed her.

"I'll keep an eye on him."

"Good. Now, where is the swamp water you're trying to pass off as coffee around here?"

• • • •

Jodie listened to the chatter on the radio while studying a map of the town using Google Earth. With the search and rescue software developed by the Ontario Provincial Police, she drew circles on the map with Francine's home in the centre. Using GPS trackers synced with the software, each officer leading a group of volunteers would track, real-time their location and progress. The idea was to have people on the ground searching and moving outwards while other investigators were called in to canvass for witnesses at the surrounding homes and collect available video at plazas and residences with anti-theft cameras hanging above their garage or side door. The trick was to do multiple tasks simultaneously while not diminishing the quality of the work. You had to rush without rushing. While drawing the circles, Reggie stood beside her talking to another detective who had just walked in. Jodie listened to them while completing her task.

Reggie said, "They say if they noticed anyone watching them? Maybe the same car driving by more than once or the same car parked on the street? Anything?"

"Nothing. We got nothing on this Staff. It's like she stepped into another world or something. She just vanished."

Jodie said, "Bullshit."

The detective said, "I know it's bullshit. But we got nothing."

Jodie said, "There's always something. The how is the most interesting. He walked into a house, into a little girl's bedroom and took her? Why didn't Francine scream? How did he get her out of there without waking anyone up? I checked the weather report for here last night and I have to say, he did pick a good night for it. The falling snow covered any tracks he might have left which indicates some planning. Only the front door had been left unlocked, which it normally wasn't. That was luck, not planning. That indicates impulsivity. What does that say about the guy? An impulsive planner? I would say the guy knows Francine. To have a complete stranger in town checking houses for unlocked doors doesn't fit. He randomly picked a home with a small child in it? I don't think so. So if he knows Francine, someone around here knows him. We gotta figure this out and quick. I know the search is helpful, we need to do it but I don't think we'll find Francine outside. Someone took her and has her and we gotta keep the pressure on him so he stops to think before he does anything that can't be undone. We need something. Anything that will point us somewhere. You know? What we need is an old-fashioned clue."

The door to the RV opened and a red-cheeked patrol officer said, "Staff? You need to hear this."

He stepped inside and following behind him was Nadine of the Giant Tiger.

–4–

Nadine told them the story of the strange man and what he had bought. When she mentioned the rope, duct tape, padlock, and chain, all the officers leaned in close to her and she tilted her head back under all the scrutiny, her eyes roving from face to face.

Jodie said, "Do you know who he is?"

"No. Never saw him before and believe me, I'd remember."

Reggie said, "Nadine, you know everyone."

"Not this guy. I'd tell you if I did. I mean I'm here now aren't I?"

Jodie said, "What did he pay with?"

"Cash."

Reggie said, "Well, that's not helpful."

Jodie turned to Reggie and said, "Talk to your guys on the radio. Ask any of them if they know who the guy is. The description is very distinct. Someone has to know him."

And she was right. Someone did.

•   •   •   •   •   •

Two summers ago, Officer Benoit ran into Nadine's stranger. Purely on accident. Officer Benoit tried not to run into anybody. On a quiet Sunday, he'd hop in his cruiser and head over to Eddie's Honky Tonk and Eatz, with a 'z' because the owner thought poor spelling would bring in a younger crowd. It didn't and they needed to do something about that before they lost all their money and had to collect unemployment. Eddie, the owner, would rather die than have the government give him money. The whole idea stunk like charity to him. Eddie and his wife Selena decided the bar life wasn't for them. They were early morning people and because Eddie could cook an egg and fry half decent hash browns, they re-opened the place as an all-day breakfast restaurant that didn't actually stay open all day. They closed every day at two in the afternoon and weren't open on Mondays. That didn't hurt their business any. Officer Benoit knew about the history. He didn't care about it, but he knew of it. Officer Benoit didn't care about the food either. The reason Officer Benoit liked to go to Honky Tonk and Eatz was because it sat on the very border of his patrol zone and if a supervisor wanted to catch him out eating breakfast, they'd have to drive forty-five minutes away from the station to do that. For some reason, Benoit forgot that all police cruisers were equipped with GPS and all a supervisor had to do to check on him was search his call sign and the location of the cruiser would pop up on their computer screen. Officer Benoit had been around a long time and the GPS capability of the police cruisers happened to be a new thing, something that passed from one ear to the other without being absorbed by his grey matter in between.

The truth of the matter was, all the officers went to breakfast on Sunday but they went together, neglecting to invite Benoit because Benoit had a habit of picking his nose. He'd do that while you were eating, while you were talking to him and then he'd examine the find on the end of his finger before crushing it in a napkin. No one wanted to see that while eating eggs. No one wanted to see that at any time. They stopped inviting him: to anything. Benoit didn't know any of that. He thought he was pulling a fast one on the bosses and gloated about it in private.

On the morning he met Nadine's stranger, after he ate his breakfast, he paid and got into his cruiser. He picked up a coffee from Tim Horton's and headed to his second spot he thought was secret but because of the GPS he'd forgotten about, was a well-known fact. He'd found the trail patrolling a few years ago and decided to investigate it because it looked like a place he could disappear in. An opening in the trees caught his eye. It didn't appear to be a natural opening and when he glanced at the ground under the arch of branches, he saw indentations in the dirt looking very much like old tire tracks. Nature was in the process of reclaiming the path but Officer Benoit saw it as an ideal hiding spot. Weeds swayed, leaves littered the dirt and tiny saplings strained for the sunlight. Benoit eased down the path, cringing with every branch-scraping squeal on the cruiser's exterior and the intermittent bumping of the undercarriage against something hard. Glancing into his rearview mirror, he watched the foliage close behind him and he smiled. It made him feel as though he were driving into the Batcave or something. No one would find him there. It became his Sunday-after-breakfast-napping-hole and that is how he thought of it: all in one long word.

Officer Benoit had just settled into his spot and adjusted the seat back as far as it could go (which wasn't far because of the metal shell they put in the back of police cars to transport prisoners). It suited him fine on that day with the coffee cup steaming beside him, country music on the radio, the air conditioner on and a western by Louis L'Amour in his hand ready to read if he couldn't nap right away. Benoit opened the book and after a few lines in, he felt the old familiar feeling of lethargy about to dip him deeper into the utter relaxation of sleep. Snapping twigs startled him. He sat upright, checking the rearview mirror, the side mirror and glanced out through every window. He didn't want to end up on the front page of some newspaper because some jerk with a phone took his picture while he napped in a fully marked police cruiser. Officer Benoit thought that'd be just his luck. Every fool out there had a cell phone now and because of that, privacy was something lawyers said people had a right to although there was no way to expect such a thing nowadays. He didn't see anything and opened the Louis L'Amour book. When he heard another twig snap, a surge of fear-drenaline kicked in, drying out his mouth and pinching his heart in his chest. It took a few moments of silence to calm his over-taxed heart. His usually quiet spot was very active this morning. He sipped on his coffee, cracked open his book again, and caught the shape in the rearview mirror. He jerked, startled, and hot coffee shot out through the small, sipping hole.

"Fuck!"

He wiped the spilled coffee off of the laptop in the cruiser with a wet-wipe and considered the shadow. Officer Benoit thought the figure had been a man. No real reason other than the size of the person and the way the person moved. The person struck him as masculine, and he thought, so what? Benoit shrugged and turned back to his book. The man was moving away from him so what did he care? He turned his attention back to his book and then he frowned, not seeing the words on the page. Benoit wondered what was the person doing way out here alone? Benoit thought the man had been wearing a backpack too. The frown deepened at the corners of his mouth. What if the person was out here burying something, like drugs? Even worse, what if the person was burying a body while Benoit sat here doing nothing? How good would that look? An officer sitting nearby while a crime occurred or was covered up while he read a Louis L'amour? He'd be in a world of shit if they found out. It didn't occur to Benoit that it'd be close to impossible to show he had been sitting in that exact spot at the exact time while knowing someone was up to no good and he chose to ignore it. Benoit, thinking he'd be found out sighed because that was how he saw the world, as something out to get him and he closed his book muttering, "Just my luck isn't it? Right when I was getting comfortable."

Benoit turned off his car, thought about driving away and remembering the backpack on the man's back and the potential of all the ominous items contained within, he stepped out of his cruiser, tucked the keys in his pocket and turned on his portable radio and walked after the man.

He parted the dense foliage with his hands, his heavy boots crunching through leaves and snapping twigs thinking if the man he was following didn't know someone was coming towards him, he'd have to be deaf.

Benoit stumbled onto an old game trail and followed it. He didn't have to travel far before the woods gave way to a pond. He smelled the water before he saw it. A deep, earthy smell like worms on a road after a heavy rain. The glassy and smooth water reflected blinding light at Benoit. He squinted against it and put a hand across his brow to act as a brim. When he could focus he saw the man standing ten feet from him, staring at him with a fishing pole in his hand. Yup. The man had heard him coming.

Benoit said, "Hello. How are you doing today?"

"Fine."

Benoit walked closer. The man had slurred the word, garbled it and Benoit thought the man might have been drinking.

"What are you doing out here?"

The man held the fishing pole out.

"Yeah. Any good fishing here?"

Benoit closed the distance to five feet. The sun was low in the sky behind the man, putting the man's face in shadow. Still, Benoit could see something was wrong with the shape of his head.

The man spoke in a slow deliberate manner and said, "The lake overflows into this pond. And it's harder to get here so most people fish in the lake rather than here. So, yeah. Good fishing."

The man's backpack sat open by his feet on the ground. In the bag was a metal water container and a paper bag.

"You have a fishing license I can look at?"

"Yes."

The man set the pole down and reached into his back pocket. Benoit didn't know why, but when the man moved his hand to retrieve his license, he tapped the butt of his gun. The man handed over the license and Benoit ambled to the side so the sun didn't obscure his sight as much. That was when he saw the man's face. Afterward, Officer Benoit would feel bad about his reaction only he had been caught off guard and his initial reaction was to flinch and wrinkle his nose as though he smelled something offensive.

The man stood there, waiting with his hand outstretched and the license in his hand, his misshapen face and empty eye socket revealed by the daylight. His stoic expression stating he knew what he looked like and had to deal with reactions like Benoit's all the time. It was nothing new for him.

Benoit took the license and said, "Thanks."

He wanted to return the license after a quick glance and leave. He wanted to go back to his cruiser and not be under the sad eye of the victim of his unprofessionalism. But that would be worse because maybe the man would see his hasty retreat as a sign that Benoit, an officer, someone who is supposed to treat everyone with respect, couldn't stand to be near his marred features. Instead, he wrote the man's name into his notebook along with the listed address and license number. Then Benoit called to dispatch from his portable and told them where he was. He asked the dispatcher to run the man through the system. Benoit hoped the man wasn't wanted or anything. He just wanted to get out of here. Find another place to read his book and drink his cooling coffee in peace. He wiped a line of sweat off his brow and sighed. Besides, all the paperwork would ruin his day and what if the bosses began to expect more work out of him? When the dispatch told Benoit the man was clean and there were no warrants for him, Benoit's mood lightened. He even smiled. He returned the license and said, "Thank you. You have yourself a good day."

"I'm working on it," said the man and he smiled. Benoit's smile wavered and he struggled to suppress the urge to cringe. The man had one ugly grin. There were some teeth missing and Benoit decided that was the reason for his deliberate speech. He was an easy man to remember. Of course, when Benoit told Jodie about the man, he left all the lazy, hiding from work methods out and his reaction to the man. Jodie just wanted his name.

•　　　•　　　•　　　•　　　•

Jodie said, "So you have his name in your notebook?"

"Yeah."

"Do you remember his name?"

"I got my notebook right here. I can find it."

"You carry your old notebooks around with you?"

"No, no. This is the same one."

"From two years ago?"

Benoit turned red and said, "Yeah." He started flipping through the pages.

Jodie and Reggie shared a look. A guy who didn't go through a notebook in close to two years didn't do too much. Most officers, even rural ones, would go through a notebook between five and six months. Two years? A guy who took two years to fill a notebook was actively avoiding work and Benoit had turned red because he knew it. When he found the name, he sputtered it out with relief. He said, "Uh, Graham. Graham Richards."

The address Graham had on his fishing license was actually a P.O. Box. The mailbox was at the post office in town right beside the Subway, about a block away from the Giant Tiger. Jodie asked Reggie to talk to the postal guy, see if they could find the registration card, but was told they'd need a warrant for that information. Reggie then assigned an officer, Eddie, one of those guys good with computers, to do a complete background check on Graham Richards.

Jodie said, "I want everything you can get on the guy, but what I want first is an address."

Eddie, nodding and popping a Fisherman's Friend lozenge into his mouth said, "Not a problem."

Eddie found through land registry files in the City's database an address for Graham Richards.

Reggie said, "Don't we need a warrant for that? We needed one for the post office."

Eddie said, "Nope. The land registry information is public record. We're good to look."

Now that Jodie had an address, she requested a surveillance unit to go to the place and see what they could see. Preferably, without letting Graham know they were watching.

When that was done, Jodie asked Reggie if they had a drone nearby to do some silent reconnaissance from the air. Reggie said, "I'll look into it," and started punching numbers into the desk phone.

Jodie got in touch with Barbara, their go-to warrant writer, to get her started on the warrant framework, in case they needed one. Jodie was being told by Barbara that what they had was circumstantial, at best, and not enough to get into anyone's house when she received another call from the surveillance team leader, Bryce.

To the warrant writer, Jodie said, "Hey, Barbara? I got another call I have to take. Can you start on the warrant anyway? At least get it rolling in case something more compelling comes in? Great. Thanks."

Jodie clicked on the flashing line and said, "Bryce? What have you got?"

"Nothing. There isn't even a road into this guy's place. I don't even know if there is a place. Could be a cave or a thatched hut for all I know. There is a trail, kind of, and I can see a snowmobile but we can't get any closer without this guy seeing us. He's like, in the middle of nowhere. And that's not an exaggeration."

"Okay. Is there any place you can watch to see if someone arrives or leaves?"

"Well...I can put a couple of guys on snowmobiles, have them sit where they could see anyone leaving the general area of Graham's place but I gotta tell ya, if this guy sticks his head out, he's going to see us. We're as noticeable as a seal in a speedo."

"If that's the best you can do then do it."

"Alright."

"And call me if you see anything worth sharing."

"Like little Francine waving from a window? Will do. After I get her back, though."

"As long as we get her back, Bryce."

•   •   •   •   •   •

The drone Reggie was trying to wrangle their way cost the Ontario Provincial Police $250,000. Correction, it cost the taxpayers that much for one of them. The O.P.P. had three drones and they had proven useful in locating missing people in rural areas and so for that reason, they were well worth the price. The drones had saved the lives of many elderly people who had wandered away from their retirement homes. The onset of dementia or Alzheimer's can be slow or fast. So the staff at these homes, having trusted Big Bob to go for long walks on his own because he had always returned before, were unprepared when he didn't come home at the time they were expecting him. Big Bob hadn't displayed any signs of either degenerative disease. The scary part about it was that a person with dementia could walk forever. Always walking ahead and not stopping for anything. The danger to these lost people came from the environment. When they started walking, they may have been wearing clothing appropriate for the weather at the time, but when the sun drops, the temperature follows and that fall coat and light gloves Big Bob had been wearing when he left would no longer cut it. Sometimes these confused people would walk in a straight line and if they hit a wall, they would walk along it and until they hit another obstruction and then walk along that. A few years ago, Jodie read of a woman with dementia walking straight into the woods, wearing only her night clothes until she got stuck in thick brambles. People with dementia tend to be less verbal. The search parties looking for her passed within twenty feet of her. They never heard her. They never saw her. The poor woman died from exposure. The drone would have seen her. It would have registered her body heat on the infrared camera and they would have freed her from there and returned her home safe if not a little worse for wear. Up until now, the drones had been used to save lives. And now they would use the drone for surveillance. But maybe that would help save Francine's life. Thinking about it, Jodie wondered if using the drone in such a way was a privacy breach? Was using the drone more intrusive than surveillance? As long as the police and the drone stayed off the private property of Graham Richards, was it even trespassing? Whatever. The lawyers could argue over that. All Jodie wanted was the little girl back. Jodie, waiting to hear if they could even get a drone, was holding onto her coffee cup, listening to the radio, hoping to hear some good news.

Reggie said, "Jodie?"

"Yeah?"

"A drone is on the way."

"Good."

They were lucky that afternoon. One of the three drones had been a hundred and twenty kilometres away. A nice easy highway drive would bring it here in little over an hour.

When the drone operator arrived she told him what she wanted. If possible, she would like the drone to circle the property and not to go on it. She didn't want the the drone operator using the drone camera to zoom in to see inside any windows, but if he happened to see a little girl on or around the property, like by accident, that'd be great if he could let her know.

Scratching his beard, the drone man said, "By accident? What does that mean?"

Jodie said, "It means, if she's there, I want you to find her, but don't be so intrusive about it. Don't be so damned obvious, is all."

"Okay. I guess."

Drone man left the RV and Eddie, the computer guy who had been researching Graham Richards, turned around from his computer and said, "Jodie? You should probably look at this."

Five years ago, Graham Richards survived a massacre. The killer didn't intend for Graham to survive. The killer, Brandon Voorhees, had shot Graham in the face and the chest which is not something you'd do thinking the person would live. At the last second, Graham flinched and turned his head. The bullet went in under his right eye plowing through teeth and the roof of his mouth. It carried on out his other cheek and into the skull of his wife, Meghan. Brandon shot Graham again in the upper chest. The bullet nicked his lung on the left side. Graham fell, unconscious, bleeding out onto the cold floor. The killer then shot his son Evan in the chest and then the old man hiding with them behind the counter. Brandon Voorhees killed twenty-three people and wounded forty-three that day. He was shot and killed by the responding police officers. He wouldn't drop his rifle and when the barrel of his rifle started creeping up to point in the direction of the officers, they shot him.

It had all started with a bad day. Brandon, a travelling salesman who, in the words of his boss, "couldn't sell water to a man dying of thirst in the desert," returned home after getting fired to find his wife, his high school sweetheart, involved in a threesome with her yoga instructor (Belinda) and her husband (Carl). His wife didn't even flinch when he walked into their bedroom to find her giving a blowjob to some strange dude while straddling a woman's face. He couldn't even remember the last time she gave him a blowjob. It was like that joke where the guy gets married because he thinks he'll be getting BJ's for life while at the same time, the wife is smiling thinking she'll never have to give one again. In his case, the joke wasn't a joke at all. Oral sex stopped as soon as he put the ring on her finger. Well, him receiving it had. On the day he walked in on the sex play in which he wasn't a participant, she stopped long enough to tell him to close the door on his way out. He did close the door. But then he went and got his rifle from the safe in the garage, loaded it and returned to the bedroom and shot everyone in the room. The room stunk of blood and the acrid scent of gunfire. Brandon, nodded, left the bedroom and closed the door behind him.

Remembering he was supposed to pick up for his wife vegetarian protein powder from a supplement store, Brandon returned to his gun safe. He sat on a stool and calmly loaded four rifle magazines and stuffed them in his coat and pants pockets. He didn't know why he did this. His brain was buzzing white noise, like a radio tuned to a spot in between stations. He looked at his hands doing what they were doing but they didn't feel like his hands. Almost like they were gloves, as though he was wearing another person but not controlling that person. No. It was more like he was just along for the ride, as though he was taking a piggy-back ride on himself.

Why was he getting the vegetarian powder for his wife? She wouldn't be eating ever again. A giggle snorted out and he buried the thought. She wanted the powder and so he'd get it for her. In the closet he picked up a black helmet. He stared at it in his hands. He had bought the helmet when he briefly considered joining a paintball group. His wife didn't approve and so he put the helmet in the closet and forgot about it until today. He put the helmet on. Sweat from his hairline ran down the right side of his face. He stared out of the window. The sky was so blue. He sighed. It was so quiet in his house. He glanced at himself in a mirror, saw the helmet on his head and couldn't remember why he put it on. But then he remembered it wasn't him wearing it. He was a passenger in his own body. He wasn't the driver and so it didn't matter what he did or didn't do. He walked to his car and putting the rifle on the seat next to him, he drove to the new outlet mall. He received a flyer in the mail and knew the supplement store his wife preferred had opened another place there and was having a sale. When he thought of his wife, the image of her face pulped from a bullet pushed itself to the front of his mind. He swiped it away by waving his hand in the air, as though shooing away an annoying fly. He chuckled. That hadn't been real. And if it had been, he hadn't done it. No, sir.

When he arrived at the outlet mall he circled the lot, trying to find a place to park. The new plaza was busy that day and he had to brake more than once as people walked in front of his car. He scowled under his helmet. They didn't even look at him. Like they had every right to walk wherever they wanted, whenever they wanted. Or, scary thought, maybe they walked like that, not even looking at him because they couldn't see him. Maybe he wasn't even here. Maybe that was why people talked over him or stepped in front of him in line as though he didn't occupy any space at all. Taking one hand off of the steering wheel, he stared at it. The hairs on his fingers were dark and coarse. He hadn't noticed how coarse they looked before. Or had he? Blinking, trying to dispel the fog in his mind, his distracted self wasn't paying attention to the road and his right tire side-swiped a curb. He stomped on the brake and slipped the car into park. Images crowded in on him: his wife giving head, the other woman's breasts sliding to either side of her chest, the man smirking at him, as though he was less than nothing, a non-human and then his bedroom painted in blood, soaked in it, and the screams, the gurgles and the pleading. He laughed, shaking his head and he said, "What a strange thought." He smacked the forehead of his helmet and said, "How did that get in there. Can't be real, it just can't be. I wouldn't do something like that. Not me."

He continued to mutter as he stepped out of his car. He opened the back door and making sure his rifle was loaded, took it out, closed the doors on his car and locked it using his key fob and laughed again. Why was he locking it? Habit, muscle memory, oh, who cares? None of this was real. He gazed at the blue sky and thought it was a beautiful day.

He patted his pockets for the loaded magazines and smiling because they were there, stalked towards the center of the plaza. Taking aim at a man with a Lego bag, he started shooting.

•　　•　　•　　•　　•

Jodie said, "I remember that. Jesus, that was Graham? One of the survivors?"

"Yeah. Probably why his face is so messed up," Eddie said.

"Sad."

"Yeah, but this could help with the warrant."

"How so?"

"Well, he lost a kid. Francine is around the same age. Maybe, he wanted a kid again."

Jodie frowned and said, "That's a stretch."

"Maybe so. But who knows how fucked up the guy is? That would mess up anyone. Anyway, it is a theory and not a fact. As long as it's presented as a theory, it can be used."

Jodie wasn't comfortable with the idea. It wasn't entirely honest. Although the idea was plausible it didn't feel right to her. For one, Graham had lost a son. If the loss was so profound would he take a girl to replace the boy? Wouldn't that destroy the illusion of replacement? Still, he lived in the woods, far from prying eyes and he had bought those weird items from the store the day before Francine went missing. The only thing missing from the abduction kit Graham had bought was a gag. Giant Tiger didn't sell those.

"Huh. I'll think about it."

Reggie said, "Don't think too long. The clock is ticking."

-6-

Bryce didn't like the woods, didn't like the cold and he didn't like the snow. And because he didn't like snow, he didn't like winter sports and that included hockey. He had been accused of being un-Canadian from time to time, and he didn't take offence to it, because liking hockey doesn't make someone Canadian and besides, what was he supposed to do? Start liking the cold? Start liking the snow? Pick up a stick and start skating? No thanks. To hell with that noise. Give him a beach, sand, sun and someone to bring him drinks, colourful ones with the stupid umbrellas in them because, why the hell not? That was his ideal vacation. But here he was, freezing in the snow because he was here to do a job and even though he hated the environment, he'd do the job. And he'd do it well. Bryce sent two of his six-member team back to the nearest detachment to get snowmobiles and the sled suits and helmets to go with the machines. Bryce just bet those sled suits were warm. Warmer than what he was wearing anyway. The rest of his team was spread out around where they thought Graham's place was. They didn't know because they hadn't seen it, not with their own eyes at least. They were operating blind. What was that line from the *Naked Gun* film? Like a blind man at an orgy, they'd have to feel their way around? Bryce smiled and then frowned. He hated the cold. His teeth chattered and he closed his mouth tight to stop his teeth from clacking. He wondered what happened to the drone that was supposed to be on the way. The drone might have done reconnaissance, but Bryce had no idea. No one told him if it had spotted a home or a base or a freaking tree-house and he didn't hear the damn thing buzzing nearby so who knew?

What he did know was that he was stuck in a trifecta of misery. He had to leave his car on the side of the road and approach on foot through the cold woods coated in snow. He expected to be sitting in his car waiting for someone to move so he and his team could follow them because that's what they normally did. In his car, he'd be warm and he could talk to his team on the radio. They'd yap at and make fun of each other over their encrypted radios and attempt to decide the veracity about the newest interdepartmental gossip. Fun shit that passed the time. He did not expect to be out in the snow and the cold, and because he didn't think of that possibility he hadn't dressed for it. Instead of winter boots, hat, mitts, insulated pants and a heavy coat, he was in running shoes, no hat, thin gloves, jeans and a parka. He was dressed for an afternoon at the pub, flirting with a waitress and sipping on pints of imported beer. His lack of foresight left him freezing and unhappy.

Leaving his car and trekking through the snow to his spot in the cold, wet nowhere with the snow getting into the tops of his shoes having no idea what or who he was supposed to be looking for other than a creepy man and a little girl. Even if he did see something, what would he call out to his team to pinpoint his location? I'm by a tree with snow at the base? There were a gazillion trees out here, all with snow at their damn bases. At best, Bryce guessed he was south of the target's house. That's it. But even that was a guess because no one had seen the house. Bryce shivered as cold air slid down his back. Bryce wished he had worn his kevlar vest. Not only would it protect him from bullets, it would have kept him warmer. His teeth clattered again. He didn't hear the steps approaching from behind him. He didn't know he wasn't alone. Not until he heard the voice behind him.

"Hello."

Bryce jumped, and his one foot slipped as running shoes weren't the best for this terrain, and at the same time he clicked his radio as his hands and body tensed. Over the air, his team and Jodie and all the other officers in the command vehicle who had been listening on that channel heard him squawk "Ahhhh!"

Bryce scrambled to this feet while keeping the man who had appeared out of nowhere in front of him. Bryce had a gun on his hip in a holster but his coat was covering it. Seeing the man's hands covered in giant mitts, Bryce thought he would have enough time to get his own gun out if the man shucked off his mittens to open his heavy coat to grab a gun of his own, or even a knife. The man wore a heavy coat with a fur-lined hood shadowing his face.

From the radio in his hand, "Bryce! Are you okay? You need help"

He clicked the portable button, eyeing the man in front of him and said, "Give me a minute."

To the man, Bryce said, "Can I help you?"

Slow and deliberate the man said, "I was wondering if I could help you. You're looking for that little girl, right?"

The hair on Bryce's body stood. And this time, it wasn't because of the cold.

• • • •

After they heard Bryce's yelp, everyone in the RV stared at the portable radio tuned to the surveillance teams frequency. All chatter in the RV stopped and brows furrowed. Jodie touched the gun on her hip and Reggie hugged his elbows. Then Jodie said to Reggie, "Call the dispatcher and find out who is assigned to that portable. Then have them call everyone on the surveillance team on their cell phones to check in."

Eddie, sitting at his chair put his coffee down and said, "I'm on it, boss."

Jodie heard Eddie on the phone getting the information. Over his shoulder, he said, "That's Bryce's portable," and he continued to chat on the phone to dispatch. Jodie picked up the radio, asked Bryce if he was okay and he told her to wait and once more the group stood around looking at the portable, waiting for Bryce to speak.

Eddie hung up the phone and spun around in his chair. He said, "The rest of the surveillance team is accounted for and they are fine. They think Bryce is south of Graham's property."

Jodie frowned and said, "Think?"

"Yeah. That's the best they can do. They're in the woods, no line of sight to each other so they set up in a general way to cover the compass points without going on Graham's property. Not effective but it's the best they could do."

The radio chirped, "Jodie? I'm going to call you."

Jodie picked up the portable and said, "10-4."

She pulled the phone out of her pocket, waiting for it to ring. Everyone around her quieted. It buzzed in her hand. She answered it and said, "Bryce?"

7

Graham sipped a coffee while sitting at his kitchen table with a Sudoku puzzle from the local paper in front of him. The voices on the radio were updating constantly about the search for little Francine. Snow decorated the bottom of his sliding glass door and condensation made beaded triangles in the corners. On the wall of the kitchen, close to the ceiling, hung a TV monitor. It flickered on. It did that from time to time. Graham installed motion sensor cameras on his property and most times an image of a deer or a family of raccoons would flash on the screen, ambling across his lot in that bum shimmying way that raccoons have, and he'd go back to doing what he was doing, secure in his isolation. Once he had seen a bear walk through. It had been fifty feet from his house. He saw it stand on its back legs and swipe a furrow into a tree with one large paw. It sniffed the air, dropped to all fours and disappeared from view.

After what had happened to him and his family, Graham didn't think he was being paranoid by installing all those cameras on his property. He preferred knowing what or who might be coming to visit. It had taken him some time, but he was starting to care about his life again as he knew Meghan would have wanted him to. And for that reason, he wanted to be prepared to protect it.

In the afternoon while the hunt for Francine heated up with pleas for volunteers to help with the search, Graham saw a man walking along the fringes of his property on that hanging TV monitor. Graham frowned. The guy looked like he was dressed for a night at the club and not the minus ten-degree weather outside and the shin-deep snow on the ground. The man was holding something in his hand. Graham moved closer to the TV. It looked like something with a long antenna. The man moved towards Graham's place, crouch walking and staying behind trees as much as possible. He did it in a stumbling way, like an inept spy. Then it hit Graham, *cop.* Why were the police here? Behind Graham, the radio announced there were no new leads for Francine.

Graham turned to the radio and frowned. They were here for him. For some reason or another, they think he has Francine.

Graham stood and poured the rest of his coffee in his cup down the sink. He put on his boots, coat, and mitts. In the top right of the screen, the camera projecting the image was identified by S4. Southern camera, fourth one which meant it would be the most eastern one on the southern side.

The cop out there looked cold. Graham stepped out of his house and closed the door behind him. Time to introduce himself and invite the cold policeman into his home. The idea was strange to him. He'd never had a guest in his house before and he never wanted one. But if he wanted to continue living the way that he was living, off the grid, he'd have to make an exception for the police. Graham would have to invite them into his home so they can poke and prod and tear apart what seclusion he managed to carve out for himself. To regain his privacy and his hermit lifestyle, he'd have to be inviting. Graham hands clenched into fists. Why couldn't people just leave him alone?

8

Jodie, Reggie, and three uniform officers stomped through the snow, kicking it in fanning sprays as they were lifting their feet and putting palms on passing trees for balance. They filed into a small clearing around Graham's house. Smoke chuffed from a chimney from the top of the small home built of logs and stone. The residence reminded Jodie of a rustic frontier home nestled in the woods in a dramatic Western film. Two other structures were separate from the home but were of such a similar style you could discern the same hand had built them. The snow-covered roof was marred by fallen branches from barren trees. Other than the isolation of the home, it had a happy family gathering vibe rather than a backwoods *Deliverance* feel to it.

As they approached, the door opened and Bryce stepped out with a steaming cup in his hand. Behind him stood a shadow. As she walked closer, Jodie could smell the coffee.

She smiled at Bryce and said, "Making yourself at home Bryce?" There was a light tone to it but Bryce, looking at the coffee in his hand, knew it had been meant as a reprimand. He hadn't wanted the coffee, but he'd been damned cold outside and the pot had been freshly made and he thought it couldn't hurt, right? Jodie made him think he had been wrong.

"He offered me a coffee while we waited for you. I was cold and uh, I didn't want to be rude."

"Of course." She extended her hand to the man behind Bryce, "Mr. Richards?"

He nodded and stepped back to let them in.

Jodie stopped at the door and said, "Before we come into your home," she looked at Bryce when she said 'we', "I have to make you aware of a few things okay?"

Standing behind Bryce she could see an outline of Graham. To Jodie, it seemed he moved where the shadows would be and because of that, all she saw was the nod.

"Before we come into your home, I need to let you know that you don't have to let us in. This is purely voluntary on your part and that you are inviting us in without any coercion from the police. Is that correct?"

He nodded and Jodie shaking her head said, "No, I need to hear you say it. Are you inviting us in?"

"Yes." The word sounded weird as though half of his mouth had cotton in it.

"Have the police in any way intimidated you so that you feel you have to let us in?"

"No."

"You understand that if we find anything criminal in there after we were lawfully invited in, you could be held accountable?"

"Yes."

"You also have the right to revoke your consent at any time. Do you understand that?"

"Yes."

"Are you still inviting us in?"

"Yes."

"Do you mind if I have some K-9 dogs with their handlers out here? To look, actually, smell around the property?"

"No."

"Well, okay then. Thank you."

Bryce and Graham stepped out of the way and Jodie and the other officers walked in behind her. Jodie noticed behind the door a plastic bag from Giant Tiger. In it were the items Graham had bought the previous day. Minus the padlock and chain.

• • • • •

In the kitchen, Jodie removed a digital audio recorder from her backpack and placed it on the kitchen table. Graham sat across from her and waited. Bryce stood behind Jodie, leaning against the glass door with his coffee. Jodie removed her notebook and saw Graham's face out of the shadows for the first time. Graham's jaw bulged on the right side giving it a swollen look but at the same time, the thinness of his face made it appear sunken. A pink scar bisected his face disappearing into the beard lining his jaw. Parts of his cheeks and nose were as melted wax. And the missing eye, that was a showstopper. The eyelid, covering nothing, appeared nothing more than a fleshy depression in his skull. The other eye, clear and so dark it was almost black, measured her, making her feel almost naked under the knowing glare.

Graham saw her and for the first time Jodie felt like how a criminal must feel when she was interviewing them, as though all her secrets were not secrets at all; merely a poorly constructed facade. She swallowed, looked away and turned back, taking in the broad shoulders and the callused hands resting on the table between them. She paused and forcing a smile, opened her notebook and removed a pen.

"Do you mind if I audio record all that stuff I said outside? Since we're in your house now?"

"No."

Jodie turned on the audio recorder and restated what she had said outside and also made Graham aware of his rights. Graham had agreed to let the other officers search his home, his two outbuildings and anywhere they wanted.

Jodie said, "Behind the front door I saw a bag from Giant Tiger. You were there yesterday, right?"

Graham nodded.

"I didn't see the padlock or chain in the bag. I was told you bought those items, is that right?"

Graham said, "Yes."

"I might have missed the items because I didn't search through the bag. Are they in there? The chain and lock?"

"No."

"What did you do with them?"

Graham stood and Bryce dropped one hand to his waist, where his gun sat. Jodie frowned at Bryce and he stuffed his hand in his pocket as though that was what he had meant to do all along and took another sip of coffee. Graham kept his eye on Jodie. He must have noticed Bryce's reaction but looking at him, Jodie couldn't tell if he did.

Graham said, "Follow me."

Jodie and Bryce trailed Graham down one hallway lined with bookshelves. Jodie noted books written by Joe Abercrombie, Walter Mosley, J.K Rowling and other authors, ones whose names she didn't recognize. The hallway ended at stairs going into a basement. At the bottom was a door. The chain and padlock shone on the outside of the door, shiny and new.

Jodie said, "Do you mind opening…" but Graham had already removed a key from his pocket and slid it into the lock.

Jodie shared a look with Bryce, wanting him to chill and to reassure herself he didn't have his gun out and naked in his hand like some overzealous rookie. Bryce's hand was resting on the butt of his gun. She didn't like that, but at least it wasn't out and pointed at anyone.

Graham pulled the chain out of the brackets and held it in his hand. The stairway was narrow and after he pushed open the door, he stood back to let the officers go before him.

Jodie stepped down the stairs, aware how close Graham was to her. She turned sideways and entered the earthy-smelling room.

A bright light hung from the low ceiling. She pulled her head into her shoulders and took her flashlight out of her pocket. She shone it around the room and realized she stood in the center of a shrine. Framed photographs crowded the walls. The smiling face of a woman and a young boy stared out at Jodie and she suddenly felt dirty for forcing her way into this room and into this man's most private pain. On a table before her was a kid-sized baseball glove. A hardball, the surface scuffed and ragged still showed an autograph decorating one side. In one picture, she saw the woman and Graham standing beside each other. He wore a suit and she glowed happily in her wedding dress. The Graham before her seemed such a different man to the one in the picture. The man in the picture had both his eyes and his flesh was smooth and unmarred. His expression and bearing portrayed that of a confident man, happy about his place in the world.

Jodie left the room and closed it behind her. To Graham, she said, "You can lock it up."

Back at the table, Jodie said, "I'm sorry for all this but you know why we have to do it right?"

In a deliberate way Jodie was getting used to, Graham said, "Yes. I'm your Boo Radley."

Bryce said, "What's that mean? Did he say, Boo Radley?"

Jodie said, "He's saying we got the wrong guy."

Bryce chuckled and giving Graham a dark glare he said, "They all say that don't they?"

Looking at Graham, a suggestion of a smile at the corners of her mouth, she said, "Yes, they do."

•   •   •   •   •

Jodie and all of the other officers left Graham's home. She walked at the back of the group and turned her face up to the darkening sky. Snow spiralled down. The staggered falling flakes made her think of seconds passing by.

Francine was running out of time and they were no closer to finding her. She stopped and turned back to Graham's home. She smelled woodsmoke on the air. In the window, she saw Graham watching them leave. He raised a hand, acknowledging her and she raised one back. They returned to their cars and drove to the RV without speaking. They walked towards the command vehicle appearing like a group defeated.

They entered the RV, passing news people shouting questions. They ignored them and closed the door shutting out the voices and the chaos. They had a media officer specifically trained to deal with the group outside. Right now, Jodie sensed no one had the energy to issue statements that didn't state anything. Once inside, Jodie started a pot of coffee and the aroma filled the small interior. On the whiteboard was a picture of little Francine, the one Jodie had given to the media to circulate. Francine smiled at her from it.

Jodie said, "Well, back to square one. Reggie, we're going to need an update..."

Bryce said, "Wait. We're backing off the cabin in the woods guy? Just like that?"

"What would you suggest? We searched his house, his lot, hell, we even had the dogs go through. One of them was a cadaver dog. And nothing, nada, zilch. I think there is a better way to utilize our resources than snooping on a guy without any reason to snoop on or from a place from which to snoop. So yeah, back to the start. Review the data and create a plan accordingly."

"I don't like it."

Jodie, crossing her arms said, "I know you don't like *him*. You made that very clear. But like has nothing to do with anything. We follow evidence. And your dislike of him is not evidence."

"He's fucking weird! That's evidence to me."

"And that's why you work surveillance and not cases. And by the way, I think if you got shot in the face and then woke up to find your family dead, you'd be fucking weird too. Anybody would be."

Bryce stood and left without another word. The door slammed at his back.

"Ok, let's see what the searchers have turned up. And do we have anyone watching any of the video we gathered?"

They worked into the darkening night and Jodie kept seeing that picture of Francine. A happy child, expecting to be safe in the night, expecting to be safe at home. Jodie feared they would never see her again. So the next morning, when Francine showed up on the doorstep of her home, ringing the doorbell, when Jodie learned of it, she was so surprised she went into the washroom of the RV and cried. Jodie hadn't expected a happy ending. She'd seen so few of them.

After the police left, Graham poured himself a glass of water and shook out a couple of Tylenol Fours from his prescription bottle. His head hurt from being around people. A stabbing pain would begin behind his eyes (both eyes which seemed like a cosmic joke to Graham considering one eye was gone) and move out concentrically until his entire head throbbed in grating misery. It felt like two plates of bone grinding together under his skin and sometimes, when the pain got so great it buckled his knees, he thought he could hear the scratching inside his skull like the sound of a fork scraping against a plate. Sometimes, it would get so bad he would have to crawl from where he had been trying to ride it out to his bedroom where sound and light were blocked. Graham had built his own isolation chamber in his bedroom for that purpose. While the police were here, looking in his house, in his outbuildings, in his yard, and into his *life*, he could feel the stirrings of pain awaken and knew it would swell into the debilitating kind if he didn't get on top of it. The Tylenol Fours helped if he ingested them early enough. As soon as he closed the door behind the police, he had hurried to the kitchen for the Tylenol Fours. After he swallowed them, he walked to the window and watched them leave while making slow circles with his index fingers on his temples.

He saw Jodie turn her face up to the falling snow and he smiled. Graham remembered the first time Evan saw snow. His wide eyes like bright jewels nestled in his ruddy cheeks watching the fat white flakes drift on currents to land on his gloved hands he had held out while seated in his stroller. Graham choked on a sob and pressed the hurt down. The pain of his loss dropped on him when his brain idled and he had time to think and to remember. He wondered if that would ever pass? He didn't think so. He couldn't stop thinking about Evan and his last seconds on earth. What must he have been going through after his parents were shot in front of him and the smoking barrel of that rifle turned to him? God, he needed a drink. He stopped doing that maybe three years ago? That sounds about right. And truth be told, for the most part, he didn't miss it all that much. The only time he thought of drinking was in times of stress because whatever was bothering him didn't seem as important when the alcohol saturated his blood and spun his brain into welcoming nothingness. And this was a stressful time. All those cops in Graham's house bothered him. All those cops thinking he'd taken a little girl bothered him. But he'd get over it. He usually did. And without alcohol. He finished his coffee and left the window glad to be alone again. Well, as glad as he could ever be. He didn't like to be around people. It hurt his head. It burned his eye that wasn't there. With the way the one cop, the one he'd found snooping in the woods, looking at him, Graham had a strong suspicion the police would be back. Or maybe they'd never left. They could be out in the woods right now watching and waiting to see what he would do. They wouldn't leave him alone now. Not until Francine was found. Grimacing and standing before his closet with all of his cold weather gear on hangers, he thought he should probably do something about that. He told himself the reason he would venture out into the cold, starless night was to get Francine back so the cops would leave him alone. So everyone would leave him alone. Remembering Evan's face and how much the loss of Meghan and his son destroyed the hopeful part of his soul, he also knew if he left his warm cabin, he'd be doing it for Francine and to save her parents from the anguish he knew intimately. He didn't want anyone to go through what he had survived. Because you never really survive the death of your child. Not completely. After the death of Evan, Graham viewed the world through a different lens. Everything appeared grey and drab. That's why he had pad-locked and chained the room of memories. Graham couldn't throw any of their belongings or photos away. He could never do that. But he couldn't stand to look at them either. Sometimes when he couldn't sleep he'd be tossing and turning in his bed and then in a blink find himself in that room surrounded by *them*, the people he loved, the people he failed by surviving. Then the anger would get on top of him until he couldn't breathe and following the anger would be the pain. There was always pain. Graham thought of himself as breathing, but not alive, not in the way he used to be when Meghan and Evan walked beside him. He was trying to find his life, because to quit now would be to fail Meghan and Evan again. But that loss of hope he had felt after their deaths? Graham wouldn't wish that on his worst enemy. Graham plucked his heavy winter coat off the hanger.

10

Francine didn't remember a whole lot of the night that she'd been taken. She awoke for a brief moment to a man in her room. The nightlight in her room made his shadow huge on the wall and backlit him so all she could see was the impression of a coat and a wool hat with a pompom dancing on the top. The cloth he pressed to her face stunk and made her think of the glass cleaner her mom made her use to wipe the mirror in her bathroom with. It burned her throat and stung her eyes and she sucked in a lungful of air to scream and inhaled more of the foul substance and before she could expel that air, darkness dropped over her eyes.

She awoke in another room although she didn't know that, not right away. Her comforter, the one with Rainbow Dash smiling at her while jumping over clouds lay on her and she thought the man in her room had been one of the worst nightmares she ever had. Francine shivered with the image of the dark man and the stinky cloth. It had been so real. The previous reigning champion of a nightmare involved her brother and a bag of Jolly Rancher's candy. The candies belonged to her brother and he had caught her stealing them from his room. In the nightmare, her parents decided to make her eat the whole bag as punishment only the bag never emptied. She'd reach, pull out some candy, eat it and when she'd reach in again, it was like the bag was full, as though she had just opened it. Her stomach got bigger and bigger and just before it would burst open and Jolly Ranchers would spill out of the gaping hole and fill the entire house, she'd wake up. Francine was convinced stealing wasn't for her. Not with nightmares like that as a consequence. But the man in her room with that cloth, well, that one made the Jolly Rancher one feel like a comedy in comparison. Francine sighed and rubbed her eyes. She gazed around her and didn't recognize where she was. A sinking feeling in her guts made her eyes bulge and her breath hitch in her throat. This wasn't her room.

The walls in this room were painted sky blue. On one wall, My Little Pony stickers were posted everywhere. On another wall, white puffy clouds were divided by an arcing rainbow. She pushed the comforter off and made to stand and noticed a metal cuff encircling her ankle. The other end of the cuff was affixed to a chain secured to an eyebolt in the floor at the center of the room. There were no windows. The light in the room came from a table lamp beside the bed. She pulled on the chain with her hands, not believing the realness of it, the solidity of the silver loops. The chain rattled with the movement, a tinkling sound. In the corner of the room, affixed to the ceiling was a white plastic circle that held a black, reflective dome. She knew it was a camera. Her brother pointed them out to her before when they were trailing behind their parents in a Wal-Mart. He told Francine it was how they caught thieves. She blushed, remembering the dream and her role as a Jolly Rancher thief, but she studied that camera, curious about what it could see and how it caught thieves. Francine pushed down on the metal cuff, hoping she could slip it off. It hurt when the solid metal scraped against her ankle and tears blurred her vision.

She heard the scratch of a key against a lock. She retracted her legs and pulled her blanket up to her chin. Rainbow Dash's smiling face was wrinkled in her fists. The door opened and a man was silhouetted in the frame. At least she thought the person to be a man. He filled the door with his bulk, standing there, his breath heavy through the mask he wore to cover his face and head. His hands clenched and unclenched by his side. His shoulders heaved with every inhale.

Francine said, "Who are you?"

His breathing got faster. He put a foot into the room.

Francine closed her eyes and whispered, "I want my mommy. Come get me, mommy, please come and get me, please, please." Francine pulled her knees to her chest and began rocking back and forth. "Mommy, come and get me, please, please, please." Tears collected in her eyes and were absorbed by her blanket. It seemed he stood there forever, a terrible dark statue of monolithic menace. From behind him, she heard a TV. She knew it was a TV because she recognized the jingle for a commercial. After the song ended, she heard her name and something about a search. The man's head turned toward the sound. He closed the door and she heard the sound of the lock engaging. She hadn't seen him since and wished she would never see him again. She would. But she would also see another man. And the other man would be very angry.

•   •   •   •   •

Francine did not know how long she had been in that room. She drank the chocolate milk in a mini-carton and ate the Dunk-a-roo cookies left on the bedside table. She didn't want to eat them. Her mother would never let her have treats until she ate something healthy. To eat it, she felt she'd be betraying her mother and maybe her mother wouldn't come and get her because she ate those cookies and milk. Besides, she wanted nothing from the man in the dark. What if he put something in it? Like he had on that cloth that smelled so bad? Francine fought the awful hunger cramps for as long as she could. The hungrier she got, the stronger the scent of the food became. To her hungry self, the food was soon the only thing of interest in the room and her widened eyes studied the offering. Francine reached for the food with a palsying hand and when she grasped the milk, she tore open the top and she sucked it back, tears shining on her cheeks the whole time. When she finished with the milk and cookies, she turned her back to it and tried to fall asleep. When she slept, she didn't have to think, she didn't have to be scared. She was tired of being scared. With her eyes closed and her brain burning with images of the man standing in the doorway, she felt the need to use the washroom. Then she remembered the chain on her leg.

She opened her eyes, turned and surveyed the room. In the same corner of the room with the camera above, she saw a bucket. Next to the bucket on the floor was a roll of toilet paper. She didn't want to use that bucket. It was right under the camera. What if he was watching? She really had to go now, though. There was a pressure she couldn't ignore. Worrying about the man watching her, she used the bucket with her blanket wrapped around her. She encircled the bucket with the blanket and staying within it, she relieved herself. After, she returned to bed, her face to the wall and alternated between crying and hitting the wall with her palms. At some point, she fell asleep but didn't remember doing it. It snuck up on her unsuspecting like the dark man had.

A bang woke her. She popped up in her bed and turned to the door. Closed. The lamp projected the shadow of the door handle onto the wall. The shape of it reminded Francine of a clown nose. Another bang. The door shook in the frame. A man grunted on the other side and Francine screamed and then stuffed a corner of the blanket into her mouth. She didn't know why, but she didn't want to be heard and she wanted to catch her scream the next time one tried to escape her. She heard thumps outside the door. The walls shook and rattled her bed. A man squealed, high pitched and keening. Francine took her hands off the blanket and clapped them over her ears.

Even though her hands cut off the sounds from outside the door, the walls shook the bed she sat on and to her, it felt like the one time a plane flew low over their house. The violent passing of the plane had shaken a picture frame off the wall. The wall bowed in a the chocolate milk bounced on the side-table and when it hit the floor, the shaking stopped. Her eyes bulged from her head as they studied the door handle. She could smell her sweat. It slicked her skin. She heard her heart from the pulse in her ears. She removed her hands from the sides of her head and spit out the blanket. She heard the metallic strike of a key. She saw the doorknob turning.

Francine pressed her back to the wall and muttered, "No-no-no, don't come in, don't come in here."

A man entered the room wearing a coat with a dark hood with fur around the collar hiding his face. A different man, taller than the other one, leaner and with wide shoulders. He froze when his hood turned to her and she heard him expel a sigh. His head followed the chain to the cuff looped through a link. He held up a key ring to the light. She saw an eye in the shadow of his hood. He picked one and held it between his index and thumb and moved towards her.

She pressed herself further into the wall and she heard him say, "Shhhhh," as he grabbed the cuff and held the key up to her eyes. She extended her foot and held her breath. She smelled the cold on him and the freshness of winter on his clothes. He un-cuffed her ankle and stood back from her and waited. Behind him in the doorway, a shadow moved.

Francine screamed and the man turned to the other shadow and they grabbed each other and fought in the small room. One man fell to the ground and tipped her pee bucket. The man standing tripped on a leg and fell on top of the other man with an 'oompf'. The contents splashed up into the air and onto the men grunting and grappling on the floor. The smell of her urine permeated the room.

The man who had freed her rolled the other man onto his back. In doing so, his hood fell back and exposed part of his jawline. He grunted and struggled to one knee. He pushed the other man flat to the ground with one hand and started punching him in the face with the other. Every punch, punctuated with grunts, was knocking the other man's head into the hardwood floor. The man on the floor cried out, "Stop! Stop it!"

The man who had un-cuffed her didn't stop. The scent of blood rolled over Francine erasing the smell of her waste in the tipped over bucket. In the weak light of the lamp, red spatter followed a hard thump. The hits kept coming until the man on the ground could only gurgle. The man stopped hitting him. Francine could hear his ragged breaths. Then the man on top tilted his head back and screamed until his breath ran out. Francine covered her ears again and ground her teeth. When the screams faded, Francine's hands dropped from her ears. The man was shaking. With the noises coming from him, Francine realized the man was crying.

·   ·   ·   ·   ·

The man pulled his hood up and turned toward Francine. He motioned for her to follow him and waiting until she heard his steps recede far enough away, she left the bed and tiptoed to the hallway. She heard the rattling breath of the man on the ground. She paused to look at his face but the poorly lit room and his bloodied and pulped features made him unrecognizable.

She poked her head out in the hallway and the hooded man waited for her at the bottom of a set of wooden stairs. When he noticed she saw him, he walked upstairs, his heavy tread creaking as they receded and he waited for her at the top. They made their way outside the house this way. She stood in the open back door, looking at the cold ground and wiggling the toes on her bare feet. The man was squatting in the snow in the backyard. He stood and walked towards her holding a piece of folded paper. He held it out to her and staring into the darkness of his hood, she pulled the paper from his grip. The blood on his gloves stained the paper but she took it anyway. On the front, she read, *Det. Reyes.* She noticed red blood droplets on the snow by his feet. He then pointed through a fence. She followed where he was pointing and saw part of her own house. It was the backyard of her home! She knew it because she could see the swing set her dad tried to assemble, couldn't and left it for her mother to do, which her mother could and did put together. It had a rainbow awning on it. Her mom had made the awning herself after finding the material at the Len's Mill Store. Home! And it was so close!

Francine turned back to him with the glow of the dawn lighting her smiling features. He waved for her to go. He then pointed to where his eyes would be in the hood and then pointed back to her house. She understood. He'd watch her get home. She said, "Thank you," and ran home, her bare feet crunching through the snow with the blanket wrapped tightly around her shoulders.

11

Everyone freaked out. Including Jodie. After returning to the RV from Graham's dejected and tired, Jodie had fallen asleep in the RV planning for the next day. The search parties were recalled when it got too dark and too cold to continue late into the night so Jodie looked over the areas that had been searched and was deciding where to move the groups next. She studied the GPS overlays of the group and planned a route for the groups that would be, in her opinion, the most effective. She also had an officer watching all the video they had copied from gas stations and convenience stores looking for strange vehicles, strange people or strange anything. She couldn't decide what the criteria for strange was and so the officer she chose to review the video was a local one. Reggie had left at nine in the evening after making sure the entire team had been fed and there was nothing more that he could do as a supervisor. The video officer had left shortly after Reggie and before she knew it, Jodie was sitting in the RV alone with a cold cup of coffee in front of her while trying to make sense of all the data they had acquired. Jodie remembered looking at her watch a little after one in the morning and then nothing else until a banging on the RV door woke her from a sleeping state into a confused one. At first, Jodie had no idea where she was. This wasn't her bed. Was that her drool on the table in front of her? The banging continued and she heard a tugging on the door handle and it all came back.

She wiped the side of her mouth, patted her hair and opened the door. The jerk officer from yesterday stood there, bouncing on the toes of his feet.

"She's home!"

"What?"

Yesterday he had been a sullen, rude man who didn't hide his prejudice very well. Today, he was smiling and for a brief second, Jodie forgot to dislike him.

"Francine's home!"

"Holy shit!"

The officer laughed, "Holy shit is right! Walked home and rang the doorbell and well, there you go."

• • • • •

Jodie fled into the washroom and cried. She hadn't realized how much she was worrying for the little girl until then. Most of the time, she'd been focused on how to get her back while in the back of her mind the clock was ticking. They were already past the time in which most abductors had killed the child they had taken and Jodie knowing that, fearing that would be the outcome based on the statistics, was working on her and adding to her stress. She splashed water on her face and stared at her wide eyed reflection. She patted her hands dry and deciding the lines from the awkward sleep running across her forehead weren't going away anytime soon, stepped out of the RV and walked to Francine's house.

A large crowd of people stood out front. Officers, news people, and neighbours alike, all were smiling, united in their relief. A carafe of coffee and cups were being handed around by a husband and wife and were received gratefully by the recipients. Jodie excused herself past a group on the driveway and knocked on the door. It swung open and Jodie recognized the face of the older brother, the one who had left the front door unlocked and before she could finish saying, "I'm Detective Reye..." he wrapped her in a hug and cried into her shoulder.

• • • • •

Jodie walked into the kitchen. Francine was sitting on the lap of her mother while her father, Terry, played with her hair. His quivering lips and shiny eyes made Jodie think that he was touching her like that to make sure she was real. Bernice, her face a wet mess, was rocking Francine back and forth and every few seconds, she'd kiss her on the cheek. The brother walked to stand beside Terry with his hand over his mouth and his eyes continuously leaking tears. Francine held the blanket tight around her and in one hand she clutched a white piece of paper. As Jodie moved closer she saw that it had her name on it.

"Hello. I'm Detective Reyes."

Jodie squatted in front of Francine and Bernice clutched her tighter.

Jodie pointed to the paper in Francine's hand and said, "Detective Reyes. That's me. I think that paper is for me."

Francine held it out to her and Jodie removed hospital gloves from her coat pocket (she never attended to any investigation without them) and slid one on. As Jodie reached to take the note, Francine said, "The man who saved me. He gave that to me."

Jodie, smiling said, "I'll take good care of it."

Jodie took the paper, stood and unfolded it. Her eyes scanned the neat block letters and when she came to the end of it, she ran out of Francine's home.

•   •   •   •   •

The letter provided the address of the house where Francine had been kept. The writer stated the police should get to the house quickly. The man who had taken Francine might be dead or he might have fled from the home. The police didn't have much time. Marshalling the crowd of officers on the front lawn, Jodie asked if any of the local officers knew the address. One of them, a tall woman with bright red hair pointed to a snow covered roof and said, "Yeah. It's right there."

Jodie said, "You lead, we'll follow."

The woman ran through Francine's backyard and out the gate at the back. Following behind Jodie saw small foot prints in the snow. They were smudged, as though by a pencil sketch artist's thumb and she said, "Don't ruin those prints!"

They continued after the woman for a short distance, the snow crunching under their feet, and their breath pluming above their heads, before the officer in front stopped outside a small, chain-link fence. The beige-bricked home had a thick carpet of snow on the roof. There were no lights on, but the back door stood wide open.

Jodie, exhaling a breath not from exertion but from her spiking adrenaline, opened the gate. The tall woman officer said, "Don't we need a warrant."

Jodie said, "No. Someone may be dying in there. We have to go. Have someone get an ambulance rolling."

Jodie glanced behind her. About six police officers and fifteen neighbours stood in a ragged group behind her. She pointed at the officer at the back of the group and said, "You stand by the gate, no one gets in." Pointing at another next to him, she said, "You go to the front, keep everyone off the property, got it!"

They both nodded. In a loud voice so the crowd could hear it, "Anyone coming onto this property without my say-so is to be arrested for obstruct, got me?"

The crowd groaned and Jodie, nervous about how long it took for the note to be found and how loud this crowd was becoming outside the house said, "The rest of the officers follow me and be careful where you step."

Jodie crossed the backyard, onto the back porch and stepped into the dark interior.

12

The floor creaked under her feet. Jodie winced. She wanted to be quiet in case the guy was still in the house, sitting in the corner of a dark room with a rifle pointed at an open doorway waiting for a person's chest to line up in the sights before pulling the trigger. She shook her head, thinking the people crowding outside and their blind run to this house had destroyed any possible stealthy approach. They had to go in fast.

Jodie said to the four officers behind her, "Two of you go upstairs and clear it. We'll wait here watching the main floor and guarding this exit until you get back before going further into the house."

They nodded and Jodie moved so they could walk past. They clomped up the stairs with their guns out and mouths open, breathing heavy. Jodie thought the officer at the back, the one with the stomach hanging over his gun belt better take it easy. His face shone red and glistened from the run over here and he still hadn't recovered his breath. Jodie turned her attention to the end of the hall, her gun pointed that way but held in a two-handed grip at the waist. She'd be able to fire that way and be accurate because of the stable grip and the narrowness of the hallway. And this way, her arms wouldn't get tired from holding the handgun out and away from her body.

Footsteps sounded above her head. She heard doors squealing open on old hinges and muttered curses. She turned her head to the tall woman officer behind her. She read the name tag on her vest: K. Bowles. Jodie heard a thump and someone upstairs say, "Fuck." Jodie rolled her eyes and Officer. K. Bowles smiled.

The heavier officer took his time coming back downstairs. He held onto the rail and the way he leaned on it, Jodie knew he needed it to keep him upright. Looking at his face, Jodie didn't think the guy was over thirty-years-old yet. Working his way towards a heart attack if he didn't start looking after himself soon. He blurted, "Nothing..."

Officer Bowles shushed him and the man's already red face turned a deeper shade.

Jodie nodded and leading off, they walked down the hallway away from the stairs. Shades covered all the windows. Weak daylight filtered in through the gaps but the house was dark the further in they went and Jodie took out her small flashlight and turned it on. She crossed her left hand with the flashlight over the hand with the gun. Now the light would follow her muzzle and add some stability as opposed to aiming with one hand. Dust drifted through the beam. The further into the home Jodie walked the scent of the place became stronger. It smelled like damp socks and old potatoes in a cupboard. She wrinkled her nose at the scent and wandered past a kitchen and into a living room. An empty aquarium sat on a half wall. A large TV, not a flat screen but the older kind with a tube inside and requiring four burly people to move it anywhere was sitting against a wall. A coffee table littered with dirty glasses and a bag of goldfish crackers within arms reach of the love seat in front of the older TV completed the room. A door stood open to the left of the TV. Stairs lead down.

Jodie tread down the stairs. She tested each step with her foot and eased her weight slowly onto the boards to minimize any creaks all basement stairs seemed to make. She reached the bottom. The creaking steps of the officers behind her stopped as Jodie glanced around the open room. Jodie saw wooden studs outlining rooms that were planned to be. Pink insulation and plastic covered the exterior walls. Photos were taped to the insulation. They were photos of children Francine's age. The pictures were taken at different places. Children at splash pads, at a park and outside of a school. A lot of different pictures and a lot of different kids. The kids weren't posing either. They weren't looking at the camera or seemed to be engaging with the person taking the picture at all. These pictures were taken by a watcher. By someone who didn't want the kids or the parents to know the pictures were even being taken. Right in the bottom corner, Jodie saw a picture of Francine.

Behind her, Officer Bowles said, "Jesus. That's my son there. Brady. What the fuck is my son doing there?"

Jodie said, "Let's go."

Jodie continued to shine her light around the basement until she found a hallway of unpainted drywall. She saw two doors. One of them was open.

Jodie stepped across the dusty floor, her gun and light pointed at the open door. She peered around the corner and saw a dresser with a lamp on it, a bed against the wall and a pair of handcuffs attached to a chain secured to an eyebolt secured to the concrete of the floor.

Jodie inhaled a deep breath and went to one knee to be lower in the doorway. Standing, if the man was in the room holding a gun, he'd be pointing at where her chest might be so she didn't want to be standing when she entered the room. She kept her flashlight high for that reason, to potentially trick him into aiming high. She moved into the room low and fast and was hit with the stench of blood. She had been to so many sudden death scenes and murder scenes, she knew the smell of blood. She wrinkled her nose and her beam lit upon a man lying on the floor. He was on his back and Jodie thinking he was dead and in the mean part of her mind, glad he was dead because fuck him, she started to holster her gun and the man coughed. Blood sprayed from his mouth in a mist and Jodie felt some of it land as a light spatter on her face. And once again she thought, *Fuck him*.

Jodie kicked everyone out of the crime scene and let the ambulance people in to collect Ned Grough, the kidnapper. The fire department wanted to come in as well because they were curious and gossipmongers, but Jodie forbid them entry. No one fucked up a crime scene more than the personnel of the fire department. Not only did they like tromping through a scene with their big boots, moon-eyed and mouth agape, they also enjoyed ripping down drywall for some reason. They made a real mess of any crime scene and if they didn't need to be in the home, no reason to let them near the place at all. Once Ned was out and safely on his way to the hospital with a police escort, the forensic identification officers descended with their evidence bags, swabs, and cameras. Francine was safe at home and now, because of the stranger, Ned's goose was cooked. While securing the scene and arranging for the identification officers and more resources, Jodie was also thinking about the good samaritan stranger. Jodie had a strong suspicion, bordering on certainty, that the mysterious stranger had been Graham. So far, there'd be no way to prove it.

After she left the scene, Jodie was driving home to have a shower and get some much-needed rest, and the more she thought about it, the more confident she was that the stranger was Graham. She didn't know why she was so certain, but she was. Especially after the formal interview with Francine under the watchful eye of her parents. While the forensic identification officers were doing their thing at the house, Jodie went back to Francine's home. With the permission of her parents, Jodie interviewed Francine using a video camera on a tripod. This was after Francine had been checked out by ambulance personnel. A follow-up doctor appointment was made for the following day. The interview was very interesting. Jodie couldn't help but comment on how brave Francine had been throughout the whole ordeal. The intriguing portion of the interview had to do with the mysterious stranger. Francine said she hadn't seen the man's face, not fully, but what she had seen made her think the shape of it was wrong. Jodie, leaning in asked what Francine meant by that. What did she mean when she said the shape was wrong? Francine couldn't explain what she meant by it being wrong, only that the shape was different. This vague yet perceptive description made Jodie think of Graham. Did Graham have an odd-shaped head? Check. Did Graham know he was a suspect in the disappearance of Francine? You bet. And did Graham, who lived out in the middle of nowhere, want anyone, especially the police, bothering him? Nope. How to make all that go away? Get Francine back, that's how. The problem with her theory was the how of it. How did he know where Francine was? How did he find her, free her and leave without leaving a trace of himself behind? There were no other fingerprints in the home other than Ned's and Francine's. So, Graham must have worn gloves. In the fight with Ned, even if Graham had bled and they collected that unsoiled sample somehow from the bloody mess left on the floor, Jodie would need a DNA warrant to get a sample of Graham's blood to compare to the blood at the scene. And how would they get that? What judge would sign an authorization to compel Graham to submit his DNA based upon the word of a traumatized little girl as evidence? She could ask Graham for a consent sample but why? What was the main goal here? What could she do? More importantly, should she even *do* anything? There is an alternative theory here. Graham could've been involved, felt that the cops were getting too close to him and wanted to return Francine to her home. When he went to the home to do that, he got into the fight with Ned because maybe Ned wasn't ready to return her. But, if that was the case, why didn't Graham just kill the guy? Why leave a witness behind who could put you in the cell right beside them for a long, long time? If you were going to abduct a child from her home, would you get squeamish about murdering your partner to prevent going to jail? Jodie never would have known where Francine had been held captive if he just dropped her off at home and left. And besides, Ned hadn't said anything about a partner. It could only help him in whatever deal he was trying to swing to stay out of jail and be the target of all other prisoners. Child predators were not well-liked in prison. They usually had to be placed in protective custody. He definitely would have told on a partner. It wouldn't make sense to stay silent on that information. And then there was the evidence. All the evidence of the offence was in Ned's home. Beside the computer in the basement was printed instructions on how to make your own chloroform. A DIY for rapists and child molesters. And on a table beside the computer desk were the ingredients and a capped bottle of homemade chloroform. From what she understood, it was tricky to get the mixture right. Ned had been lucky he hadn't killed Francine with it. Still, the stranger aspect was a problem.

The more Jodie mulled it over she knew she would have to investigate that avenue and show that she did all that she could to identify the stranger. If she didn't do that, the defence would suggest it had been the mysterious stranger who had been the kidnapper and had planted the evidence on Ned when the searches and the news coverage had made him nervous. Considering all of the evidence, it would be a ridiculous counter theory. But Ned was looking at a long, long time in jail and so the defence would be obligated to try anything. It would be better for her to close the door on that nonsense. So, Jodie would have to look into Graham. He was the only one in her mind who could have saved Francine. She had no evidence other than the unclear description of a scared little girl but she would have to try. Jodie had to admit, she was painfully curious to find out how Graham had located Francine. At this point though, that part of the investigation would have to wait. She still had a lot to tidy up at the scene and this would give her plenty of reason to forestall interviewing Graham again. All she had was a hunch and an indefinite description. She had nothing substantial, and besides, Graham wasn't going anywhere. In the end, it took her a week to clear up her investigative task list before she had the time to pay Graham a visit.

-13-

Jodie walked through the thick trees towards Graham's home kicking crusted snow so it dispersed into powder in front of her boots. Puffs of air escaped her mouth similar to an old-fashioned train fuelled by coal chugging along a rail line. Eyes were on her and not just those of the forest animals. She could feel them. Graham had cameras set up out here. She had seen the screens in his home.

Bright sun penetrated the tall spikes of trees. The white snow threw the light into her eyes and she was grateful for the sunglasses perched on her nose. She crested a small rise and on the other side stood Graham with an axe resting on his shoulder looking at her. A pile of wood lay about his feet, neatly chopped. Smoke from the chimney drifted lazily into the air and Jodie thought the scene would make a great cover for a romance novel about the lonely lumberjack in the woods hoping for love. Graham's damaged face ruined the illusion. He glared at her with one eye, the hood on his coat thrown back as though daring her to take a good, long look at him.

She smiled and taking her hands out her pockets eased her way down the slight decline to stand before him.

"Hello, Graham."

He nodded. No smile, no warmth of any kind.

"It sure is cold out."

No response.

"Well, aren't you going to invite me in?"

He sighed and swung the axe blade into the chopping log. He turned his back to her and said over his shoulder, "C'mon then."

•   •   •   •   •

Again in the kitchen. Graham placed a cup of coffee in front of Jodie, picked his cup off the counter and sat across from her. Jodie glanced at his hands holding the mug. The knuckles were bruised and raised on the right hand. On his left hand were dotted-line scratches. Graham saw her glancing at his hands and a corner of his lips lifted briefly and then returned to being a straight line in his face.

"What can I do for you officer?"

Jodie removed a voice recorder from her pocket, held it up and said, "Do you mind?"

Graham said, "No."

She placed it on the table between them and hit the record button. She stated the date, time, where they were and who was present. She asked him if she was coercing him to speak with her. He said she wasn't. Did he understand he could conclude the interview at any time and that the interview was voluntary? He did.

Jodie said, "So. I don't know if you heard the good news but little Francine has been found and is safe at home."

Graham pointed to the portable radio by the sink, "I heard."

"Do you know the details of how she was found?"

"A good Samaritan found her? Something like that."

Jodie nodded and said, "Yes. Something like that. The same night we talked to you."

Graham sipped his coffee.

Jodie said, "Aren't you curious how this person found her?"

Graham shrugged.

"I am. And not just because it's my job. Countless cops and volunteers running around searching for little Francine, and nothing. This guy finds her, or knew where she was, and the best part is, instead of calling the cops he breaks in there, beats on the guy holding Francine, puts the guy in the hospital actually with a broken orbital bone, some fractured ribs, then points Francine in the right direction to get home and poof! The Good Samaritan disappears. Have you ever heard such a crazy thing?"

"I've seen crazier."

Jodie, eyes flitting to the hole where Graham's eye used to be, nodded.

She said, "Can you offer any reason why the guy wouldn't call the police?"

"Why would I know anything about that?"

"I think your insight would be invaluable."

"Again, why do you think that?"

"I'm just curious as to what you think about it all. We were at your house one night, and the next morning, Francine shows up at home. I want to know if you can think of any reason why this person wouldn't call the police?

The person would be at no risk. An anonymous phone call, that's all it would have taken."

"I have no idea why this person did anything. No insight. Nothing."

"Nothing?"

"Nothing."

Jodie said, "There are two reasons, in my mind, why a guy wouldn't call the cops and wouldn't stick around afterward. One: the guy wants nothing to do with anyone. A real loner. The type of guy who builds a home in the woods that no roads lead to. But still, that person could have placed an anonymous call." She smiled at him and continued, "Two: the guy was a partner in the deal. He didn't call the cops because we would ask all of the questions we like to ask so we can understand. And if the guy stuck around, we might find out he was involved after all and then, well, that wouldn't be good for that guy would it?"

"I don't care either way since I'm not either one of them. However, I do prefer direct questions. From what I understand of interviews, someone asks questions and someone answers. I haven't heard a lot of questions from you. Just statements."

"Alright. Your hands. How'd you hurt them?"

"I do all the maintenance around here. Building, repairing, chopping wood." He shrugged and said, "It happens."

"Did you find and rescue Francine?"

"No."

"She described the man who saved her as having distinct features. She said the shape of his face was weird. What do you think of that?"

"Nothing. Sounds to me like the guy could have been wearing a mask. Since he didn't want his identity known, it would make more sense if he had worn one."

Jodie smiled. Mask. She hadn't thought of that.

"One last question, if you had any information about this crime, would you share it with police?"

"Yes."

"Unless you have any questions, that concludes our interview."

"I have no questions."

Jodie turned off the recorder. She said, "Can we go off the record here?"

Graham sighed and folded his arms, "What do you want?"

Jodie sipped her coffee and placed it down. She leaned forward and said, "Look, I'm not here as a cop. Well, yeah I am, but right now, not really. I didn't actually expect you to tell me anything. Not with all the elaborate steps taken to remain anonymous. You're a loop I had to close and I closed it. I don't think you had anything to do with Francine's disappearance, okay?"

"Okay."

"But I am dying here. I need to know how you did it?"

"Did what?"

She smiled and said, "I know it was you. And it was fucking awesome."

Graham didn't move. He sat as a statue, staring at her from his one dark eye. When she didn't continue, he shook his head and stood saying, "I have a lot of work to do and I'd appreciate it if you'd leave."

"How did you find her? Half the town, police officers trained in searches, canine dogs and even drones couldn't find her, but you did. How?"

"Maybe I wasn't being direct enough. Please. Get out of my house."

Jodie stood and picked up her coat from the back of the chair. She put it on and said, "Graham. I'm not here to arrest you..."

He laughed and then grimaced, sucking air through clenched teeth.

"Are you okay?"

"I get headaches. Now go."

"Okay, okay." She backed towards the front door and she thought if she left she'd never know and it was too much so she started talking, trying to convince him of her intentions to learn and she realized she was babbling, but the door was getting closer and if she walked out, he'd never let her back in so she talked to forestall what she knew to be inevitable; her ejection. She said, "I just need to know how you did it. I've been thinking about it all week and I know you want to be left alone and I'm here as, uh, as a person, not a cop, because you did something wonderful and you don't want the world to know and you know how rare that is? Everyone wants their fifteen minutes, hell, the whole world seems to chase that dream and it's like people don't do good things anymore just because they are good, no, they want a payoff of some sort. They want a pat on the head, a parade and some cash in hand. But you, you find a girl that would have been murdered, that would have had terrible things done to her before she died and you want...nothing. That's amazing to me."

"Your boots are on the mat."

She slipped on one boot and continued, "But that's not the only amazing part. I don't have any idea how you found her. None at all and I think that if I don't know, it'll bug me for the rest of my life. I swear, whatever you tell me, stays with me. I won't tell anyone. I respect your privacy."

He raised his eyebrows at her and she put up a hand and said, "I know, I know, me being here and not leaving kind of means I don't respect your privacy, but I had to show up at some point. It's my job after all. But don't you see? I have to know."

"I don't care."

He reached past her and opened the door. The gust of wind pushed snow across the mat. She slipped on her other boot and handed him a card from her pocket and said, "I'm sorry. I'm sorry for coming out here and bothering you. Take my card. And if you want, you can call me and you know, invite me next time."

He took the card and nodded at the open door.

"I mean what I say, Graham. If you told me something, I wouldn't tell anyone. My word means something."

"I know it does Detective."

"Jodie."

"Alright. I know it does Jodie."

"Unless of course, you told me you murdered someone or something along those lines, then you know, I'd have to do something. Just, I don't know, I can be a good friend Graham. We all need friends."

"I don't. Goodbye Jodie."

She stepped out and he closed the door behind her. He watched her walk away and when she passed over the hill and out of sight, he smiled. She was amusing and as far as people went, he didn't mind her. He returned to the kitchen, swallowed a couple of Tylenol and got back to work.

14

Graham woke early every day with a headache threatening to ruin it. To prevent the headache from morphing into a debilitating migraine, he followed a routine. And he followed it this morning. He woke up and stared at the ceiling, thinking about the list of chores he had to do. He rolled out of bed, stood, stretched and walked into the kitchen and turned on the coffee maker. He poured himself a glass of water, placed two Tylenol in his mouth and washed them down. He shook the container. A few rattled inside. He would have to get more soon. That meant another trip into town. He sighed.

After a quick shower, Graham ate oatmeal with brown sugar and raisins while drinking a coffee, listening to the radio and reading a paperback. He used to be able to read for hours at a time. After the incident though, he could only read for half an hour to forty minutes before his head would begin to ache. Then he would need a few hours off before he could read again. He folded a page down and put the book on the table. He cleaned up his dishes and the general mess that comes along with any meal and reviewed his list of today's jobs he needed to do. He'd cut enough wood for the furnace to last him another month or so. He should check on the solar array and the batteries. If the solar panels weren't pointed just right, he'd lose efficiency and he wanted his buffer batteries to always be full. He couldn't afford to be inefficient. He had purchased a software program that moved the solar panels so that they followed the arc of the sun for optimal efficiency and so far, it was working. He would have to keep on top of it though and he might as well make sure the wiring was still good. One time, he'd found a cable gnawed on until the wires showed under the plastic coating. The poor animal probably that had done the chewing must have had a nasty shock.

After he checked on his electrical energy, he would look after his hydroponic garden. In one of his sheds, he had constructed a makeshift greenhouse. Inside were long cylindrical tubes with the components needed to grow his plants and fruits. The tubes had proven to take up less space and optimized his yield. With trial and error (mostly error), he had perfected his garden and even though it took up hours of his time almost daily to maintain it, he enjoyed it. It kept his brain still. Thoughts on improving his set up prevented memories of THAT TIME from creeping up on him. Waking up in the hospital with tubes everywhere, machines beeping, strange faces behind half masks and why couldn't he see from one side of his face? Trying to ask questions, wanting to know what was going on, except there was something wrong with his face. His jaw wouldn't work, his tongue felt strange and swollen in his mouth and why wouldn't anyone answer him? And then the anger, out of nowhere, spilling out him and compelling him to get up and pull at the wires and wanting to know and trying to ask, WHERE WAS HIS FAMILY? WHY WAS EVERYONE TRYING TO HOLD HIM DOWN? And the rage overcoming him until blackness crowded the edges of his vision, throbbing with his frenetic heartbeat, and in the centre of his circular sight, the nurse who wouldn't listen to him, who just wanted to hold him down and put him back to sleep oh, how he hated him. He remembered his hands reaching for the nurse with the bald head and sweaty upper lip, wanting to grab that nurse's head between his hands and squeeze, squeeze, squeeze until his eyeballs popped out of his skull because FUCK HIM and his non-answers. Before his hands could clamp onto the nurses head, the nurse stumbled back, glaring at Graham with terror swollen eyes and then more people rushed in to hold him down and plunge a dripping needle into his arm.

He shivered at the table. Push those thoughts away. Swipe them off the screen of your mind. You have work to do.

He dressed and stepped outside. On the front step sat a package. Graham frowned and looked around him, searching through the bare branches of trees, not sure what he was looking for, maybe another person wanting to catch sight of the freak and snap a photo to plaster across the internet. The anger rose up from his stomach. He closed his eye and breathed. He imagined the rage seeping out of him with every exhale. With calm reasserted and a tiny pulse of pain behind his eye to signal the onset of another headache, he picked up the package and walked back inside to the kitchen. He set the plain brown box with tape across the top of the table. Graham tore off the tape and opened the box. A book, *Cuckoo's Calling* by Robert Galbraith rested inside. Under it sat a note:

I saw you had all the Harry Potter books by J.K. Rowling and it became clear to me that you have excellent taste. I'd be inclined to believe you are a

Shaking his head, Graham understood Jodie would become a pest. He
didn't know whether to smile or scowl. He did neither. He went back to
work.

• • • • •

In the evening, Graham made dinner using the components from his
garden. Tomatoes, leafy greens and potatoes were tossed into a salad. He
added tofu for the protein and added a nice balsamic. The last two items he
purchased from the store and he didn't like that. He was striving for self-
sufficiency here. He resolved to learn how to make his own tofu and dressing
at some point. He hated going into town. After the incident at the mall,
Graham could no longer eat meat. Couldn't stand the smell of it and the one
time he tried to force himself to eat some bacon (because who doesn't like
bacon?) he gagged it down and within minutes he was puking it back out.
He didn't understand why. And no doctor could tell him either. There was
nothing physically preventing him from eating meat. It hurt his head to
think of it and so he didn't.

With a glass of water by his elbow, he ate with the radio playing in the
background. Outside his window, snow drifted to the ground in thick flakes.
Graham liked the way the snow lightened up the night. The white on the
ground caught the moonlight and gave the snow a blue luminescence he
thought quite beautiful. In the summer months, it would be dark outside.
The earth and trees swallowed what light the moon spilled from the heavens
and most times all he would catch would be his own reflection in the
window and he didn't want to see that. On the counter under the window
sat the book from Jodie. He didn't want to read it. It would be like
consenting to her showing up and intruding into his life. He knew he would
read the book though. Graham didn't know what to do about Jodie. She
wouldn't be going away. She had the stubborn set to her eyes Graham knew
all too well. Meghan wore the same expression. He had no idea how to make
Jodie go away but what bothered him more was that he wasn't sure if he did
want her to get out of his life. There was nothing romantic in the notion.

That inclination had been shot out of him. Graham did appreciate intelligence and good humour and Jodie possessed both in ample amounts. And for some reason, his head didn't hurt around her, not in the way it did around so many other people.

He put down his fork, stood, grabbed the book and sat down again. Opening the front cover, he read the summary inside. J.K. Rowling, huh? He was definitely going to read it. Damnit. He didn't want anyone in his life. Not anymore. Did reading the book mean he would have to let her into his life? It was just a book, right? He needed to talk to someone. So Graham called the one person who had all the answers. And if she didn't, he'd at least be pointed in the right direction. He called his mom.

"Let's recap shall we?" His mother, Sonya said after he told her his problem. No phone line reached where he lived and cell phone reception was non-existent. Graham had to buy a satellite phone. It was expensive and he bought it for emergency purposes. The thought behind the purchase was to have a number in case his parents needed him or his ex-in-laws needed him for something. He didn't talk to either group much. It hurt his head to talk to people. From the pain came the rage. He didn't trust he could control himself when the anger rode through him. He thought of the dinner he had at his parents after he had been released from the hospital. They made him a meatless meal because he'd been complaining about the smell of meat when he was in the hospital. His parents drank wine. He drank coffee. He couldn't remember what it was they were speaking about. It was something stupid though, something that shouldn't have caused him to get so angry but then he couldn't control it. The rage rolled over him in waves, crashing against and dismantling his control. He remembered being enraged at his dad. He wanted to stab him in the chest with the butter knife by his hand. What had his dad said? He couldn't remember, even now. Graham did know that whatever his father had said, it had made him mad, so mad he broke the ceramic mug in his fist. The hot coffee spilled over his hand, shards of the mug dug into his hand spilling blood droplets onto the tablecloth. His dad stood on shaky legs and clamped his head with his hands with gritted teeth shiny and huge like piano keys. His dad grunted, a stream of drool shot from his mouth and he dropped to the floor. Graham blacked out at the table, his face dropping to the plate with a crack. What had his mom thought at the time? The two men in her life collapsing in front of her. When Graham woke up with one killer of a headache, an ambulance worker was shining a light in his eye while they secured his dad to a gurney and rushed him to the hospital. The doctor said his dad had suffered a stroke. No lasting damage had been done but it took the doctors awhile to make that assessment, but still, Graham was grateful that he hadn't crippled his dad. They suggested his dad change his diet. But Graham knew it hadn't been a stroke. It was another thing he could do. A new and terrible thing. But it wasn't so new, was it? There had been that nurse. The one who stumbled back from him when he woke up in the hospital with terror shining from his eyes. From that moment at the hospital with his dad hooked up to beeping machines, Graham knew he couldn't be around people. Even those he loved weren't safe around him. When he told his parents what he would be doing, moving out into the middle of the woods, they did the normal parent thing. Instead, they wanted him to move near them, be closer, spend more time together. Except for his dad. Although his dad said he wanted him around, he didn't mean it. He felt what Graham had done. Although he couldn't explain it and wouldn't say it out loud because it sounded crazy, his father knew Graham was responsible for his stroke and he was afraid of Graham. Graham needed to be on his own. He needed to keep away from people because he was dangerous.

More significant, his isolation helped him deal with his guilt. He wouldn't have to look at his parents and know he wasn't strong enough to protect their grandchild. And his in-laws? Not only did he survive the death of their grandchild, he survived the death of their daughter. Deep down he knew they didn't see him that way and it was a manifestation of his own guilt projected onto them. Didn't matter. The guilt was real enough for Graham.

Sonya continued, "We have a young lady who thinks you're someone she'd like to know. A young lady who doesn't make your head hurt, right?"

"Right."

"Not like your dear mother does anyway..."

"Mom..."

"Or your father."

Silence. He didn't like to think about the dinner. Sensing his unease, Sonya deflected and said, "How does that work again? How do I make your head hurt?"

"It's hard to explain, I see things..."

"Oh that's right, you see emotions. Like colours or something right?"

"Not exactly."

"Did I mention I know a wonderful therapist?"

Graham was starting to regret calling his mother. He said, "Mom..."

"Alright. Fine. Back to this young lady. Would it be so bad to have a friend? Everyone needs a friend."

"That's what she said."

"Did she? She's smart too. So, can you explain the problem to me because I'm not seeing one."

"I...I don't know. I'm afraid I guess."

"Is that all? Hardly seems like a reason at all."

"I don't know if she wants to be my friend. It's more complicated than that. It's like she wants something from me. And being my friend is the only way she can get it."

"How did you meet this young lady detective? Did you find that little girl? I saw something about it on the news. Young girl rescued by a mysterious stranger. Quite a story. Was that you?"

He didn't want to talk about that. His mother knew portions of what he saw and because he was unsure of it himself, the reality of it, he didn't feel comfortable sharing that with anyone. Not even his mom. "I..."

"I knew it. That had you written all over it. That was a great thing you did. Almost heroic..."

He groaned, "Jeez mom, you're killing me here."

"Settle down. Of course, she's interested in you. Anyone in her position would be."

"But she's not interested in me. She's interested in what she thinks I can do. Like I'm some sideshow freak or something, like all those media fuckers with their cameras and their fucking questions and their..."

"Language, dear. Breathe please."

The anger came upon him like that at times. Snuck up on him like a lion to its prey. Unknown and unfelt until the moment it struck. He inhaled through his nose. A headache lurked on the horizon.

Sonya said, "So what if she wants something from you? That's what people do, my dear. All relationships are based on personal gain. To think otherwise is juvenile and naive wouldn't you say? And that's not a bad thing. Sometimes the thing you seek in another is something you're trying to find in yourself. And sometimes it's as simple as needing to feel present. Do you know what I mean by that? By being present?"

"Yes. Being present is like being real."

"Exactly. A person cannot live in a vacuum. Not in a healthy way. So if she wants something from you, let her try to find it. Maybe you'll find something in her of value although I suspect you already have. Otherwise, you wouldn't have called me. So call her. Meet her for coffee. Do something. Don't be the creepy hermit in the woods. So cliche."

"I'll think about it. Thanks."

Before hanging up she extracted a promise from him to call her in a week or so to update her on his decision. He went to bed, opened the book Jodie had left for him and started to read it.

15

Jodie read through her file at home. Coffee cooled at her elbow as she scanned the reports on her computer with a pair of reading glasses perched on the end of her nose. The Crown attorney had read through the Francine file and was starting to send all the follow-up requests that Jodie, being the primary investigator, would be responsible for supplying. She wrote down the ones she would need to look after and forwarded an email to the Forensic Identification unit requesting the reports the Crown was seeking. She smiled. The Forensic guys were usually behind a few months on reports. Their specialized training required detailed reports that took some time to complete. They would not be happy with having to rush the reports on the Francine file for the Crown and she pictured her one friend in the unit, Trevor, throwing up his hands, cursing and threatening to leave the unit and go back to pushing a cruiser and slogging calls. He never would. He loved what he did and was good at it, but he did like to put on a show every once in a while.

Her cell phone trilled on the desk. She glanced at it. Unknown number. Usually, that meant a call from work. Most of the higher-ups had cell phones with blocked caller ID. Jodie had the same feature on her phone.

"Hello?"

"I'm looking to speak with Detective Reyes."

The measured speech, slurred tongue, Jodie knew who it was and smiled. She said, "Graham. How are you?" It had been almost two weeks since she had left the book at his front door. She thought he would have called sooner if he was going to and when he didn't, she hadn't expected him to call at all.

"I'm fine. I'm calling to let you know you were right."

"Right? About what?"

"The book. It was good."

"Great! I'm glad you liked it. Normally, I hate detective type novels because they are so often wrong but this one, it's hard not to like Cormoran isn't it?"

"Yes."

Silence. Two people letting an awkward quiet grow. Graham said, "Well, I wanted to thank you…"

Jodie jumped in, "I have the other two books lying around here. You want me to bring them by? Maybe have a cup of coffee?"

"Uh, Yes."

"When would be a good time for you?"

"Doesn't matter. I'll be here."

"Okay. How about…" Jodie squinted at her work calendar on the wall and said, "Sunday morning? Is that good for you?"

"Yes."

"Great. I'll see you then."

"Yes. Okay."

He hung up. She frowned at the phone in her hand, shrugged and drank her coffee. She felt a tingle in her gut and looking forward to Sunday, found the two books and stacked them by the front door to be sure she wouldn't forget them. She even added a new appointment in the calendar on her phone with an alert to remind her.

PART TWO: SUMMER

—1—

Claire, known as Violet to her clients, was picked up in Scarborough, in front of a convenience store by four men in a Dodge mini-van. She was told to sit in the back and she squished in beside an effeminate man named Mickey. In front of them were three men, two up front and one seated on the middle bench seat. The driver wore a dirty ball cap and a heavy beige coat. Beside him, a heavy man wore a blue tank top, the shoulders white and forearms a sunburnt red. Perched high on his head was a *Bass Pro Shops* cap. The one in the middle wore a *Blue Jays* cap and a red T-shirt underneath a jean jacket. Looking at them, Claire thought, *Shit-kickers...great.* Guns n' Roses *Sweet Child of Mine,* played over the speakers at a low volume. The inside of the van, although clean and newer looking, smelled of oil.

The one in the middle spoke to her and Mickey. He had an unlit cigarette hanging from the corner of his mouth. Claire didn't like him. Her likes and dislikes didn't matter too much in her job but she'd seen enough assholes in her time to pick them out pretty quick. Her danger meter had been fluttering the second the guy on the middle bench turned around in his seat to talk to them. Maybe other people found him charming, Mickey didn't seem to mind him, but he had a look to him that made Claire think of a nature show she'd once seen of a python swallowing a rabbit. It had crushed the rabbit first, wrapping itself around the struggling animal with its liquid-like moving coils. The rabbit's eyes protruded and the snake stared at it, a flatness there calmer than a small pond on a windless day. With the same dead eyes, the snake opened its mouth and pulled the rabbit into its maw. The back paws of the rabbit twitched. The snake's eyes reflected nothingness. Under the man's eyes talking to her and Mickey, she felt like that rabbit.

They talked for some time, the songs changing as they continued on the highway, the unlit cigarette or as her stepfather had called them, coffin nails, dangling from his lip.

Claire asked, "Aren't you going to smoke that?"

"Nah, the jerks up front don't like it."

Mickey said, "Either do I."

Smiling, the man said to Mickey, "Who asked you?"

Although delivered with a smile, the statement contained an undercurrent of violence. The man held Mickey's eyes. Mickey turned away from the glare.

Seeing a passing sign, Claire frowned and said, "Where are we going?"

The man in the middle said, "To my house."

"I thought we were going to a local hotel. That was the deal. We go to a hotel, have our fun and then you take us to the nearest subway."

Raising one eyebrow, the man said, "The deal has changed."

Claire, not liking the man's lizard eyes and his friend's silence up front, realized she might be in some real trouble here. Her voice shaking, she said with a placating smile, "Oh yeah? That'll cost you more you know. I don't make house calls. I sure as shit don't leave the city. I don't know about Mickey here but I certainly don't. A girl can't be too careful you know? So although you guys were going to pay me well, I'm going to have to say no to the new deal. If you could drop me at the nearest subway station, that'd be great."

The man laughed, "Hear that? She's telling us the deal is off!" To Mickey, he said, "How about you pretty boy? You don't like the new deal?"

The words themselves held no animosity and Mickey watched Violet (Claire had introduced herself as Violet) and the man talking, a line drawn between his eyebrows because something was going on here. Something he wasn't seeing but he could sense it. A tenseness in the van. The driver turned the volume on the music down. Mickey didn't care about the old deal or the new deal. He needed the money. He needed meth. His body and mind wanted it. If the new deal meant he could get more money to appease the itch for an even longer time then he was all for it. Mickey said, "Whatever. I'm good."

The man laughed again, "You're good? I'm glad. I really am. I was worried we were about to be turned down by both of you. That would hurt my feelings terribly. A couple of prostitutes turning us down? You'd have to be a special kind of pitiful if that happened."

They continued in silence. The man in the middle with the half smile on his face, shifted around in his seat so he could keep an eye on them. Them wasn't right, though. He wasn't looking at them. He was staring at her. Her hands clenched tighter on her purse. She could feel her phone in the thin bag and feeling it gave her comfort in the same way seeing a life buoy on a boat would. They passed the next exit, the one for Yorkdale plaza. The plaza had a main subway hub attached.

Claire said, "You passed my exit."

"Did we?"

"Yeah, you did. Remember? The subway?"

The man frowned and said, "Now that you mention it, I do remember you saying you wanted off this ride. What I don't remember is the point in our travels where you became the boss. Now, you said you wanted to be dropped off at the next subway station and I do remember you saying that quite clearly, but I don't give a fuck what you want little lady. Not one bit. We're going to get our money's worth out of you two. Yes, we will." And then he winked at her. The danger meter zipped into the red zone with the wink. If a wink could convey evil intent, well, this man had perfected said wink.

Smiling, she said, "Look, I've had this happen before. Picked up, taken out of the city, the evening is over and guess what? I'm out of the fucking city and does my date want to take me home? Hell no. When they drop their cream, they go to sleep and dream."

The man laughed loud at that little quip. A real belly-shaking kind of laugh. The cigarette jumped around on his lip and then popped right off. That made him laugh louder and his friends in the front of the van joined him. *They sound like a pack of hyenas*, thought Claire and then, *Oh god, how am I going to get out of this one?* Because she knew this was something more than a little slap, tickle and greasy cash. These men had other plans. She clutched the phone through her purse tighter in her hands. Keeping her hands in her lap and out of sight of the man, she slipped one hand inside to pull out the phone.

"Goddamn, that was clever. Made me lose the cigarette right out of my mouth." And seeing her shoulders move while she offered a frozen smile he said, "What you doing there, missy?" He leaned over the back of the seat. He sat back, shaking his head. "We can't have that. No. We can't have that at all. Hand it over now."

"My purse?"

"Yeah. Your purse. And you too Mickey."

Mickey said, "I don't have a purse."

"Your phone man. Give me your goddamn phone."

"Why?"

The man moved fast. Claire heard a whap and in her peripheral saw

Mickey's head snap back. Not until the hit did she notice the man's fist retracting. She hadn't seen it coming. Neither had Mickey. She turned to Mickey to see his hands bordering his nose. Blood leaked down his chin and in the darkness of the van and the passing sodium lights, it looked like black liquid, like ink.

"What the fuck, man!"

With uncanny speed, the man slapped Mickey on the side of the head. Blood sprayed on Claire's hand. She felt the warmness of it.

With teeth clamped tight the man said, "Give me your phone. And you too, little lady. I want both of your phones and I want them now. "

Claire, her teeth clacking from the sudden fear coursing through her handed over her phone with shaky hands. Mickey's phone followed.

To Claire, he said, "I want your purse too."

After seeing what happened to Mickey when he asked why she passed her purse to him. He searched through her purse and once satisfied he handed it back to her but kept her phone.

"Just wanted to make sure you didn't have a knife or gun in there."

Mickey, offended said, "What about me? I could have a knife on me. In one of my pockets."

"Do you?"

"No."

"Good. Besides, if you pulled a knife on me I'd stick it up your ass sideways."

"Oh."

"Yeah. Oh."

The man handed the two phones to the passenger. Over the man's shoulder, she saw the passenger doing something with them in his lap. The window rolled down a small crack. Hot air filled the air-conditioned interior. Four pieces were pushed out the gap. Four pieces? Claire realized he pulled the batteries off of the phones. Her guts churned. A tear rolled out of her right eye. The man saw it and reached over and brushed it away with his thumb. A gentle touch. He smiled at her the entire time. Claire shivered. She was in the shit this time.

Bruce and Lynda with a 'y' as she was fond of telling everyone she introduced herself to, lived in a small town named Kauffman's Vale. There was no vale or valley to speak of. When the town had been established in 1904, the people settling there were predominately German and they just liked the way vale sounded. The name gave the impression the town was a pretty place and in the summer, it could be. Dark trees surrounded the city and the scent of pine and earth always hung in the air. Beautiful purple, yellow and white wildflowers grew wherever they could, dotting hills and ditches with a pastoral aesthetic any painter would love to capture on a canvass. There were two streets in the town that bisected exactly in the centre. The town's founders wanted the city to grow outwards from there until it became a booming metropolis to rival Toronto. It didn't because although the summer days could be nice and the scenery beautiful and idyllic, the winters were brutal, unrelenting and not worth the one and a half months of warm weather you might get in the summer. Kaufmann's Vale sat right in the middle of a cold belt. The geography of the land funnelled the cold air from the great white north to the town and it would settle in quickly causing snow to fall at an alarming rate and generally cause town-wide misery. When the short summer ended you would spend the rest of the year bundled up from head to foot in thick clothing. The snow piles on either side of the driveway grew taller than most people and if you didn't have a snowblower, you were in for an awfully long sore-lower-back kind of winter. The main reason the town didn't collapse was because of its location. Smack dab between Sudbury and North Bay, the townsfolk didn't have too long of a commute to either city and the roads were well maintained and plowed regularly for inter-city travel. For someone who didn't want to live in a small home on an even smaller lot of land, Kauffman's Vale was ideal. A person could buy a two thousand square foot home on an acre of land for half of what you'd have to pay for that in Sudbury or North Bay. If you didn't mind the snow and the cold, it would be perfect. The trouble with the small town was there wasn't a hell of a lot to do. There were excellent snowmobile trails, cross-country ski trails, eight hockey rinks and a good sized pond for those inclined to ice fish. But those activities cost money and not all of the people could afford such luxuries. So for the young people in town when they were bored, they'd drink, smoke drugs and have sex. Consequently, there happened to be a lot of young mothers in Kauffman's Vale.

Bruce had an opportunity to play in the Ontario Hockey League which was a stepping stone to the big show, the NHL. In order to realize his dream, he didn't drink (much), never did drugs, didn't have a snowmobile or a fishing rod and so the only form of entertainment left to him that wouldn't mess up his chances to be drafted was sex. Provided he didn't get someone pregnant. That would be one hell of a speed bump on his road to potential riches but being a teenager, that wasn't much of a deterrent. He'd be careful and he knew he could rely on his girlfriend Lynda to be the same.

Lynda wanted to have sex with Bruce but worried he might do something stupid, like ask her to marry him or something. He was a bit of a silly romantic. If everything worked out for him, and she hoped it did, he would be leaving to play hockey in another town. She wouldn't be going with him because that would be absurd. She knew the statistics on high school sweethearts and marriage. They were dismal and truthfully, Lynda didn't think she even wanted to get married. Why would you need a license and a ring to be with someone? Just be with them. Simple. And she liked her last name. She didn't want to give that up for anybody. What for? It seemed so outdated, like you take the man's last name which to her, implied ownership. Subtle implication but to Lynda, it was there all the same. Must have been thought up by a man. So although marriage and pregnancy were out of the question, sex with Bruce was not. He was fit, good looking and for a popular jock, he also happened to be a nice guy. Not a bad choice considering the other barbaric teenage alternatives. She didn't want to go to university a virgin. They had petted each other in the back of his mom's Toyota SUV and once she showed him what to do to her and not to grab and stroke so hard as though he was trying to rub her clitoris off, it was nice. Really nice. She was ready for the big event and she told him so.

They had told their parents they were going into Sudbury to catch a movie. That would give them at least four hours of alone time. Bruce's dad offered him his car, a Honda Civic but he wanted his mom's SUV (he thought he'd need the room in the back) and his mom tossed him the keys and told him to at least not bring the beast back empty. Bruce stuffed the keys in his front pocket and feeling the condoms there, he put them in the other pocket. He didn't want to poke a hole in them by accident. He shivered at the thought.

He picked up Lynda and they drove to the Tim Horton's and got coffee, bagels, and timbits before driving to their spot. Bruce's mom was an accountant who worked from home. She also dabbled in real estate on the side. She was handling a property in town, a small house on a big lot. The owner had passed away and now the family wanted to sell it. No one lived there. Her mom had the lawn mowed regularly and the home's heat and electricity going to keep the air conditioning on for the potential buyers to walk through without sweating through their clothes. Lights on a timer made potential robbers think someone might be home and they'd be on now, shining yellow light from the windows and above the garage making a glowing halo around the home. The driveway was long and dark and screened from the road by big evergreens. The perfect spot for their romantic interlude. They wouldn't go into the house because that would be wrong and also because Bruce didn't know the code for the alarm. They'd park in the driveway, eat their food and drink their coffee and engage in awkward, nervous small talk while both thinking of what they were about to do. They were going to do 'it'. And that was supposed to be a big deal. And they would both treat it as such.

•   •   •   •   •

They were going at the preliminaries fairly well. They were making out to the hum of the air conditioner. It was a wonderful hot summer night without a cloud in the night sky to diminish the brilliance of the stars overhead. Mid-July weather and both of them were looking forward to a summer of backseat fun provided tonight went well. Bruce kept trying to French kiss Lynda because he thought it'd be cooler and turn her on more except he had coffee breath. Every time he slipped his tongue in her mouth she suppressed an urge to gag. Instead, she disengaged and put her lips by his ear and pressed her cheek to his.

"Ok. I'm ready. You have the condoms right?"

"Does the Pope wear a pointy hat?"

She rolled her eyes and said, "Just get them already."

Leaning away from her and reaching into his pocket he said, "I got them right here."

He held one up, the shiny wrapper reflecting the glowing lights from the house. He grinned and waggled his eyebrows and she laughed, happy in the moment, excited to be finally doing 'it' and with someone as cool as Bruce. Her fingers pushed back his hair and he put his hand on hers. Behind Lynda, a face appeared in the window.

All at once, Bruce screamed, Lynda flinched, a hand banged on the window behind her head and a voice screamed, "Please help me!"

Claire estimated that they had driven close to four hours north. She could see the time on the dashboard clock over the man in the middle's shoulder. It was a long, awkward and silent drive with Claire staring out the window and Mickey scratching the small red scabs on the inside of his forearms until his arms were a red mess. The blood from his nose had dried all over his face. He had to breathe through his mouth because his nose was swollen and clogged. Claire couldn't think of a way out of this, whatever this was. Scared, she turned over ideas in her mind and rejected them before they could form. She thought of getting the attention of other motorists but couldn't think of how. The windows didn't roll down at the back and even if they did, the man with the fast hands would be on her in an instant. She considered scrambling over the seat and if by some miracle she made it past the man in the middle, maybe she could yank the wheel, cause an accident so the cops would have to show up. Traveling on a highway at one hundred kilometres an hour the accident would more than likely result in her death. She didn't want to die. There had been times when she thought of where she was in life and because she couldn't see a way of getting out of selling her body to stay off the streets, sure, she thought of taking her own life. Especially after a client left her, leaving the spent condom on a side table in whatever hotel hell she happened to be in on top of the cash paid to her. The client fucking her twice by leaving the goopy mess on top of the money like that. To any client, she was an itch that needed to be scratched and that was all. She had no other value than the hole between her legs. You don't get feeling that worthless without also thinking about ending your life. Uselessness and death. The two ideas hold hands in your head and if your value degrades below zero, what are you clinging to life for? In those recurring moments, she knew desperation. They had become the best of friends. But right now? She wasn't thinking of dying. She was thinking of living and cursed herself for getting into a van full of hillbillies. But how could she have known? Claire couldn't predict the future. If she could, she wouldn't be in this van right now would she? She imagined what awaited her at the end of this ride and her eyes pooled.

These three men, taking her and Mickey out of town to who knows where after she told them she didn't want to, well, that was a good indicator of what was coming. And it was not something good. In a situation like this, death was a strong possibility. If she had any chance of getting out of this alive she had to be calm in her mind but had to outwardly play another role. She would have to be the wolf wearing the meek little lamb cloak. She would do what they said and she'd do it with a trembling lip and liquid eyes. She'd be accepting to their direction and give them the impression she was weak and not worth worrying about. She would wait and when the opportunity arose, she would be out of there. Mickey would have to take care of himself. In this instance, the notion of caring for a fellow person would get her hurt and maybe killed. Sentimentality is a useless tool when your own life was at stake. Claire studied the men, trying to discern the leader by word or by deference in body language. Since silence was the companion for most of the trip she couldn't tell. She'd watch and wait. And so thinking, they left the highway and traveled roads with the occasional home breaking up the landscape of trees, rolling hills and fields of crops. They passed by these trees and the sporadic placement of homes invisibly. No one sitting in their home would think twice about passing headlights in the night. Such a sight would be expected. And when something is expected it fades into the background, like it almost isn't there. Claire could expect help from no one. There would be no one looking for her. No one calling her. No one to go to the police and file a missing person report. It hit Claire then. Why she and Mickey were chosen. They were the expendable litter of society. And if you're expendable, does it even matter if you disappear? No. A shiver ran along her arms. The hairs stood on the raised goose-bumps like flags on a hill.

They slowed and turned down a driveway. Branches scratched along the sides and the roof. The van rocked from side to side over the terrain. The van stopped in front of a wooden cabin, the porch light a bright jewel in the darkness. Surrounded by a hill and dense trees, the place stood isolated. A perfect place to kill someone. Or two someones.

The man in the middle said, "Home sweet home! Now let's get out for a stretch and get this party started!"

He slid open the side door and hopped out, his boots crunching on the gravel driveway. He raised his arms above his head and groaned while he stretched. The two in the front exited and stood beside him and Claire thought, *the man in the middle, he's the leader.*

He lit the cigarette in his mouth, turned to them and said, "Okay. C'mon out now."

Claire exited first and Mickey followed at her heel. Mickey's eyes darted everywhere and every few seconds his face would twitch.

The man said, "Oh-oh. Looks like someone needs a fix."

Mickey's face lit up and said, "You have something?"

"Sure do. It's right on inside."

The man in the middle led, Claire and Mickey followed and the other two were behind them, penning them in. The man in front flicked the cigarette off the porch into the darkness. He opened the door and flicked on a switch in the front hallway. He moved into the hallway and took off his boots and stared at Claire and Mickey, waiting for something. Then he said, "Jesus guys, have you no manners? Take off your shoes."

Claire pulled off her Converse sneakers and Mickey kicked off his black boots.

"Alright now, follow me."

The two men pressed up close behind her. She could smell the cigarette smoke from the man in front of her. She walked after him with Mickey snuffling the blood in his nose. The man in front turned a corner out of her sight and she heard his steps descending on creaking stairs. They were going into a basement. Of course, they were. A tear sprung from Claire's eye.

•   •   •   •

The basement walls were covered in wood paneling and posters of old horror movies. Christopher Lee as Dracula threatened a young lady from one of them with burning eyes behind a dark cape. A couple of couches with saggy, worn seats were placed in an 'L' pattern in front of a stereo raised on cinder blocks and wood. The stereo was silver, shiny and big. She hadn't seen one of them in a long time. Most people she knew had wireless speakers connected to their phones or listened to the music library on their phones with earbuds. The more well-to-do people used the over-ear headsets made by Dr. Dre. This ancient entertainment unit played cassettes. Actual analog cassettes. Claire had only seen them in old movies. Otherwise, she'd have no idea what they were. The passenger brushed passed Claire and Mickey and after pressing a couple of buttons on the stereo, heavy metal music filled the room. The man turned around and played air guitar while staring at Claire.

"Turn that down a bit would ya?" Said the man from the middle bench seat.

"It's Bon Jovi."

"I know who it is. I like to be able to hear a person talk if that's all right with you."

The music lowered.

"Violet? That's your name right?"

Claire nodded.

"Don't look so sad. You're bumming me out here. You want anything to drink?" He waved his hand at the mini bar behind him, "We have alcohol, the hard stuff. Beer too, but if that's not up your alley, we have soda too."

She shook her head and the man frowned. He said, "You're going to have a fucking drink and loosen up a bit or we're going to have a problem Debbie Downer. You got me?"

"A Coke would be nice. If you have one. Please."

He smiled and she saw the young man he used to be in that smile. He might have been handsome once. The flatness of his eyes detracted from his looks.

"Was that so hard?"

To Mickey, he said, "What about you young fella? What's your poison?"

Mickey, rubbing his arms as his eyes roved around the room said, "I uh, was hoping you had some harder stuff."

He walked over to the small bar with a shiny black counter and bent behind it. When he stood he had a can of Coke in his hand.

"Catch." He tossed it to Claire and she cradle-caught it to her stomach.

The man placed a small black lockbox on top of the bar. He unlatched it and lifted the lid. He turned it around so Mickey could see what's inside.

"So, we have some meth, some cocaine, heroin and my personal favourite; marihuana. What would you like."

Mickey's eyes bulged. His tongue darted out over his dry lips. His right hand tapped the top of his thigh. He said, "Meth. I'll take the meth."

The man winked at him, smiled and said, "I just bet you will."

The group of men moved to the bar and beers were passed out. Mickey retired to the couch with his meth pipe and lighter. Claire eyed the stairs. She hadn't heard a lock click. Doesn't mean there wasn't one. She could imagine running up those stairs to find the door locked while the three men crowded the stairs behind her, smiling with hard eyes. Their casual violence was bad enough. What would happen if she really pissed them off? She'd have to wait for her moment. She pulled her gaze from the dark stairs and found the man from the middle bench staring at her. He nodded at her and smiled as though he knew what she had been thinking and approved of her choosing not to run. He was the dangerous one. He was the one to fear the most.

•   •   •   •

The cassettes were changed with regularity. Prince's *Purple Rain* was replaced with Bruce Springsteen and then older Tragically Hip albums blasted late into the night. The driver of the van was focusing his attention on Mickey. Seducing him with a liberal dosing of drugs and alcohol. He escorted Mickey to the washroom to clean all the blood off his face and when they returned, they sat on the couch side by side with the man drawing circles on Mickey's inner thigh. They laughed and joked and Claire could see Mickey's fear had gone. With his bright eyes, smile and animated conversation it was easy to see that Mickey was enjoying himself. Having a grand ole time. Free drugs and booze? Yes please!

The other two men insisted Claire sit between them at the bar on fake bamboo stools that swivelled to offer a view of the room. They talked to each other over the head of Claire, drinking beer and discussing football, baseball, and people they knew who were breaking up or cheating on each other. Normal talk being repeated in bars and living rooms everywhere. The scene had a touch of normality to it, but underlying it all wasn't anything normal. Whether they pretended otherwise, these men were holding Claire here against her will. Something bad was going to happen here. Her phone had been tossed out of a van. No one knew where she was. Worse, no one cared where she was. Her legs moved from side to side with nervous energy. The can of Coke warmed in her hand.

"Take off your clothes."

"Huh?" Claire's head turned to the man, the one from the middle bench in the van. The sudden request startled her out of her reverie. She was watching Mickey and the driver make out on the couch and wondering what to do. They were in the shit and Mickey, making out with the man on the couch and getting into it, he didn't realize it. Didn't even seem to care. Thinking about all that, the craziness of Mickey's actions and the fact the two men had been talking over her, not to her, but over her, for the past hour or so, she wasn't prepared for the demand.

He took a swig of his beer and said, "Take off your clothes."

Staring into those flat eyes, the suggestion of a smirk curling his cheek, Claire knew he wasn't asking her. He was telling her.

"Okay."

She stood and moved back a few steps and pulled off her top and dropped it to the floor.

The other man said, "I like bigger titties."

The leader said, "Nah. Those are perfect."

She continued to strip until she stood naked in the room, her clothes in a pile at her feet.

The leader said to his friend, "You want her first?"

"Hell, she's got three holes I can see. We can both have her."

"Alright."

And that's what they did.

•   •   •   •   •

In the end, exhausted, bruised and in pain, the men dragged her and Mickey to another room in the basement. Her left eye was swollen to the point she could hardly see out of it. She had protested another round of anal sex with a mumbled 'please no' and had been punched in the eye for it. Micky was no longer smiling. She didn't know what he had done to displease the man but she had heard him scream a few times. She heard him plead. She heard him beg. None of it helped. He cradled his right hand to his chest as though it needed the support. Blood encircled his mouth and his nose was off centre on his face. He whimpered with every step. They were being led to the far corner of the basement and Claire thought this was it, they were going to kill them both because she could see no restraints or cages to contain them in the room. So she was surprised when the leader pushed on the wall and it moved in slightly before popping open. The door had been concealed by the wood paneling on the walls.

"Get in."

Claire had to duck-walk to get in and the pain in her back from bending that way made her hiss through her lips. A windowless room, with smooth stone walls and a small mattress on the floor. The feeble light came from the open door. And it stunk. Like stale sweat, cheese and strangely, since the floor was smooth paved stone, dirt. It smelled of earth. She paused. Once they closed the door, Claire knew she would be in complete darkness. She stopped. Mickey bumped into her from behind. She whispered, "No, no, no..."

"We haven't got all fucking day. Get in there!"

Mickey crashed into her and she fell onto the mattress. Mickey cried out and Claire had the breath taken from her when his elbow sank into her stomach. Clothes hit her face and rolled off. She recognized her shirt. At least she wouldn't be left naked in the dark.

The leader leaned his head into the room. He said, "Get some rest. Round two begins when we return." He laughed. The door closed and the darkness swallowed Claire and Mickey.

—4—

Claire put on her clothes in the dark. She hoped she hadn't put any on backward or inside out and then thought who gives a shit? She tried to talk to Mickey but he ignored her. She knew he was alive because she could hear him breathing beside her. He had curled into a ball on the small mattress beside her. She had felt him move around and heard the soft sounds of cloth and she thought he must have put on some clothes. Later in their dark cave, Claire brushed against him when she turned. Under her hand, she noticed Mickey had put on pants but not his shirt. Weird. But then it was very warm in here. Clothes were protection though weren't they? Basic protection against the elements. Had Mickey given up completely? Claire spoke to him, trying to draw him out by asking if he was hurt or needed help. He whimpered, moaned and moved his position now and again on the mattress but he wouldn't talk to her. What did they do to him to make him give up like that? He had been hurt. She had seen him and he looked hurt, but they hurt her too. Orifices burned, bruises blossomed, cuts bled and the way they had bent her stretched and tore her muscles. It wasn't enough to make her give up. She wanted Mickey to talk to her so they could develop a plan together. Figure some way out of this mess. If they didn't get out of here on their own, she knew it wouldn't end well for them. She pictured being dumped in a shallow grave on top of Mickey with the leader shoveling dirt onto their open lifeless eyes and tangled and bruised limbs. She saw him smiling down at them with a blue, uncaring sky over his shoulder teasing them with a promise of freedom they'd never have. She shivered. A blood clot from her nose fell into the back of her throat. She reached out, found Mickey sweating beside her and she spat the clumpy mess away from him. She was on her own. That might have scared another person, but Claire had been on her own since the night her stepfather crept into her room and slid his hand up her thigh. She knew the one person she could depend on was herself. She remembered the door to this hidden room opened outwards. When they came for them, they would have to pull the door open towards themselves. Why did she remember that? How could she use that?

Considering her options lying on a flimsy mattress in a midnight room, Claire dozed off.

•   •   •   •   •

Claire woke to laughing and was confused. When she opened her eyes and couldn't see anything, a fear of being blind caused a hitch in her breath and when she felt a warm body beside her, the beginnings of a scream crawled up her throat. The laughter outside the room pinched it off. She remembered. She sat up, straining her ears for more information and her body shouted at her for moving so abruptly. Claire's mouth opened in the darkness, refusing to yell or cry out while every torn and bruised muscle lit up her pain receptors. When the ocean-sized waves of pain were reduced to a trickling river, she scooted closer to the door knowing if she let them take her out of here, if she willingly gave in, she wouldn't see tomorrow. The image of the grave wasn't just a vision. It was a premonition. It would happen if she didn't fight and gave up like Mickey behind her. She didn't have a weapon or any real plan to stop herself being dragged out of this room, she just knew she couldn't quit. When the laughter died off and silence followed, Claire exhaled and felt the tenseness leave her. She listened. She heard footsteps on steps, heading away. No! Not away! A cry escaped her and her body shook all over with a sudden, violent jerk. Mickey farted behind her and she almost laughed until she heard whistling from beyond her room. She moved closer to the door as the tune grew louder. She sat on her butt with her hands on the floor beside her hips and pulling her knees into her chest, she waited. The whistling stopped. She heard the door click like it did when the man pushed on it yesterday to release the lock. A sliver of light outlined the door. Grimacing her teeth, she yelled and shot her feet out. Her heels hit the door with a satisfying slap and the door flung open. A man yelled. She heard a crack and Claire darted out of the hidden room. Blinking against the sudden brightness, she leaped over the man now sprawled on the floor and she raced for the stairs. She didn't see who the door had hit and she didn't care. She was happy he had come alone and didn't have to fight anyone. Her bare feet slapped on the wooden stairs. She pushed open the door at the top thinking how arrogant these men were to not put a lock on the door, so sure were they in their victim's complete helplessness. Claire was grateful for it and grateful too for her shoes to be still sitting on the mat by the door where she had left them. When was that?

Yesterday? Seemed so long ago now. She ran for the front door, leaned down, snagged her shoes and pushed open the screen door to the outside world, heard a "Hey! What the fuck!" and ran into the woods.

Before Claire had left home after telling her mother what her stepfather was doing and her mother somehow blaming Claire for being too pretty and wearing slutty clothes, Claire had been a runner. She had been in grade ten at the time and her phys-ed teacher noticed Claire had natural talent in the running department and actively recruited Claire for the track team. Claire had never been told she was good at anything and having a professional person, a teacher telling her she could maybe get a scholarship to a nice school if she worked at it saw an escape from her shitty town and her shitty life. So Claire worked at it. And she really liked it. It got so she not just liked it, she kind of loved it. There was more to it than throwing on a pair of shoes and running. There was technique involved. There was self-discipline. There was self-respect. Her coach told her to watch the really good long distance runners and try to pick out for herself why they were so good. Try to understand why they could run so fast for so long. Claire noticed it right away. A lot of runners kind of bounce up and down when they run. That was inefficient. You want to move forward. Your head should remain level at all times. No wasted energy. Your forefeet should propel you forward. The good ones kind of float, as though their feet never touched the ground. They made it look effortless and Claire did her best to emulate these women who, to her, had no give in them and were made of sterner stuff than most people as though they had been carved from granite and brought to life. And before the demise of her home security, Claire had been getting better. She had been getting so good her coach had told Claire the Toronto university was calling about her, wanting to know her times for certain distances.

The point was, Claire knew once she got into the woods and put some distance between her and the assholes who nabbed her, she had a chance. A good chance. When she couldn't hear anyone crashing through the leaves behind her, she paused and squatting low to the ground with her hand on the rough bark of a tree, she listened. Nothing. She had time. Claire put on her shoes and continued running with her forearms up to keep the branches from scratching her face. She didn't know where she was going and at this point, so early in her escape, she wasn't too concerned. It took her some time to find her running rhythm. She hadn't run for years and she had to work at getting her breathing right and keeping her feet light while avoiding tree roots, animal burrows and anything that might injure her and slow her down. She continued in this way for some time until she felt safe enough to take a breather and assess her situation. She listened for pursuers and listened for the sound of cars passing on a roadway. Nothing. She spun in a circle hoping to find smoke from a chimney or the roof of a cabin but only saw more trees and more dirt. Where the fuck had these guys taken her?

Claire glanced up at the sky. Through the dense leaves above she saw blue sky. She noticed the sun further along in the sky moving towards the horizon, wherever the hell that was. How long had she been asleep? She knew they had stayed up long into the night and maybe into the early morning. It could be late afternoon or early evening by now. She didn't want to be out here in the dark, wandering. Noises mean more in the night. A cracking branch could mean someone with a heavy boot was getting closer, reaching for you to take you back to the basement. Claire knew if she ever went back there, she wouldn't be leaving alive. The heat of the day and the constant running had turned her mouth dry. She needed water and she needed food. She needed to get the fuck out of these woods! She clenched her teeth and thought if she moved in a straight line, she'd have to hit something, wouldn't she? A road? A house? A fucking Wal-Mart since they were everywhere? How could she tell if she was moving in a straight line?

She checked the sun in the sky willing it to stay up. If it set, it would take the light with it. Then she'd be in the dark forest. With monsters hunting her.

Mickey needed some more meth, more cocaine, more anything to take the edge off his pain. He needed to chase away the feeling of ants crawling under his skin and the compulsion to clench his teeth until his jaw throbbed and his teeth felt soft in his gums. He swam in and out of consciousness. His body hurt in places new to him as though the pain were introducing him to previously unknown parts of his body for the first time. He couldn't move the fingers on his right hand. The skin felt hot and swollen to the touch and no matter how often he swallowed, he couldn't get the taste of blood out of his mouth. He heard Violet talking to him in the night. He knew what she wanted. She wanted his help to get out of this place. Mickey was of two minds on that. One part of him thought they had a shit-ton of drugs here and if all he had to do was give a blow-job and take it in the ass then, that wasn't so bad. The getting hit part sucked but the drugs man, they certainly sponged away most of the pain and they had so much of it! Just sitting in a flimsy old lockbox, waiting to be taken and indulged in. The drugs were calling to him, glowing from inside the metal box and to get them, all he had to do was stick around and collect them. The guys were handing them out freely last night. He knew the reason for their generosity. They didn't want him thinking too much about the situation he was in. Out in the middle of nowhere. No phone. No help. They wanted him placid. They wanted Mickey to be quiet and easy to handle. Drugs made him docile and they knew it.

In the back of his mind, the part of him that was concerned with self-preservation, arose questions and doubts. But those thoughts were unpleasant and if he concentrated on them and gave them attention, well, then he might have to do something about it. That scared him more than anything, having to decide for himself. It was easier to let someone else tell him what to do, how to do it and to reward him with a bit of crystal in a pipe. He was the horse, the meth was the carrot. He didn't want to think about why they tossed his phone out of the window. He didn't want to think about why the man, after Mickey did everything he was told, stomped on his hand and laughed at Mickey when he cried out. Mickey knew the bones in his hand were broken. He didn't think it. He knew it. He felt and heard the crack when the man's heel crushed his hand and from the swelling and his inability to move his fingers, yeah, it didn't take a genius to know that his hand was broken. And why would the man do that? After he did everything he was told to do?

Violet bothering him all night didn't help anything either. Didn't she get it? What were they going to do? Overpower three men and run off into the woods? To where? No. They were redneck assholes. They would take their fun and let them go…right? Maybe they would pay Mickey off with drugs. Drop him off at a train station with a bag full of drugs and a ticket to who cares. They wouldn't kill them. How could they expect to get away with it? When that thought slid into his brain he shook his head and redirected it. In a few hours, when they let him out of this little room, he'd get some more drugs. The best plan was to try to sleep, ignore the pain in his hand and await the wake-up call and the promise of more drugs.

The wake-up call happened to be a loud bang. The noise jerked him out of his sleep. He turned round eyes to the sound and the bright light blinded him. He squinted against it and saw a shadow pass in front, followed by brightness. Waiting for his eyes to adjust to the light, he blinked and shook. Not from the cold. The room was surprisingly warm. Mickey was shaking because he was scared. He heard feet climbing stairs fast. The slapping of feet receded with distance.

Mickey peered out the open door. The sole of a man's foot greeted him. Following the foot was a leg and the rest of the man lying on the ground. The man's arms and legs were star-fished on the floor. Mickey crawled to the door keeping his swollen hand close to his body. Upstairs the front door banged open and Mickey's eyes floated to the ceiling towards the sound. A man yelled, "Hey! What the fuck!" After that followed silence.

The man on the floor had been the one who stomped on Mickey's hand. The one he had been intimate with last night. A line ran down the centre of his forehead and down his nose. Blood leaked from his nose and a spot on his forehead. The gash was swelling. If the guy woke up, he'd have one hell of a headache. Mickey smiled and then it faded. Mickey felt a little sad. How was he going to get more drugs?

His head swivelled towards the bar. The lockbox was behind that, wasn't it? He crept out of the hole, like a rabbit scenting the air to make sure no wolves were around. The man breathed heavily on the ground. His stomach rising and falling. Blood bubbles ballooned from his nostrils. Mickey cleared the low doorway and stood massaging a spot on his lower back. He grimaced at the tightness when he straightened. Dizziness made him sway on his feet as flashing stars peppered his vision. He put his hand against the wall. Once the world steadied, he walked to the bar gingerly, mindful of his hand. Behind the bar on a shelf sat the lockbox. Mickey smiled and then coughed. He swallowed something (a bloodclot?) and retrieved the lockbox and put it on top of the bar. He pulled at the lid. It wasn't locked and when he could see all the goodies lying inside, he moaned. A bag of meth, maybe half an ounce, hell yeah! What was that? Light brown powder? Looked like heroin to Mickey. Some pills, some weed, a veritable goddamn drug user treasure trove. Mickey was so happy he thought his heart might burst. Using his good hand he crammed all the wonderful goodies into the pockets of his jeans. They slid down with his movement and he kept having to pull them up because he was so skinny and the jeans were so baggy. He bought bigger clothes because in the winter he could bundle up in multiple layers. Under the jeans, he sometimes wore two pairs of cotton track pants in the colder months when he had no place to go and hadn't made enough money tricking to get a warm place to stay and do drugs. When it came between a choice of drugs or warmth, drugs won every time.

Having stuffed his pockets full, he held his jeans up with his good hand and fast walked to the stairs. He paused at the bottom and stared into the dark room he emerged from moments before. His shirt was in a pile on the floor. The man on the floor snorted and coughed. Mickey twitched and walked up the stairs, his breath short and hot in his mouth. At the top, he paused and listened. Nothing. No creaking steps behind him or in front of him, no banging doors, and no voices near or far. Mickey stepped into the hallway, saw his shoes where he had taken them off yesterday, said, "Oh," and slid them on.

He walked out the front door with no plan and his only concern was wanting to use the drugs that were weighing his pants down. The van they arrived in reflected sun from the windshield. Birds chirped. Animals rustled. Mickey, inhaling the strong scent of pine and earth, began trekking down the road.

"Where the fuck do you think you're going?"

Mickey turned as a chill ran down his spine. Beside the small cabin was a shed. Mickey hadn't noticed it when they arrived in the night, but he noticed it now. In front of it stood one of the men who had taken him. The one who had sat on the middle bench during their long ride. The one who had smacked him in the face. Growling on the end of a leash was a large black dog. A Doberman if Mickey wasn't mistaken. It pulled on the chain. The muscles in the man's forearms bulged and writhed. The dog bared teeth.

Mickey turned back to the road and started running. He clenched his teeth and pressed his bad hand to his stomach. His good hand flew out in front of him like he'd seen sprinters do as though they were trying to row their arms faster to help propel them forward. The good hand had been holding up his pants. Within ten feet of his flight, his pants slid down. The added weight of the drugs made them slide too fast for Mickey to correct the problem. His jeans slid down past his knees and he tripped on them. He fell to the ground hard with his bare ass pointing to the sky. Behind him, he heard laughter. Dazed from the fall and his broken hand screaming in protest with its collision with the ground, Mickey rolled onto his back and pulling his knees to his chest, closed his eyes and waited for the pain to pass. The man continued to laugh. A real knee-slapping kind of laugh.

Another man's voice said, "Jesus. What happened to him? How'd he get out? Has anyone checked on Greg?"

"You should have seen..." More laughter, "His ass...hahahaha!"

"We don't have time for this shit. We ought to get rid of that clown and get on after the girl. You see how fast she ran?"

"Alright, alright. Give me a second."

Mickey's bones in his hand felt as though they were crushed glass under his skin. The dirt road had cut him up along his chest, hip and knees. That pain was dull and controllable. In his hand, the pain wouldn't abate. It kept on and on, a constant metronome of agony. He held his breath, letting it out between compressed teeth. A molar cracked and a piece of it was like a stone on his tongue. He heard the men say get rid of him and he knew what that meant. It sure as shit didn't mean call a cab and drop him off at home. It meant Mickey would never be going home again if he didn't do something. If he could get into the woods, maybe he could hide. He put a hand under himself to push himself up and had to stop with sweat now streaming off his face and coating his body. The pain wouldn't allow him to move and he crawl-squirmed on the ground towards the tree-line with rocks, roots, and branches sharp against his skin.

"What do you say? Should we let Hank here have at him? We haven't done that in a while and it may get his blood up to better track the girl."

Hank? The dog was named Hank? They were going to let the dog have him? Understanding brought new terror. Mickey, groaning, got his feet under him. His pants were bunched at his ankles, he reached down with his good hand to pull them up and in doing so, brushed the knuckles on his broken hand. He screamed.

Behind him, he heard, "Yeah. Why not?"

"Hank. Attack."

A jingling collar, claws on dirt, a deep growling and then pain as the animal slammed into Mickey. Hot breath, fur, and growls overtop of him. Claws raked him, teeth ripped at his flesh. Screaming, Mickey was swatting with his healthy hand and when the dog's teeth sunk into his stomach, he squealed and without thinking, he used his broken hand to whack at the relentless head tearing and pulling at his flesh and compounding his agony. To Mickey, the attack was never ending. The pain and terror were so much, Mickey was grateful at the end when the dog clamped slathering teeth around his neck and crunched into him, silencing Mickey forever.

-6-

Claire didn't stop moving even though every part of her thrummed with exhaustion. Her lungs ached and the breath escaping her was sharp. The sun was now low in the sky. So low she couldn't see it anymore. There was a suggestion of fading light through the screen of trees. Above her, a dark blue sky spattered with the early stars of the evening meant the the night was arriving and Claire didn't know where she was or where to go. Getting away from the men had been the priority and after she accomplished that, the goal had changed to getting out of these damn woods. The forest appeared to go on endlessly and what scared her the most was the possibility that instead of creeping closer to some form of civilization, what if she was heading deeper and deeper into the woods? She had no idea how to survive out here. Were there bears out here? She didn't know. She was a city woman. A thirsty city woman. Her saliva was like glue in her mouth. Her stomach had not had any food in some time and it protested the fasting with angry growls. Panic wormed in her guts and she closed her eyes and slowed her breathing in an attempt to keep the panic from boiling over.

Barking echoed in the valley. Were they behind her? In front of her? She heard men shouting encouragement. Claire's eyes popped open. She knew it would be too easy to get turned around out here. For all she knew, she could have circled back towards the men and all that distance she thought she made running away was an illusion. Damnit. Panic might win after all. She wiped sweat from her eyes and ran away (she hoped) from the sounds.

•   •   •   •   •

Claire's legs were heavy. Her arms and face were bleeding. Her sweat stung the small cuts decorating her exposed skin. All the branches she couldn't see in the darkness scraped against her. Behind her, flashes of light cut a swathe through the darkness. The dog was close. The men were close. She could hear them talking. Hear them offering each other some water. Claire was done in. She had given it her best shot and knew if she were in the city instead of the woods she would be safe right now. She would have outrun those middle age sadistic fucks with ease and would be sitting on her couch in her shitty, tiny apartment, watching Netflix and eating a greasy bag of microwave popcorn and sipping on a can of Coke so cold from the fridge there'd be a layer of slush in her first sip. Goddamn, that sounded good. A regular slice of heaven.

They weren't far behind her now and Claire had nothing left in her tank and even if she did, she could see nowhere to go. Darkness followed by more darkness. Wait. Was that a light through the trees? Was that a house? She squinted and ran a dry tongue over cracked lips. It could be. She gathered the last vestiges of energy and picked up her feet, doing a mix of fast-walking and jogging. Light from a window shone on a mown lawn. And she heard, what was that? A car idling. She followed the sound with her eyes and yes, right on the driveway sat an SUV. Claire attempted a smile but if anyone had seen it they would have said it was a baring of fangs with her lips sticking to dry teeth. She moved faster now as the land dipped down. The men and the dog faded from her concentration. She was aware of them but they diminished into the background like turning down a car radio when you get close to your destination. A branch ripped the skin on the top of her hand. It didn't matter. She stumbled when she broke through the screen of trees not expecting them to disappear so suddenly. The ground was also level compared to the terrain she had been running through and she wasn't used to that. Her knees wobbled.

The SUV idled. She saw movement inside. The SUV rocked on its shocks. Claire crying now, the tears coating her face in a wet sheen, used what little strength was left in her legs and ran towards the SUV. There was no plan. No thought of what the men would do once they saw her and where she was going. There were people in the SUV, someone to help her and that's all she wanted: help.

She staggered to the SUV, slapped a hand against the window and screamed, "Please help me!"

Behind her, she heard, "Hank! Attack!"

Claire turned and put her back against the SUV. She heard the jingle of a collar and a growl. Out of the dark sprang a black, bullet-headed animal speeding along the ground. She raised her right arm, screamed as she braced herself and the dog leaped into the air. Its teeth crunched into her forearm and its body slammed into her midsection knocking her back into the metal of the SUV. The abrupt violence stole the wind from her cutting off the scream. Claire dropped to the ground and the dog yanked on her arm with its teeth buried in her flesh. She felt a pop in her shoulder and a snap in her forearm. The dog dugs its feet into the earth and jerked her arm from side to side. Able to breathe again, she inhaled the hot night air and yelled, "Get em' off me! It hurts, it hurts, it hur-" the dog jerked again cutting off her yell as a fresh mountain of pain ripped through her.

She smacked at the dog's head with her other hand. Hot liquid ran down her legs and she realized in a dim way she was peeing on herself. A man snatched her hand, the free hand she had been hitting the dog with and he pinned her wrist to the ground with his knee. The dog remained still with its teeth clamped tight on her arm. The dog moaned. She could feel its tongue darting to taste her blood. She turned to the man. A dark outline against a dark night sky. He was catching his breath. He said, "You've been a lot of fucking work, haven't ya?"

He raised his arm, dim moonlight reflected off the knife in his hand. The knife stabbed down and punched through her neck. He ripped it to the side. Her blood fed the ground as the man stood. The dog growled with her arm in its teeth. She noticed the pain leaving her, like a heavy weight rolling off. She smiled in relief. She closed her eyes. She was so tired.

7

Bruce knew what it mean to be fast. To play hockey at the level he did, you had to see fast and react fast. A lot of that had to do with anticipation. Knowing when a player passed a puck and where it would go and to be there before anyone else. And Bruce was exceptional at anticipation which was why he was such a sought-after defence-man. In this instance, he had no reaction time. He sat stunned watching the violence outside the SUV, his hard-on wilting and his amorous adventure forgotten. His mouth hung open and in a dazed, daydream sort of way, hearing Lynda screaming in the close confines of the SUV, his mind was stuck in neutral while attempting to process the dog ripping into the young girl, pulling her off her feet and dragging her around as though she were a limp doll. Then the man pinning her arm down with a knee. He blinked when the man stabbed the young girl, who, just seconds ago, was banging on the window of his dad's SUV. There was no comparison, no experience in his life to draw from to help his brain understand the savagery of murder. Not movie murder, not video game murder, but real murder happening in front of him. It had borne in him a terror that paralyzed his limbs. It took a few seconds for the sensation of Lynda hitting him to reach him and when it did, he looked at her as though seeing her for the first time, like he had woken from sleep to see her sitting there and in a way, that's how it was.

"Get off me Bruce, goddamnit! We have to go! We have to get out of here!"

He closed his eyes, swallowed and when he opened them, he scrambled off Lynda and after pulling up his pants, climbed into the driver's seat. He had one hand on the steering wheel and the other on the gear shifter when the driver side door opened and two hands reached in. The overhead light turned on. Lynda screamed.

Bruce said, "Fuck!"

A hand grabbed his shoulder and a fist slammed into the side of his head at the temple. Stunned, he batted his eyes trying to regain focus and another fist crashed into his jaw. He was pulled out of the SUV and he hit the gravel driveway with a thud. A boot descended on his head and he turned away from it but it landed on his temple again and bits of rock and sand ripped into his face.

Bruce swung his arms hoping to connect with something. His movements were sluggish and slow from the knocks to his head. Kicks assaulted him from all sides. He felt his rib bend in and it took all the air from his lungs so the air escaped him in a rasp and he curled up on his side and tried protecting himself by curling his arms around his head. A kick burst his nose. His hand was grounded into the dirt by a heavy boot and he felt the brittle bones snap. All the while, in the background to his being beaten, he heard the men's grunts, the dog barking, and Lynda begging them to stop.

He heard a man who sounded out of breath say, "Enough! And stop that bitch from screaming!"

•   •   •   •

Lynda watched Bruce being pulled from the front seat. She heard the thuds and the grunts of the men as they pounded on him. Bruce's squeals of pain made her limbs shake. She was screaming at them, "Leave him alone! Stop it! Stop it!" They continued to hurt Bruce. To her, it went on forever, an eternity of brutality. She looked at the steering wheel and thinking she might be able to get away while they were distracted, moved forward, her fingers trembling and splayed out in front of her. Then a man said, "Enough! And stop that bitch from screaming!" Her heart sank into her stomach realizing she had taken too long to get moving. Retreating to the back of the SUV she spied the side door. She could get out that way. She reached for it until she remembered the dog and how fast it covered the ground to take down the other girl. She pulled her hand back as though boiling water had spilled on it.

The SUV rocked and a man entered the driver seat. Light spilled onto his face. Lynda smiled and shocked tears burst from her eyes. She was safe!

"Daddy! Help me!"

Neil, Lynda's father, spattered with blood and dirt saw his daughter and a dropping sensation in his guts made him mutter, "Fuck."

8

Lynda ended up sitting in the dark room where Claire and Mickey had been not too long ago. She at least had a Coleman's camping lamp on the ground. Her knees were squeezed against her chest. Her eyes burned and the inside of her nostrils felt on fire. A wet patch covered both her knees. When the tears fell, she'd wiped her cheeks on her knees. When snot ran down her nose, she'd rubbed that on her knees too. She wanted to know where Bruce was. She kept running the night over and over in her head. It didn't make sense. Her dad? The guy who cried at the movie *Old Yeller*? None of this could be real, could it? She ran it through her mind again.

When her dad opened the door to the SUV she'd thought she'd been saved. It never occurred to her to think what her dad was doing out here at the precise time a girl was being murdered and Bruce was ripped from the truck and beaten until his breath gurgled in his lungs. Why would she even consider the why of it? In her mind, her dad was on his annual fishing trip with her uncle Greg and their childhood friend, Ray. He was supposed to be up north on some cold lake, drinking beer, smoking cigars and eating fish over a campfire while Creedence Clearwater Revival roared out of the speakers of what her dad would call a 'boom-box'. It didn't cross her mind that her dad was the one killing that girl and beating on her boyfriend Bruce. When he backed out of the truck, his face drawn and eyes bulging and shiny like hard-boiled eggs, she furrowed her brow. Where was he going? Why was he leaving her here?

Glancing out the window, she saw three men arguing and her dad was one of them. The dog was straining at the leash to get at Bruce and then it hit her. What the fuck? Her hands shook and then the rest of her body took the queue from her hands and followed suit. Her teeth clacked together and she thought, *I have to get out of here. I have to go. I have to tell someone. Get help for Bruce.* And then the scariest thought of all, *what was her mother going to think?*

Moving slowly with her eyes wide and on her father and his friends, she slid her left foot into the driver well and gritting her teeth, willing them not to notice her, she settled into the chair and hovered a foot over the brake. The keys were still in the SUV and the engine was humming. All she had to do was put her foot on the brake, shift into drive and get the fuck out of here. *Don't see me, don't see me...*she depressed the brake. The lights flared fire in the darkness.

"Hey!"

She clutched the shifter. The door opened. Hands reached in. Lynda dropped the shifter in drive and it shot ahead. She heard a scream and it sounded like Bruce and she tapped the brake. She turned her head and Uncle Greg was at the open door. He pulled her from the SUV and tossed her on the ground. She rolled. Felt rocks scrape her skin and her wrist bent back sending a spike of pain running up her arm. She heard her dad say, "Don't fucking hurt her!" And the tires of the SUV stopped rolling over gravel.

Pushing herself onto her knees, she glanced towards Bruce. The light from the house windows caught the top of his head and upper part of his chest. She could see he was breathing.

Her dad knelt in front of her, "Are you ok?"

She tasted blood in her mouth. She said, "Mom is going to kill you." And she burst into tears.

"Yeah."

Ray approached with the dog. He said, "Hank. Sit."

The dog sat and stared at Lynda. After what she had seen the dog do she sucked in a breath and the dog glared at her with eyes as black as obsidian. She now knew what a steak felt like.

Ray with a chuckle said, "You ran over your boyfriend there."

Lynda started crying again. She couldn't help it.

"C'mon Ray! Why'd you have to go and say that?"

Ray, the one Claire thought of as the leader said, "We gotta get a move on here."

"Yeah, yeah." To Lynda, he said, "C'mon honey, let's go." He grabbed her by the shoulders and she pulled away from him, "Don't touch me!"

Neil, bending down with his hands on his knees said, "We have to go."

"I'm not going anywhere with you!"

Ray said, "That's where you're wrong. You're coming with us and there is no getting around that. The only question is, how do you want to do it? You want me to drag you by your hair-"

Neil said, "Hey!"

Ray continued without looking at Neil or acknowledging he had spoken, "or have Hank here persuade you? Or... and this option is the most pleasant, for all of us. How about you just walk your ass over to that SUV and get the fuck inside."

She looked at her dad. He dropped his eyes. She heard steps behind her. Uncle Greg.

She stood, wincing when she straightened. She said, "What about Bruce?"

Ray said, "He's coming with us too."

Bruce's chest rose and fell. A lump settled in her chest. Her eyes shone. Her lips trembled when she spoke. She sounded like a little child when she said, "You promise?"

Ray smiled and using his index finger drew an X across his chest. He said, "Cross my heart."

•   •   •   •

Lynda was taken back to the cabin, squished in between uncle Greg and Ray while her dad drove. Hank sat in the passenger seat, his tongue lolling out of his mouth. They placed Bruce in the back seat of the SUV. He groaned when they moved him, but he was unconscious. They used jumper cables to tie his hands behind his back. Even though he lay battered, Lynda thought he was the lucky one. Her dad and uncle Greg hefted the dead girl and placed her lifeless body in the trunk with grim faces. She couldn't believe it was her dad. How could it be? When she sat in the SUV, Ray took her cell phone and Bruce's cell phone. She watched him take the back off and remove the battery from both of them. He stuffed the batteries in one pocket and the phones in another. They drove to the cabin in silence. It wasn't until they emerged from the trees to see the squat little building in a small clearing did Lynda say, "Whose place is this? Does mom know about this place?"

She caught her dad's eyes in the rearview. He didn't answer. He stopped and put the SUV in park.

Ray said, "Does this truck have OnStar on it?"

Neil said, "I didn't see a sticker for it."

Ray said, "Doesn't matter. We'll have to get rid of it anyway." To Greg, "Take it to that little trail, where that boulder is with all the old carvings on it? You know the one I mean?"

"Yeah. About two miles from the cave."

"That's right. You take this truck out there and Neil will pick you up.

Before you leave, set fire to the SUV to get rid of any evidence. It should be dark enough for a while yet to cover the smoke and no one should be way out there to see the fire at this time of night. Hopefully, no one will find it for some time."

"Alright."

Neil said, "Wait a minute. Why don't you get Greg?"

"Because I don't need you getting any ideas about Lynda here before we have a chance to talk about it, that's why. Put Lynda in the room. Greg here will help me with Bruce and the...other one. Once the clean up is done, we'll meet back here to decide what to do next, alright?"

Neil said, "Alright. But you're coming with me to get Greg."

Ray said, "Oh yeah? Why is that?"

Neil said, "Because I don't want *you* to get any ideas about Lynda before we have a chance to talk about it."

Her dad escorted her to the hidden room and uncle Greg handed her the lamp.

Neil said, "We'll feed you when we get back alright, hon?"

"What are you going to do with Bruce?"

"We haven't decided yet. We'll have to talk about it."

She wiped at the tears pooling in her eyes. With gritted teeth, she said, "Don't you kill him, dad. Jesus, I can't believe I said that! Who the hell are you?"

"I'm your dad."

"No, you're not. My dad wouldn't be doing this. Not the dad who took me to judo lessons, or used to let me paint his toenails! That dad wouldn't be chasing a girl in the night with a dog! A dog for fuck's sake! And then killing her? Like what the fuck? You were supposed to be fishing with your friends! Like you do every year!"

Her mouth hung open and she brought her shaking hands up to the sides of her head. She turned her head, taking in the room, the secret room in a secret cabin and said, "Have you ever even gone fishing? Every year...were you doing...this? What is it that you're doing, dad? What have you been doing? Year after year after year?"

Neil reached in to put his hands on her shoulders and she jerked back as though he was a coiling rattlesnake and said, "Don't you touch me! Don't you fucking touching me!"

He backed away, his mouth opening and closing, his hands held out in a placating gesture as Lynda crawled away from him further into the darkness.

He pulled the door closed and before it shut completely, Lynda said, "What are you going to do with Bruce?"

Ray, winked at her from over her dad's shoulder and said, "Lynda? You should be more concerned about what we're going to do with you." He closed the door. Grumbled voices faded with distance. She curled up on the mattress and even though the room was warm, humid even, she couldn't stop shivering.

–9–

Lynda's watch showed the date and time in glowing green. So far, she had spent almost three days in this room. She was fed and escorted to the washroom regularly enough to not be uncomfortable. Ray was the one who always escorted her. She had known Ray for a long time just not to the extent that she knew Uncle Greg. Ray would pop in now and then at their house to pick up her dad to go to the local pub or wherever. She knew him to say hi and how's it going, but nothing further than that. He wasn't family. Not like Uncle Greg who had been at their house for birthdays and holidays. With Ray, she had no leverage which was why (she guessed) he was the one chosen to feed her and escort her during her washroom breaks. He wouldn't answer her questions about Bruce. He wouldn't answer her questions about when she was getting out of here. And he wouldn't let her call her mom which even though she understood why he wouldn't, it still hurt. Her mom would be going crazy by now at home. She wondered how her dad was handling it? He had to have gone home, right? When your wife calls to tell you your child hasn't come home, you get your ass home and try to help right? How the hell was he pulling this off? Then, thinking about how long he had fooled them all, maybe this part of it was a piece of cake. Another lie added to the layers of lies. Lynda moved from anger to tears to fear and eventually fell asleep out of complete exhaustion. Her mom would have the whole town out looking for her and Bruce. She was the type of person who didn't wait for others to do for her. She'd do it herself and organize an army of people to help. That was all well and good, but no one knew of this place. It was a dark secret of the professional secret keepers. She had a strong suspicion of what happened to Bruce and thinking of him brought more tears. Images of Bruce being yanked from the SUV and getting stomped on made her chest hurt. Believing what happened to him would soon happen to her, and knowing how pissed her mom would be if Lynda for one second gave up, she used the lamp to light every dark corner so she could examine her prison. If there was a way out, she'd find it.

10

Despite what Ray had hoped, the SUV was found almost an hour after Greg dumped it and set it ablaze. This was because Frank Boone and Dwight Hardy were going hunting.

Frank's braying alarm went off at 4:00am and, being a deep sleeper, he didn't hear it at first. His wife elbowed him in the back, in his kidney to be precise, and he woke up with a yelp because her elbow was pointier than a spear and she used it better than any Roman Centurion ever could. He turned off the alarm, muttered an apology and slunk to the bathroom yawning and using the flashlight app on his phone to light the way. After a quick shower, he threw the lunch he had packed the night before into his cooler and headed out to his truck. He went back inside to get his rifle and once he stowed it safely in the back seat, he drove to Dwight's. Frank was hoping Dwight would already be awake. It wouldn't be the first time Frank pulled into the driveway with the house in darkness. He hated ringing the doorbell. Dwight's hound always barked his head off when the doorbell was rung and wouldn't stop until you let him sniff your crotch so he'd know you were a friend. Frank suspected Chevy, the hound, didn't have the best eyesight but kept it to himself because Dwight got right defensive about any potentially negative comment about his dog.

From the street, he saw the front light shining above the porch. In a chair beside the door sat Dwight. A red ember flared by his mouth.

Frank pulled into the driveway, rolled down his window and said, "You're not smoking in my truck."

Dwight stood and said, "I know that. I'm smoking on my porch."

He flicked the ember into his neighbour's bushes, slung his lunch bag over one shoulder and his bow case over the other and got into the truck.

"You smell like smoke."

"Is this what we're doing today?"

"What?"

"Stating the obvious?"

"Shut up, Dwight."

"Alright."

    •   •   •   •

They were at the mid-point of deer season. They had been out four times this year and would triple that by the season's end. They hadn't been successful yet and after much beer inspired discussion, decided they were hunting where everyone else hunted. Mathematically, they were contributing to the over-saturation of hunters in a certain area. Sure, the places visited by the other hunters were popular because the trails stalked were ones used by the deer to migrate. But no one had been successful this year, well, except for that prick Toby but he went out with all the expensive tech to locate the deer. Rumour had it he had access to a satellite with infrared image capabilities and could easily track the deer and set up where he knew they would be. Now, Frank outwardly told people that was a stupid idea. Who had access to a satellite, floating in space, from their tiny one-horse town? Sure Toby was rich but that was just stupid. Some people were lucky is all and Toby happened to be one of those lucky people. If anyone wanted proof of that, they just had to look at his wife. She was stunning and Toby, well, Toby could be mistaken for a Sasquatch. But after Toby had taken home two deer in two outings, Frank inwardly thought maybe the satellite rumour wasn't so far-fetched after all. He would never admit that to anyone, especially not Dwight, but after sitting in a blind for four long days and seeing nothing, Frank began to wonder.

Looking at maps and listening to other hunters, they decided to go somewhere new and take a look around. They could get deep enough into the woods using an old service road with the truck and walk in further from where they parked it. The road was bumpy as hell and almost overgrown with misuse which is why they took Frank's truck and not Dwight's Toyota Prius. They knew the road ended at a boulder with carvings on it. The rock had been a big deal twenty odd years ago when some hippie discovered it and thought there were old Iroquois carvings dating back to some three thousand years ago on it. But the hippie was a hippie and not an anthropologist, archeologist, historian or someone who might know what the hell they were talking about and the rock was forgotten. Frank even forgot all about it until the maps showed that's where the service road ended.

Frank knew game trails ran all through that area and they would find one, wander along it and see what they would see. If they saw deer spore, they'd be in business. All they had to do was mark the boulder with their handheld GPS units and they'd be able to find it at anytime no matter how far they went away from it.

They had scouted the area the week before and decided on a general direction to travel based on the known deer migrating routes. They wanted to be ready to start their walk when the dawn lightened the sky and made black outlines of the trees. Frank saw a hill overlooking a game trail and wanted to get set up there to watch and wait. If nothing happened, they'd move to the next spot. Simple plan, easy to remember and easy to execute.

On this morning, they missed the service road entrance because it was dark.

Dwight said, "You missed it."

"No, I didn't."

"Yes, you did." Pointing out the window, Dwight said, "Notice the water tower we passed? The road was before that."

"Shit."

Frank slowed down and using the shoulder, did a U-turn. Using his high-beams, they found the entrance and drove down the trail. They traveled at a slow pace because of the encroaching trees and the deep ruts disuse and weather had carved into the dirt. It wasn't until fifteen minutes into their drive down the road that they saw a light in the distance. A wavering bright yellow glow visible through the dense trees.

Dwight said, "What's that?"

"I don't know."

They crept forward squinting into the early morning darkness at the incongruous brightness. The windows were down because of the humid summer. They smelled the smoke first. Not a wood smoke but a plastic scent, a burning rubber smell.

Frank said, "A car fire?"

"I don't know. Don't smell like no campfire."

Drawing closer, the flames became a bright focal point in the darkness. When the flaming SUV came into sight, they were hit with an aroma familiar to them both.

"Smells like roasting pig, doesn't it?"

Frank said, "Yeah. Yeah, it does."

Through the front window of the burning SUV Frank saw a distinctly human silhouette.

He said, "Oh shit."

11

When Jodie got the phone call from her boss, she was sitting with Graham on the porch he had built onto the back of his house. She held a glass of white wine with the golden sparkles floating to the surface caught by the lowering sun. Graham's steaming coffee sat on a small table between them. Off the back of the porch, the ground had been levelled and flagstone paths meandered to Graham's two sheds. The flagstones were bordered by wildflowers. Purple, yellow, white and red petals swayed in the intermittent breezes. Beautiful. Even with the bees that came along with all the flowers. The flowers smelled of summer and the sunlight made them glow. A hot summer evening, Jodie was wearing shorts, a T-shirt and running shoes. Graham wore jeans, a long sleeve shirt and well-worn work-boots. She had never seen him wear anything else. He didn't wear the same clothes day in and day out but his style remained the same. She wondered if he had other scars on him and if that's what he was hiding under the long-sleeves and jeans.

She said, "This is beautiful, Graham. Did I tell you that already? I feel like I told you that already."

"How many glasses of wine have you had?"

"This is my second and my last. I have to make my way through the woods to my car and then drive home because you live out in the middle of nowhere."

Graham grunted, picked up his coffee and sipped at it.

"How can you drink hot coffee on a day like this?"

"Like this..." He took another sip and smiled.

She smiled back. At first, his smile bothered her. The missing eye, puckered skin, and broken muscles underneath made a ghastly picture. Now she was used to it. And he didn't smile often so when he did she knew it was genuine. And those are the best smiles, aren't they? The real ones?

The reason Jodie had instigated the relationship with Graham because she had been curious. How did he find little Francine? He never admitted to her that he found her but she knew it was him. And he knew she knew. It was a weird little game they played, circling around the topic and never directly mentioning it. She also wanted to know more about him because he was interesting. Living out here, effectively alone, generating his own power, finding a well and using it as a water source and growing his own food with the use of an ingenious system of hydroponics. He wanted to be alone and although she suspected it had something to do with his scars, externally and internally, she didn't really know. She thought she should feel bad for ruining his self-imposed isolation. She didn't. She sensed his loneliness the first time she met him. A standoffish approach that made her think he was the type to push someone away because he feared closeness. All that and the fact that he had found Francine when a whole town and a slew of cops couldn't, she just had to get to know him. And she was glad she had pushed it. She considered him a good friend and she hoped he saw her the same way. They discussed books over coffee or dinner. Graham made a point of taking her through his woods and showing her the beauty of it, the solitude of it and the wonderful deep emeralds of the leaves when the sun glinted off them just right. He spoke in his quiet way and when he listened, she knew he heard her. He wouldn't mm-hmm her and glance at the screen of his cell phone. He didn't even carry one which was both strange and kind of cool. She spoke to him about her work and how hard it had been for her, a woman and a minority, to get the position she had. In policing, a lot of officers were men. And she was directing them during high profile investigations. They wanted her job and because of that, she felt like she had a target in the centre of her back ever since she had earned her position. She sometimes pictured a group of white guys in a room, rubbing their hands together, smiling while waiting for her to screw up. She hadn't. Not yet. In fact, her clearance rate outshone anyone on the force. There were over six thousand officers in the Ontario Provincial Police, so that was saying a lot. Her bosses relied on her. They counted on her to crack the tough cases. And their reliance on her was merited by her performance. She knew if she kept succeeding, she could move right up the ranks. That was an aspiration she only felt comfortable sharing with Graham.

For his part, he didn't share much. But he listened to her and wasn't that like sharing? It was a gift she had never appreciated or knew of until she had experienced it. He never ate meat and when she asked him why, he shrugged and said, "I don't like it." He didn't say it was an ethical thing or it was too expensive. He said he didn't like it and that was explanation enough for him. The dinner fare was strange because she didn't expect a man in the woods to not eat meat. His vegetarian food was creative and he did make his own bread so she was never dissatisfied or went home hungry after dinner at his home. He didn't drink either except she thought that had something to do with the frequent headaches he got. She had to leave on more than one occasion, at his request, when a headache would weaken his knees and cause a steady stream of tears to leak from his one eye. He would down a few pills and go lie in the complete darkness of his room until the pain passed.

She knew he hated crowds because they made him uncomfortable. Talking about it, she saw the way he drew his shoulders up to his ears that even discussing it made him anxious. She didn't know why that was because he didn't explain. And, she was happy he had let her into his life and she could tell by a frown or hard stare from Graham that he didn't want her to push. He wanted her to leave it alone. And she did and because of this, he let her into his life a little more each time. He showed her how he maintained living off the grid and the work it took. He was proud of his hydroponics system. He swelled like a proud father when his fingers stroked the leaves of a ripening vegetable. It kept him busy every day and she knew that was one reason why he lived that way, because he needed to be busy. Sometimes, when they were sitting like they were now, Graham's eye would tighten and she could tell he was gazing inward and whatever he was seeing made him sad. She would watch him shake his head, like a dog waking from a bad dream in which the rabbit got away, to get rid of the thought. Jodie believed he kept busy to keep such thoughts away. Whatever flashed across the interior screen of his mind hurt him. She could tell by the way he would press a palm into his empty socket and clench his teeth. He was trying not to cry. The struggle was painful to watch. When those moments happened she pretended not to see. She would stare off into space or pick up a book nearby and read the back of it and when out of the corner of her eye she noticed he had regained himself, she would wait some more and then pat his forearm.

Every once in awhile, she would think back to Francine. She really wanted to know how he had found her. It was killing her to know and she would only toy with considering asking him about it when she thought he was in a good mood. No. Not good. She thought the best moment to ask him would be when she judged Graham to be in a great mood. Sitting with him on the porch she judged him to be in a great mood because his normal scowl wasn't as pronounced. He almost wore a countenance of contentment. If she wanted to ask, and she did, now would be the ideal time to ask.

Considering it made her heart beat faster. A light coating of sweat appeared on her upper lip. She feared this could potentially be a breach of their friendship etiquette. She thought about asking in a roundabout way like, "That guy who found Francine, I wonder why he didn't come forward. The guy is a hero, don't you think?" She imagined Graham rotating his eye to her, smile, shake his head at her and return to sipping his coffee. He was always drinking coffee. To ask him straight out, she worried Graham might shut down and then shut her out. She didn't want to lose him as a friend. They were comfortable with each other and she enjoyed his company. Her regular visits at his request indicated he enjoyed her company, too. She should just ask. Get it all out of the way and into the open. It's not like he'd kick her out. At this point, he'd either tell her to mind her own business or he might actually tell her how he had found Francine. She was mulling over how best to ask him when her phone rang. She put her wine glass down and struggled to get it out of the front pocket of her shorts. The screen read a private number. Her work always called her on a private number. She sighed and answered it.

"Hello?" She straightened in her chair and leaned forward. Graham could hear a deep voice from her phone. It was too faint to hear the words so what he heard of the conversation was from her end. Jodie said, "Where is that?" Pause. "How far is that?" More deep voice responses. "So I should probably pack for a few days?""A week? I would hope we find her before then." Her eyes rolled over to Graham and then away. "You have any drones up that way?" "Good." "And search teams?""Perfect. I'll head up there tonight, then. Can you book me a place to stay and then send it to my phone?" "Great. Thanks." "Oh, and who do I report to?" "Me? I'm running the show?" "Hey, thanks. Really. I appreciate it." "Yup. I'll be on my way soon. I should be there in a few hours or so. Tonight for sure." "Thanks again." She hung up the phone and leaned back in her chair. She reached for her wine but stopped halfway and left it on the table. She wouldn't be needing it.

"That was my work. They need me to head up north to help out with a missing teenager. They're putting me in charge. I'm running it."

"That's good, right?"

She smiled and patted Graham's arm. "Oh yeah. This is good. Real good. Normally, I work under someone you know? Normally, the people I worked under would defer to me to make all the decisions and if things go well, they take the credit and if it goes bad, they can point their fingers at me. I haven't had anything go bad yet. So I'm getting a shot. This is my investigation. I'm the lead investigator and the case manager. It's all on me."

"Isn't that what you wanted?"

Her smile faded. She inhaled and rolled her shoulders, "Yeah. It shows they believe in me. And that's always a good thing. It's been so hard to earn something that is freely given to the others, mostly men, and now that I've got their belief, I need to keep it. The next promotional opportunity should go well for me and then from there, who knows?"

"Why are you so nervous then?"

"Because of two things. One: this investigation has to go well in order for that to happen and 'well' means getting the girl back alive and finding the bad guy. Two: I shouldn't give a shit about my career and be focused on getting the girl back because that's what matters in the end, right?"

"I think that's the only thing that matters. But you're human and it's natural to think about what could be. Besides, you've earned the right to be the one who brings the girl home and you should be proud of that because you earned it on merit. It means with you out there investigating, she has the best chance of being found. Don't let that distract you from your goal though. Bring the girl home to her family. And I'll see you in a week or so."

She stood, squeezed his hand and said, "Yes. In a week or so."

She turned to leave and then paused, peering down at Graham. She opened her mouth to say something and then closed it. She offered a small smile and walked away.

Graham let out a breath. The hairs on his body tingled. A line of sweat slid down from his hairline and ran into his puckered eyelid. When she paused there, a fear settled on Graham's chest. A cold stone pressing down. He thought she was going to ask him something he would have to refuse and it scared him. He didn't want Jodie to dislike him. After all this time convincing himself he needed no one and was more comfortable with no one around, he realized he had been wrong. He had wanted a friend and had convinced himself that he hadn't. Because it was easier to be alone. It was easier to not care. But now he had Jodie as his friend. And Jodie was an ideal friend. He didn't get the feelings of rage around her like he had with so many other people. When he decided to be alone, it had been for those reasons. In his anger, he was dangerous to everyone. He wanted to be free of the spontaneous fury and the skull cracking headaches. He did like his solitude and especially did not like the horrified stares at his scars, misshapen jaw, his missing eye and hearing the whispers at his back. Jodie was different. She never flinched looking at him and spoke to him directly. Even his mom turned her head talking to him sometimes because staring at his injuries was too much. Almost like looking into the sun. If the sun were a horrible scarred white guy better suited to being on the cover of a horror magazine. He liked having Jodie around. He liked feeling valued and...human. So when she paused before leaving he was scared. He thought she was going to ask him to come with her. He thought she would want him to help her find the girl. He couldn't do that and was afraid he would have to refuse her. Thinking about it, he clenched his jaw. The pain. The crowds. The people. He shivered in the hot sun.

12

Jodie arrived in Kauffmann's Vale and pulled into the parking lot of the Ontario Provincial Police station, cruising while looking for a spot. She didn't find one and decided to make one for herself. She parked her car half on the pavement and half on the grass. She turned off the car and stepped out. An officer was staring at her from the front of the building. A tall man, lean and looking like a runner. She couldn't see much of his face because of the big Stetson police hat on his head. He must have seen her pulling onto the grass because he had the glass door open as though he was waiting for her to step out of her car.

"You can't park there."

"But there is nowhere else to park."

He crossed his arms and held the door open with his back. He pointed with his chin and said, "Use the lot across the street. Like everyone else."

Jodie followed the direction of his chin and saw a CTV news van in the lot. A large antenna protruded from the roof like a dark finger pointing into the night sky. Other white news vans were crowded around it. She sighed. The boss said this would be a media heavy investigation. Most times the media impeded investigations. Jodie would have to figure out a way to use them to her advantage like she had with the Francine case. She opened the door to her car to get back in and move her car and the officer said, "Thank you."

At least he was polite.

•   •   •   •   •

After parking across the street, Jodie walked into the police station with her backpack slung over one shoulder. She stopped inside the door. A crowd of people stood in the lobby. An officer behind plastic glass wore a stoic expression as a man yelled at her, demanding information in relation to the murdered teen and the missing teen. The man yelling at her wore a nice suit and had perfect hair, the kind that looked almost drawn on. His white teeth glowed neon against his tanning-bed skin. Jodie didn't want to bring attention to herself with that clown harassing the officer behind the glass, but she would have to introduce herself so she could speak to the station commander.

Behind her, "Wasn't that bad of a walk was it?"

She turned. The officer at the door peered down at her still wearing his hat. It cast a shadow over his eyes.

"You know you don't have to wear the hat inside. As per regulations. You can take it off."

He tilted his head back and appraised her. She was used to this reaction. Being a woman in the profession was unusual. Being a black woman in the policing profession was a rarity.

"You the big detective we've all been waiting for?"

"Something like that."

"Good. Gary is going to want to talk to you quick as he can."

"Nervous is he?"

The officer removed his hat and ran a hand through his hair before putting it back on.

"Let's just say he's out of his depth on this one. We all are. C'mon, I'll take you back to see him."

"You know, you really don't have to wear the hat inside. I wasn't kidding about that."

"I know. I like it. Makes me look more official, don't you think?"

Jodie smiled and said, "I'm going to decline commenting on that one."

"Huh." He took the hat off and studied it. "You don't like it?"

Jodie, refusing the bait, said, "Where is Gary's office at?"

"I thought the ladies would like it."

He excused himself through the crowd with Jodie trailing. He kept his hat in one hand. He pulled out his wallet and held it against a pad by the door. A light turned green and he pushed through.

Before the door closed, she heard the tanned journalist complain, "Hey! How come she gets to go back? Who was that? Is she from another news station?"

•   •   •   •   •

Staff Sergeant Gary Barnes leaned back in his chair with his feet up on the table in a large meeting room. Other officers were taping notes to a map on the wall. There was a gentle susurration of sound. People murmuring, people moving, all wearing the somber expression common to funerals. A lot of pressure on a group of people who were used to breaking up field parties of high school students in the summer, domestic fights between couples and arresting the occasional drunk driver.

Gary's head swivelled when Jodie entered and his feet popped off the desk and he all but jumped out of his chair with his hand outstretched, "You detective Reyes?"

"Yes, sir."

He waved away her formality and shook her hand. His eyes reflected hope and for a moment, Jodie thought Gary was about to hug her. She broke the handshake and turned to the board. She saw a small red dot on a satellite image map and concentric circles widening out from it.

She said, "Is that where the SUV was found?"

"Yeah, yeah." He wiped a hand across his forehead and said, "A terrible thing."

Jodie said, "Can you fill me in on what you have and what you've done so far?"

"Absolutely."

•　•　•　•　•

Gary told her about Frank and Dwight and how they found the SUV. Fire trucks came and did their thing of ruining the crime scene by showering the SUV with foam and water. The abundant water turned the dirt around the vehicle into mud and their boot prints destroyed any other prints that may have been found. They left to return to their sleeping bunks and the police were left to guard the scene. Gary had arrived at the scene by the time the early morning sun was resting on the tops of the trees. Gary called for the Forensic officers to attend the scene and waited. Once the vehicle was cool enough to approach, the Forensic team found a second body curled into a question mark in the back portion of the SUV. The forensic pathologist showed up just after they found the second body with a medical bag in one hand and a lollipop in the other, took one look, ordered an autopsy, wrote the warrant for it, handed the paper to Gary and left.

There were no license plates on the vehicle but they did find the vehicle identification number on the vehicle. The owner of the vehicle was a Barbara Hanley. That's when the dispatcher told him Barbara had called in because her son hadn't come home. Shortly after that, Lynda Harrigan's mom called in to say Lynda hadn't returned either. Turns out Barbara had called Jamie first, Lynda's mom, when Bruce didn't return. They didn't know the gender of the two bodies in the vehicle but the two teens went out last evening in Barbara Hanley's SUV. Damn. Gary started to sweat. He called the hospital where the autopsy was to be done and asked them to put a rush on it. He believed he knew the identity of the two bodies in the SUV. He was right about one of them.

He drove over to Barbara Hanley's house and sent Sergeant Letty over to speak with Lynda's mom.

Gary said, "Barbara opened the door and saw me and her knees kind of went all loose. I managed to get a hand on her before she fell, but she screamed at me to let her go. She didn't want me to touch her, I think. Because she knew what I was there to tell her and she didn't want to hear it. Thank god Henry was there to help her."

Gary told Barbara and Henry they found her car. It had been burned and two bodies were found inside. The bodies hadn't been identified. A flash came into Barbara's eyes, something like hope, like maybe it wasn't her son who had been turned into charcoal. Gary got the name of the family dentist and called the hospital. Gary spoke to the forensic pathologist who said there was no smoke in either person's lungs. Shit. They hadn't died of smoke inhalation. He stepped outside the house to learn more from the forensic pathologist with Barbara and Henry's eyes boring holes into his back. The forensic pathologist gave him a short synopsis of what they had found so far in the cursory examination. Both bodies had stab wounds. The one they identified as a female had her throat cut so deep she'd almost been decapitated. The male had a knife wound directly into his heart and had a few broken ribs and fingers. The dentist had sent them x-rays of Bruce's teeth. It was Bruce. Barbara's small hope was snuffed out. When he told her, she vomited into her hands. It leaked out onto their shiny hardwood floor. Gary asked Henry to call some friends and family over for support but Henry was staring at the wall. His eyes were glazed over while he rubbed Barbara's back in small circles. So Gary walked next door and spoke with the neighbour. The neighbour nodded, her mouth a grim line and with a cell phone in her hand marched over to Barbara's while dialling for reinforcements.

Gary phoned Sergeant Letty to let her know what the forensic pathologist had said. Sergeant Letty had Lynda's dentist (the same as Bruce's dentist) send her x-rays to the forensic pathologist for comparison against the other girl. Sergeant Letty sat at the kitchen table with a cup of coffee Jamie, Lynda's mom, had made for her. Jamie's knee bounced under the table. Letty kept glancing at the door. Her husband, Neil, was up north on a fishing trip with his brother and his friend. It was a yearly thing. She had called him, asked him to come home and even though she knew he was hours away, watched the door as though she expected him to walk in at any second. She had trouble looking Sergeant Letty in the eye and every so often, a shiver would run through her body. What felt like forever, but was only thirty minutes later, the forensic pathologist called and told Sergeant Letty the other body definitely was not Lynda. Her eyebrows dropped. She said, "Wait. Are you sure?"

The forensic pathologist, annoyed at all the phone calls she was getting from the medical staff performing the autopsy and the police, barked, "Do you think I would tell you that if I wasn't sure?" Before Letty could answer, the forensic pathologist hung up. So, the forensic pathologist was sure. Letty told Jamie what the forensic pathologist had said. Jamie's hands went to either side of her mouth and her glassy orbs pulsed from under her brow. She screamed, Letty jumped, and then Jamie started laughing. The laughed choked off and she looked at Letty and said, "Where is she then? You guys are looking, right?"

"We will be. You can count on that."

Letty, with the help of the community, gathered a large search team made up of civilians and police. Hunters who used their dogs to track came out to offer their services. Almost all the student's from Lynda's high school showed up to help. For the first two days, work stopped in Kauffmann's Vale. Schools were closed, people took the day off work to help search. Gary thought it was a great thing to see the community come together and wondered why did it always take a tragedy for people to help each other out.

13

Jodie took notes of what Gary had told her had been done so far. They organized the search teams with two officers for every ten civilians. The biggest challenge had been where do they start the search? The burning truck with the two corpses was clearly a dump site. It had been driven out there and set on fire. The murders and the disappearance of Lynda happened somewhere else, or so the theory went. And what happened with Lynda? Had she been killed and left somewhere else? Should they be using cadaver dogs for the search as well? And then, if they did, they were once again faced with the question of where to start. The whole thing was an enormous mess to begin with and then when the media people descended upon the town as locusts upon a harvest, Gary needed help. The logical step was to centre the search around the dump site. It was the only real lead they had. So, for the past three days, the search team had been out from dawn until dusk, walking in ever-widening circles and at the end of the day they handed over their GPS units to the officer on scene at the site. The GPS unit serial numbers were assigned to each individual. Their tracking information would be downloaded over-night and returned to them the next day. Before they were returned, the search team leader, Thea Maines, an officer Jodie had worked with before, would review the locations searched and strategize where to push them next. They were finding odd items; combs, a sock, condom wrappers and an empty bottle of tequila which were most definitely not associated to the crime but since they couldn't definitively prove that, they were tagged, bagged and lodged into property to be examined at a later date. With the search teams, media and the lack of any real leads in the investigation, Gary was drowning and he reached out to OPP command for more help. They sent Jodie and Gary was relieved.

Jodie said, "Is there anything to suggest Lynda is still alive?"

"Nothing evidence-based. Just a mother's hope."

"Did her dad ever make it back?"

"Oh yeah. He's at home with Jamie."

"Yeah. What about his brother? Did his brother and his friend return with him?"

"Greg did. He is Lynda's uncle. I don't know about the other guy, yet. Someone might know. So, uh, what are you...what do you need done?"

"Me? I'm going to take all the reports and the interviews and I'm going to read them tonight. Then first thing, I'm going to talk to Barbara, Henry, Jamie, Neil and Uncle Greg. You have someone that can come along with me? Someone that knows all those people so I don't get the stranger treatment?"

"Uh, yeah, Kelly can show you around. He knows most everyone around here. He grew up here."

"Have him meet me at my hotel at 7am."

"What do you need me to do?"

"I need you to keep doing what you're doing. Running the search team, making sure people get enough rest and support. You familiar with the Major Case Management model?"

"Yeah. All those reports you're about to get is from the file coordinator. I got the booklet in my office on what to do and I'm trying to follow it the best I can."

"Perfect. So in those terms, you're the major case manager. If I need resources, I'll talk to you. I'll be the primary and direct the investigation. You have a good warrant writer?"

"Nothing of this experience level."

"Okay, I'll call one in. A guy I've used before. He's meticulous and fast. A unique combination."

Gary exhaled and said, "Okay."

"Everything I do will be documented by the file coordinator so you can read the reports at the end of every day to keep up to speed." She plucked a card out of her backpack and wrote on the back. "This is my cell phone number. You can call me at any time. Is there a number I can reach you at?"

"Yeah. Sure." Gary wrote his cell number on the back of his business card.

"Make sure whoever you're sending meets me tomorrow at seven in the morning, my hotel. Okay?"

"Yup. I'll do that."

A harried-looking man entered the room, peered about, saw Jodie and Gary and walked over to them.

Holding a thumb drive out to Jodie he said, "Here you go."

Jodie said, "The case file?"

"Yup."

"Encrypted?"

"Yeah. The password is on the little sticky note on the side. Don't let anyone see that."

"I know."

The man turned and left the room as fast as he had entered.

"That's Joel. The file coordinator. I don't think he has slept since this started."

"Yeah. That happens. Well, I'll call you tomorrow."

•   •   •   •   •

Back at the hotel, Jodie read through the file, watched the interviews and made notes. They hadn't video interviewed any of the parents yet. She frowned. It was a distasteful thing to do, interviewing parents. Especially since Bruce's parents were still grieving. But it needed to be done and she added it to her 'to do' list.

She reviewed the notes of Officer Wayne and saw he had been stationed at the SUV dump site as scene security. His report read that based upon the location of the dump site, the person or persons responsible had to be local. The entrance to the roadway was hidden and the dumpsite was well away from the normal area the out of town hunters frequented, he concluded that the bodies and truck had been left there by a person or persons who knew the area.

Jodie clicked on the Forensics tab and scrolled through the images until she found photos of the dump site. The Forensics officer took photos from the roadway showing the entrance to the dirt road. Tree branches crisscrossed over the entryway and at first glance, it appeared as a wall of foliage. It wasn't until Jodie looked towards the ground did she see the tire ruts in the dirt. Driving along the road, unless you knew the road was there, you'd never see it. Reviewing the statement of Dwight and Frank, they did drive past it, missing the entrance. They even scouted the area a week or so before. Even two local people had a difficult time finding the roadway and they even knew it was there. She nodded, thinking that it had been a good observation by Officer Wayne.

Jodie didn't have an entire picture of the crime in her mind yet. There was too much information to digest in one night of reading. The knowledge would have to be absorbed and mulled over. This is where her insights came from. It wasn't police intuition or hunches. She didn't believe in such things. Her ideas on how to solve crimes came from the absorption of information and based on that information, she was able to see a pattern or something that made sense. When something didn't make sense, that is what you paid attention to until it was resolved. The solving of crimes was embedded in the idiosyncrasies. What didn't make sense to her was the idea that Lynda was still alive. Two people had been murdered and left in a truck set ablaze in a barely traveled area. It was dumb luck Frank and Dwight discovered it. And although luck helped solve plenty of crimes, it couldn't be relied on. So Lynda being alive...that didn't make sense. You kill two people and leave one alive? For what reason? To hide her? To use her? But once the other bodies were found, keeping her alive would be stupid. No witnesses was always the best policy. Lynda could have been killed and for some reason they didn't know about yet, she hadn't been left in the SUV. She could be out in the woods somewhere being feasted upon by the forest scavengers for all they knew. Still, she had to operate on the belief that Lynda still lived until proven otherwise. She sighed. Jodie could be out here for some time. She worried that if Lynda was indeed still alive, the mounting pressure from the police brass and the media could change that. Damned if you do, damned if you don't kind of thing.

Jodie closed her computer, set the alarm and turned off the light. She wondered if Graham would be able to find Lynda if he was out here with her. She wondered if she became desperate enough, would she have the courage to ask?

14

The next morning, after a quick shower, Jodie put her notebook in her backpack and slung it over her shoulder. She poured herself a complimentary cup of coffee into a takeout cup and walked outside to see an OPP police cruiser idling by the entrance to the hotel.

Jodie opened the passenger door and smiled, "You even wear the hat inside the cruiser? You trying to cover a bald spot or something?"

He tilted the brim back and said, "I like the hat. I feel more official-like with it on."

She hopped into the seat and closed the door. She said, "I would think the uniform, the gun at your hip and driving a fully marked police vehicle would accomplish that. Without the hat."

"Yeah. Well. I like it. And no, I'm not going bald."

"What's your name? Since we're going to be spending so much time together, maybe I should know that."

"Kelly Wayne."

"You're Officer Wayne?"

He squinted at her and said, "Yeah. Why? Has someone been talking about me? I'm too vain to care, but I don't mind hearing more about myself."

Jodie laughed and said, "No. I was reviewing the file last night and came upon your notes. I tend to agree with you. The dump site has the feel of someone with local knowledge."

"I'm trying to get better. I've applied to the detective office about four times now and keep getting turned down. It could be because I hit on the Inspector's wife at a Christmas party but to be fair, I didn't know she was married at the time."

Jodie rolled her eyes and smiled. She said, "Oh, I get it. You're *that* guy?"

"What guy?"

"The guy who makes bad decisions in an 'aw shucks' kind of way? I mean, you were at a work Christmas party. Who did you think she was if you didn't work with her? Someone's sister?"

"Well, when you put it that way."

"Yeah."

"Look, that's a fair point. But I'm not that guy. My wife just left me, I had a few drinks...let's just say I wasn't at my best."

"Ok. So I'll be blunt. No hitting on me or people we talk to. Let's be professional."

"You got it. I can do that. Be professional."

"Good." Jodie sipped her coffee and looked ahead.

"Out of curiosity, are you married?"

"None of your business." She smiled when she said it and continued to look forward.

"No ring. But yeah. Got it. Be professional. So boss, where are we off to first?"

"Breakfast. You need to fill me in on all the families involved here and I'm hungry. Know of a good spot?"

"You ever hear of a cop not knowing where to eat? Of course I do."

"I'm Jodie, by the way."

"Nice to meet you."

•   •   •   •   •

Over breakfast, Jodie got the run down. It's all well and good to review police reports and records about people but it was always better to talk to someone that knows them or knows of them. As well as being a flirt and making good observations at crime scenes, Kelly liked to chat with people. As such, he picked up plenty of gossip but didn't spread it. Because he didn't tell the stories he heard, people tended to trust him and more often than not, would regale him with the town's juicer rumours.

In the case of Barbara and Henry, Bruce's parents, there wasn't much to tell. Barbara was an accountant and had her real estate license. Kelly said, "She does my taxes and she helped me sell my old place and get a new one. Nice lady." Henry worked at an IT firm in Sudbury and they had another child, Lucy who was going into grade six. Bruce was a hell of a hockey player. Tough, not a puck hog and possessed great positional awareness. Kelly likened him to a young Bobby Orr. Bruce had the exceptional ability of passing the puck to where the player would be and not where they were. Because of that, he was being sought by OHL teams and university scouts from the United States. Kelly thought with the skills he had, he could have gotten a free ride to a Division One school down there.

Kelly stopped talking and looked out the window. He said, "I stopped him once. He zipped through a red light so I yanked him over. A polite kid, you know? I can't believe what someone did to him. It isn't right."

"No. No, it isn't."

Neil and Jamie were high school sweethearts that, from what Kelly had heard, weren't exactly sweet on each other anymore. Neil had a mean streak in him and it was suspected he had more than once used his fists to settle a dispute between him and Jamie. It was also heard that Jamie gave it back to him as good as she got it. A few years ago, Neil, who worked for the City snow plowing in the winter and groundskeeping in the summer, showed up to work on a hot summer day limping and wearing a sweater. Anyone who knew Neil would swear they never saw him wearing anything but a T-shirt, jeans and work boots once the snow started to melt and up until the temperature dipped to five degrees below zero. On this particular day, not only was he wearing heavy jeans, he also had a scratch mark above his right eye and a shiner to go with it. He told people he fell down some stairs. And maybe he did. But the same people saw Jamie with bruised knuckles peeking out of a wrist wrap. Add that to the fact that the neighbours had heard them yelling the night before, well, it didn't take a rocket scientist to put it together.

Jodie said, "Why are they still together? Do you know?"

"Beats me. Maybe it'd be too expensive for both of them to split up. You get used to living a certain way...I don't know, really. Could be there is comfort in living with someone you dislike. You're never disappointed by them are you?"

"That's a sad way to live."

"People do it all the time. I'm pretty sure my ex-wife hated me for a full two years before she had had enough. Of course, it could also have taken the viper that long to find someone else before leaving me."

Jodie smiled, "You call her the viper? She that bad?"

Kelly shook his head, "Not really. We were young and I think both of us expected something different from the marriage. She's not really a viper. She's a good person but not a good person for me, I guess. Although leaving me for my first cousin? I still think that was in bad taste."

Jodie laughed, then pulled it back not wanting to offend Kelly but he waved it off, "It's okay. It is a little funny. It'd be funnier if it happened to someone else, but I can see the humour in it now. Needless to say, family gatherings are awkward."

Jodie choked on her orange juice. When she cleaned herself off, Kelly said, "Who do you want to visit first?"

"I'm thinking we'll talk to Barbara and Henry. Get more background on the relationship between Bruce and Lynda. See if they know anyone from out of town who knew them, try to get an ID on the Jane Doe. After that, we'll talk to Neil and Jamie. But first, we have to let the file coordinator know, what was his name again?"

"Joel."

"Right. We'll let him know what we are up to and he can create action tasks for it in the case file. Major Case protocol."

"Gotcha."

"Can you do that? You know him right?"

"Yeah. I'll call him before we go."

15

The house of Barbara and Henry sat on a rectangular lot with golf-course-worthy grass and a stamped concrete driveway. A large maple tree stretched its leafy canopy over the lawn and onto the driveway. Hydrangea climbed the light grey brick surrounding the garage. Four cars filled the driveway and more lined both sides of the streets.

Kelly said, "Family and community support. Bruce was a well-liked kid."

They parked on a side street two blocks away and walked towards the home on the sidewalk. Floral scents competed with fresh cut grass. A lawnmower could be heard rumbling in a backyard. In these small towns of the north, the population was predominately white. Jodie knew she would be stared at. Some people would stare with curiosity, others with suspicion and thankfully, just a small minority would outright hate her for nothing more than not being white. The red door of the Hanley residence loomed before her. She wondered what type of greeting she would receive. Although she was used to the varied welcomes, it still caused a fluttering in her stomach. She exhaled and in her peripheral, sensed Kelly looking at her. Her feet carried her to the front door. She patted the gun on her hip, made sure her badge was visible on her belt and she knocked.

A young girl opened the door wearing blue jeans and a dark shirt. From the pictures of Bruce Jodie had seen, the young girl resembled her brother but with feminine features. A softer jaw and a thinner nose.

Jodie said, "Hello. You must be Lucy. Can I speak to your mother?"

Lucy said, "She's been crying a lot." After saying that, her lower lip quivered.

Jodie said, "I know. And I'm sorry. Only it's important that we speak with her and your father."

Lucy said, "There are a lot of people here."

A man stepped into the hallway behind Lucy and said, "Hey Kelly."

Kelly nodded and said, "Henry. I'm really sorry."

Looking at Jodie, Henry said, "Now is not a good time."

Jodie said, "Okay. Can I leave you my card? Can you call me when there is a better time? I'm sorry but it's real important I ask you some questions, to help Lynda."

His brow furrowed and he said, "Like you helped Bruce?"

At the mention of Bruce's name, Lucy left the door and after a few walking steps, ran up the stairs.

Henry's head turned to follow her. When he turned back to Jodie, his face burned red and he exhaled. He said, "I'm sorry. I don't know why I said that. We'll help. I uh, there are a lot of people here. I'll call you later. I promise."

Jodie handed him her card after scribbling her cell phone number on the back. She said, "No need to apologize. I'm sorry to have intruded."

"Yeah. Okay." Henry closed the door.

Kelly whispered, "That was intense."

"Death usually is."

They walked back to the cruiser, both quiet and preoccupied with the aftereffects of a parent's confused grief. Definitely, the worst part of her job was dealing with the bereaved and the almost tangible quality to the emotion of their loss. What was worse was that she knew she would have to talk to them again. After Jodie met Neil and Jamie though, speaking to the Hanley's moved to the bottom of her to do list.

•　　•　　•　　•　　•

They arrived at Lynda's home a little after nine in the morning. Not as affluent as the Hanley's, the house was smaller with red brick and siding that had once been white but was now a flaking pale yellow. The sloping roof was missing shingles yet despite the somewhat rundown appearance, the lawn was well kept and the driveway shone black with freshly applied sealant. At this home, no cars lined the streets with supporters.

Jodie said, "Doesn't look like they have many friends."

"I told you they fight a lot right? When they aren't physically fighting, they are chipping at each other with insults and they don't seem to care who they do that in front of. Makes it awkward to be around them."

"I guess that would."

Jodie climbed the few steps leading to the front door. She raised her hand to knock and the door whipped open before she could. A man stood behind the screen wearing a tank top, shorts, and no shoes. His cheeks and chin were dark with unshaven hair. Sweat dotted his brow.

In his right hand, he held a can of Busch beer. Looking at Jodie, he said, "Yeah?"

"Hello. I'm Detective Reyes with the Ontario Provincial Police. You're Neil, right?"

"Yeah."

"May we come in and speak to you?"

"I don't know you." He took a swig of beer.

Kelly leaned into Neil's view and said, "You know me, Neil."

"Hey, Kelly." He turned his gaze to Jodie, waited and said, "Alright then," and turned from the door.

Jodie caught Kelly's eye and he returned a tight-lipped nod. Jodie opened the door and stepped inside. The house smelled of Pine-sol with an undercurrent of carpet cleaner. Following Neil down a hallway, she passed a woman in the kitchen scrubbing the floor on her knees with a brush. As Jodie passed the doorway to the kitchen, the woman looked up and yelled, "Hey! Who are you?"

Behind her, she heard Kelly say, "Hey Jamie."

Jamie rushed the doorway with the scrubbing brush in her hand leaving a trail of soapy water on the floor and said, "Have you found her?"

"No. Jamie. I'm sorry, but we haven't."

Jamie dropped the scrubbing brush and palmed her eyes. Her shoulders shook and when she dropped her hands, she said, "I'll get back to cleaning, then."

Jodie said, "We'd really like to talk to you. Anything you can tell us could help."

"I don't know what I could tell you. She's a good girl. Better than me and definitely better than Neil, the slug. I wouldn't know where to start."

"Look. I'm going to talk to Neil in the living room and when you're ready, you can join us. You know more than you think you do and I need to know it too."

Jamie squinted at Jodie and said, "You do this a lot? Find missing people?"

"Yes. And I'm good at it."

"Yeah." Jamie turned her red eyes to Kelly and said, "Jesus Christ, Kelly! You're in our house. Take off your hat would ya?"

Kelly pulled the hat off his head and said, "Yes, ma'am." He smoothed his hair out, his face glowing crimson.

From the living room, Neil said, "Are we doing this or what?"

Jamie's eyes pointed at the sound of her husband's voice and until then, Jodie had never seen disgust described by a gaze before.

•   •   •   •   •

The interview, if it could be called that, took place in the living room with Neil and Jamie sitting on the same couch but on opposite ends. If they tried to get further from each other, they'd drop off the couch and onto the floor. Jodie would ask Neil a question and either Jamie answered it for him or chortled at his reply. Neil, for his part, cut Jamie off every chance he got and even did the classic move of repeating what she said in a sing-song voice for the sole purpose of annoying her. Jodie had to draw on all her skills of diplomacy to keep the interview from disintegrating into a contest of insults. She was able to get them to agree to answer her questions separately and not to interrupt the other. She reminded them the answers they provided could help her locate Lynda and they needed to focus on that. Normally, both people would be interviewed separately and on video to have an accurate record of what was said and so that the answers the interviewees provided were not influenced by the other. Jodie's intention had been to do just that. She wanted them to get to know her a bit, build some rapport and then have them attend the station for a video interview. She knew Jamie would go, but Neil, he'd already been drinking and for some reason, seemed resentful at the police even talking to him. More than once he said, "What are you doing here for? You should be out there finding my daughter!" Jodie reminded him that the search teams were out there trying to do just that. Her role was to investigate and potentially uncover information to assist in finding Lynda. Neil muttered, "Fat lot of good that's doing."

Jamie said, "Maybe if you'd been home for once, this wouldn't have happened."

"Don't start on that again. Like I have control over what Lynda does or who she dates."

Jodie noticed he used the present tense when referring to Lynda.

Jodie said, "I read that somewhere. You were away with your brother and friend?"

Neil scoffed and said, "Some detective."

Jamie said, "He was off on one of his fishing trips with his two butt buddies, Greg and Ray. They do it the same time every year. No matter what. The year my father died, Neil here didn't even cancel the trip! I went to my father's funeral by myself."

Neil rolled his eyes, "Jesus, Mary, and Joseph, will you never let go of that? We already paid for the trip, I go every year and it's not like your father even liked me!"

"You weren't supposed to be there for my father! You were supposed to be there for me!"

Jamie's red face turned crimson and to forestall the bitter vitriol about to spill from her mouth and because she was genuinely curious, Jodie said to Neil, "Where were you?"

"Fishing. Up North."

"Where?"

"Little town, Woodborough. They have a freshwater lake. Great fishing. We've been going since I was a teenager."

"Where'd you stay?"

"The same hotel we stay at every year."

Jodie glanced at Jamie and returned to Neil, "Can you tell me the name of the hotel?"

He squinted his eyes, slugged back the rest of his beer and said, "The only hotel in town, the Woodborough Hotel."

"Who did you go with?"

"My brother Greg and our best friend, Ray."

"Okay." Jodie noted the name on her notebook. To Jamie, she said, "Normally, we interview everyone in a formal setting. On video and at the police station. That way, it is a true and accurate representation of the interview. I'd like to get a better picture of Lynda. Who her friends are, what she likes to do, that sort of thing. We haven't identified the other person with Bruce and any help in doing that would be great. Would you be able to do that?"

"Anything to help. I, uh, just don't want to leave here, in case Lynda comes back. I want to be here."

Kelly said, "We can bring a camera here. We have the equipment at the station."

Jamie said, "That'd be a lot better."

Neil said, "You need to interview us again?"

Jodie said, "It'd be very helpful. This is informal. I wanted to meet you first and have you meet me before we begin the whole formal part of it. In my experience, it eases the information gathering. So. What is the best time for you? We can come back with the equipment later. Just let us know a time that works for you."

Jamie looked at Neil, shifted her eyes to the beer in his hand and said, "Six o'clock tonight? That will give one of us time to be more presentable."

Neil grunted. Jodie stood and soon after, so did Kelly. She handed Jamie her business card with her cell number on it. Jamie walked them to the front door. Neil sat on the couch, staring out the window.

•   •   •   •   •

Once in the police cruiser, Kelly started the car and they pulled away from the curb. Jamie watched them from the front door, arms crossed under her breasts.

Jodie said, "Was that typical Neil behaviour?"

"He is a shit-kicker. Known to run his mouth in the bar, get in a punch up now and again but not a bad sort as far as that goes. I always thought of him as a good dad though. He coached Lynda's soccer team for a few years and from what I heard, he was good at it. Not the overbearing yelling at the kids kind of coach. Patient with them. Wasn't too helpful now though, was he? Considering we are looking for his daughter who was last seen with her murdered boyfriend."

"That's what I was thinking. An uncooperative cooperative. He answered the question but it took him some time to get around to it."

"What are you thinking?"

"I don't know. I didn't like it, that's for sure. We should call that hotel. See if we can figure out why he didn't want to tell us the name. Also, talk to Greg and Ray. See what they have to say."

"Cheating on his wife maybe?"

"Maybe. I can't see why it would matter where he stayed, but it did to him."

16

After the officers left, Neil went to the washroom. He heard Jamie return to the kitchen and her cleaning, something she obsessively did when stressed and knew he'd be left alone while she was preoccupied. He locked the door behind him, something he never did and considered unlocking it in case Jamie checked on him and found it odd. He kept it locked. He didn't want her to walk in on him, not now.

He sat on the toilet and pulled out a throwaway cell phone Ray had purchased for each of them once the shit hit the fan and the police had found the burning truck. Of all the damn luck. No one went to that spot, not ever. They thought they would have a few more days to sort it out and cover their tracks but then Neil's cell phone blew up with calls from Jamie, telling him to get his ass home because Lynda was missing. And then they found the truck with the two dead bodies in it and Ray wanted to talk to him about what to do with Lynda, how she had to go, how she had to disappear because it wasn't just about him was it? No, it was about all of them and if he thought she wouldn't tell anyone, that she would keep their little secret, he was fucking kidding himself. Well, Ray was fucking kidding himself if he thought he would allow anyone to kill Lynda. Not his little girl. Neil didn't come right out and say that. Ray was a stone cold killer. Just like him and Greg. It wouldn't be prudent to tell him that. He'd kill Lynda for sure. Neil had to stall for time. He didn't know how to fix this or if there would be any fixing this. Not to the satisfaction of everyone. While they sorted this out, he and Greg had to go home. There was no getting around that. It'd be too suspicious to do otherwise. Except for Ray.

He had no one to report to. His mother lived with him and for all of his life, she never gave a shit about Ray and wouldn't care if he never returned. As long as the bills were being paid and there was food in the fridge, she never gave Ray any thought at all. And because someone had to stay and look after Lynda to make sure she was fed and looked after, Ray was the one to do it by default. Neil hated leaving Ray with Lynda. It left a cold pit in the hollow of his stomach. Neil was more certain about his brother, Greg. He figured Greg would stick with him on whatever decision he made. He was reasonably sure of that. But then again, who knew what someone would do when looking at a life sentence behind bars.

He dialled Ray glancing at the doorknob expecting it to turn and hear his wife bitching at him and wondering why the door was locked.

"Yeah?"

Neil said, "The cops were here."

"And?"

"A detective, one I didn't know, showed up. She was asking questions."

"Well, that's what they do."

"She asked the name of the hotel we stayed at. To go fishing."

"Huh."

"Yeah. Huh is right. Can you call that guy? Make sure he answers when they call?"

"Kind of risky. We only ever told him to say we were there if one of the wives called. The cops are a whole different kind of trouble."

"Will he do it?"

"I can ask him. He is one of those Freeman of the Land dudes, so he just might, if only to stick it to the cops. But once I call and ask, all he has to do is watch the news and although I don't credit him with too much intelligence, he could guess why we're asking."

"What do you think then? Is it worth the risk?"

"Riskier than keeping Lynda around? No."

"We're not talking about Lynda, Ray. She's not open to discussion."

"We're going to have to talk about it sometime. You going to keep her locked up the rest of her life? Is that your plan?"

"Once shit cools down, we'll talk about it. Figure something out. Shit man, I don't know, but she's off limits, you got me?"

"I got you, Neil. Speaking of her, are you able to bring her some clothes or something? I got toiletries but she's getting kind of ripe."

"I uh, I'll try. Fuck man there's a lot going on. The cops are coming back to do a formal interview. That detective, she looks at you man, she's a sharp one."

"She? Is she hot?"

"She is but not your type."

"Why's that?"

"She's black."

"A hot woman is a hot woman, man. I don't care about that."

"Would you take her home to mom?"

"Hell no! But that's not what we're talking about is it?"

"Yeah, yeah. Listen, the cops might come looking for you though, to verify our trip. Can you call Greg and let him know too? My wife is all over me. I can't take a shit without her asking where am I or what I am up to."

"Yeah, yeah."

"And Ray?"

"What?"

Neil growled, "Be nice to Lynda."

Benny Salamanca, or Benny the snake to those who knew him well, was the owner of the Woodborough Hotel in the small town of Woodborough, Ontario. Benny ran into trouble years ago with the government because he didn't want to pay taxes. He'd rather use the money for something important: like beer, fishing poles, actually for anything other than giving the money to the government for services he didn't see or use. In his greed, he conveniently forgot about the free healthcare he used and the upkeep of the roads he drove on, the kind of stuff people paid taxes for. One evening he received a notice from the government asking for more money. Sitting behind the desk in the back office of his hotel, a cigar smouldering in the ashtray at his elbow and a glass of Wild Turkey with melting ice in his one hand, he read the letter that began with "Dear Mr. Salamanca," like they were friends or something and hadn't talked in a while. He had submitted his taxes a couple of months ago and according to his calculations, he finally broke even and didn't have to pay them more. Using the tax software on a clunky laptop, he smiled thinking finally something worked out for him for once. For a brief moment, he had been happy. He should have known better. If you're never happy, if you always expect the worst, you can never be truly disappointed. According to the government, his calculations were way off. When they ran the numbers, he owed $1348.14. What pissed him off was the fourteen cents added on at the end. Did they really need that fourteen cents? They couldn't round it down? Would they financially collapse if they didn't get their fourteen cents? He crumpled up the notice and not satisfied with that, he used his lighter and set fire to it in the washroom while holding it over the toilet. When he couldn't hold it any longer, he dropped it into the water and flushed it. The tax notice was another turd on the crap show his year had been. His dog dying had been the first bad thing to happen. And when his dog died it surprised him how much it hurt. The damn beast followed him around with his tongue lolling out of its mouth half the time. It left slobber stains on his pants, on the couches, on damn near everything and when the old beast didn't get up one morning, he thought, no more dog crap to pick up. Except when Benny knelt down to pick him up intending to unceremoniously leave him at the dump, his knees buckled and tears spilled from his eyes as though he had turned on a faucet. Chest heaving wails echoed in the small hallway. He picked up the dog, Chimo, and put him on his lap and petted him until the sun climbed in through the window to sting his sore eyes. Sitting there in his own misery, knowing he loved the dog and the dog, had loved him, he wouldn't be taking the dog to the dump.

In the end, he had had him cremated, put in an urn with a placard on the front and didn't even blink at the exorbitant cost. Next thing, his truck crapped out on him. He blinked at that bill. Goddamn mechanics had him over a barrel with his pants down getting ready to fist him. He needed his truck. He used it to haul away trash from the hotel, carry new furniture and a whole myriad of things to help make his crap life a little easier. When you need something though, it ends up owning you doesn't it? You're working for it instead of the other way around. With Chimo dying and the truck on its deathbed, he was out of money and he remembered thinking, after finishing his taxes and breaking even, *finally I'm catching a break.* He should have known better. He wasn't rich. If you're not rich, you don't get those secret tax breaks that people say is good for the economy because of some trickle-down economic theory no one but the rich understand. What? So the rich get to keep more of their money on the belief they'll invest it in more jobs or more spending? Pfft. No one clutches their money tighter than the rich. It is their insulation against being a nobody. Instead of trickling down, their stacks of money grew. If they saved enough, maybe they could purchase that private jet and go on more vacations while slugs like Benny paid and paid and paid. Benny didn't want to pay. He was goddamned tired of it. Researching online on how to somehow get out of it, he read up on a group of people called the Freeman of the Land. To Benny, it seemed like a clever loophole to either get out of paying taxes or at least forestalling it.

The Freeman believe that statute laws were contracts. Since they never agreed to the contract, didn't sign them, then they were not subject to them. Tax laws, traffic laws, and even criminal laws have no authority over them because they were born into them and did not agree to them. They believe in doing no harm to others, no harm to other people's property and not to use fraud or mischief in their own contracts. They used maritime law and common law language and did not recognize the authority of the courts because, in common law, equality is paramount and since that is true, no government official or court personnel is above the law and so they must obtain the consent of the governed. Benny read up on it, researched it and sent a letter to the Canadian Revenue Agency telling them they had no authority over him and as such, could demand no more money from him. He declared his sovereignty from Canada and said he would be paying no more taxes.

Benny was not the smartest guy or the bravest. He should have foreseen the shit-storm his declaration would cause. No government would ever allow anyone to not pay taxes. And since the Freeman was becoming a popular group, the government was getting more and more of these notices. It needed to stop. So the Canadian Revenue Agency sent another letter telling Benny what would happen if he didn't pay his taxes. Clearly it had been a scare tactic, but it was one based on fact and it did scare him. It scared him a lot. Benny reviewed the chart of growing penalties for non-compliance and considered how far did he want to go with this? Don't pay and eventually, they *will* take everything from him. His hotel, his truck and if his dog was still alive, they would have taken him too. If he stalled for too long, the interest would climb and climb and he wouldn't be able to pay even if he wanted to. The government was holding his balls in their hand and if he resisted, they would squeeze and twist them. Benny paid and forgot all about being a Freeman of the Land. Except, because of all the noise he had made about being a Freeman, people still thought of him as one.

Benny thought of himself as a businessman. But not one who kept meticulous records. If someone wanted to remain anonymous, pay cash for a room, he wouldn't even note it on his ledger. He'd pocket the cash and keep his mouth shut. And if the customer happened to be a young female, he would sometimes receive sex as payment. A lot of young prostitutes came to his hotel usually with a pimp waiting for them in the car while they checked in and if they wanted a room for the weekend, well, depending on how attractive they were, they could pay with their flesh. He made enough to stay afloat and keep a little extra and yes, continue to pay his taxes. The regular sex was a bonus too. Relationships were hard. He didn't like the idea of reporting to someone every day and having them ask you why you left your shoes outside of the closet instead of putting them inside. They ask the rhetorical question in a passive-aggressive way and how are you supposed to respond to that? If you get mad, you're wrong, if you reply in a passive-aggressive manner, you're accused of being sarcastic. The only real answer was to put the shoes in the closet and wait for the next complaint of what it was that you were doing wrong. Who needed all that? And all he wanted was the sex anyway so this worked out best for everyone. In order to have the criminal type of customers return, Benny learned discretion was his best tool. When the cops showed up, he didn't see anything, hear anything and he didn't know anything. And it helped that he wasn't the curious sort. For almost twenty summers, he had rented three rooms to three men who never showed up. Benny didn't know why and he didn't care. They paid. End of story. And he could rent the empty room and get paid double for that one booking. All they asked him to do was to tell whoever called looking for them that yes, they were there but out of the room at the time. Then Benny would phone one of them and tell them who the person was that called for them. Pretty simple. And not once in twenty years did anyone call to ask.

Benny was in the manager's room smoking a cigar when his phone rang. He squinted at the screen and it read: unknown number. Not unusual. Anyone who ever called him did so from an unknown number. He didn't know why he bothered looking anymore.

"Hello?"

"Benny?"

"Yeah."

"Ray here."

"Who?"

"Ray."

Silence.

Ray said, "The guy who rents the three rooms every year? For going on twenty years now?"

"Oh, yeah. How you doing Rick?"

"It's Ray. Look, someone is going to call and ask if we stayed up there the past week. I need you to tell them yes, but you saw us leave on Monday morning. Got that?"

"Monday morning. Got it."

Benny didn't ask why or who. He didn't care. This guy paid every year and he got to pocket the cash. That is what he cared about.

Ray said, "We left in a pickup truck and a dark van."

"Okay," said Benny. He blew a smoke ring and watched it float to the ceiling. He wasn't listening to Ray about the vehicles. He was thinking about what to get for lunch. Poutine, which was bad for his waistline but good for his mental health or a chicken salad from Wendy's which was more expensive than the poutine, far less satisfying and generally a huge disappointment but in the end, better for his waistline. He heard Ray or Rick say something else and he said, "What was that?"

Ray said, "I said, can you give me a call after the person calls? To let me know how it went?"

"Uh, sure. What's the number I can reach you at?"

Ray told him and Benny hung up.

He put out his cigar, stood, winced when his right knee cracked and limped out of the office to talk to the front desk clerk. He opened the door and saw the clerk speaking on the phone, feet up on the desk and one finger knuckle deep in his nostril.

The desk clerk, Darryl, hated being a mechanic, was tired of all the grease under his nails, on his skin and the smell of the garage sickened him. It got to the point where walking into the shop made him nauseous. A cold line of sweat would headband his skull and his breath would be short little hiccoughs of sound. He knew Benny from fixing his truck up and how pissed Benny had been at the price. After the truck was fixed, Darryl quit the garage, walked straight over to Benny and said he'd clerk for him for a couple of bucks above minimum wage and act as a general handyman. What sealed the deal was Darryl offering to be his personal mechanic and promising to keep the truck running at no extra cost. Except for parts of course. Still stinging from the giant bill, Benny hired Darryl and almost immediately regretted it. And he would have more cause to regret it today.

Darryl said, "No, no it shows they were here. The room is paid for and those are the names the rooms are under but they were never here."

Benny stumbled to the front of the desk, waved his hands in front of Darryl, put a hand over his own mouth and shook his head, miming, adequately enough for Darryl to understand, that he needed to shut up.

Darryl furrowed his brow at Benny and turned from him to better concentrate on the phone. He said into the phone, "How do I know they weren't here? Well, not only were they not in those rooms, someone else has been staying in them. I thought it was weird, but the short dark haired girl staying in one of the rooms certainly isn't named Neil."

Benny rolled his eyes and reached for the phone. Darryl leaned away, covered the mouthpiece and whispered, "I got it, boss."

"Darryl, give me the damn-"

Darryl spoke into the phone, "Yeah. I'm positive those dudes never checked in. The records show they paid, but they were never here." He listened and then said, "Sure, I'll give a statement. Send someone over and I'll talk to them." Pause. "No problem. Glad to help. You have yourself a great day."

He hung up the phone, spun back to Benny to find Benny's hands reaching for him with a very red face and unhappy expression.

"What the fuck Darryl? Don't you understand basic sign language man? I told you to shut up and give me the damn phone!"

"Hell boss, what's the big deal?"

"Who was that?"

"The cops."

"The cops! Holy hell! Are you a complete moron? Stupid question, of course, you are."

"What are you all upset about?"

"Listen man, you just told the cops that I double book rooms. You just told them I collect money from one group and then rent the rooms to other people. Can you see how there might be a problem with that?"

Darryl returned a blank stare and then he blinked and turned red.

Benny said, "So you do get it? Finally."

"Sorry boss. I didn't know."

"I know that! That's why I was trying to tell you!"

Benny exhaled and closed his eyes. His heart fluttered a bit in his chest. A painful pinch and he knew he would have to calm down or else risk collapsing on the rug. He didn't want his face touching that nasty rug and he didn't want Darryl to be responsible for getting him help. The moron. When his heart stopped jigging, he opened his eyes and he said, "What did they want?"

Darryl said, "They asked about rooms 203, 204 and 205 and the dudes who rented it."

"And you told them they never showed up and we rent the rooms to other people in their place?"

"Yes."

Benny pinched the bridge of his nose and said, "Anything else?"

"Well, they asked how far our computer records go back on these guys and I said six years. And I told them the same dudes rented the same rooms around the same time every year. Then they asked if they always never showed up but I was like I don't know because I've only worked here for a few months. Then they said they would send a cop over here to get a statement from me, to tell them what I just said."

"Alright. I gotta think."

"The cop on the phone was really interested in those guys. Like, real interested."

"Yeah?"

Nodding his head and squinting his eyes, Darryl said, "Oh yeah. Like they were up to something."

Benny reached behind the desk and pulled out a box of receipts. He rifled through them and found what he was looking for. The charging address for those three rooms on the credit card showed that they were from Kauffmann's Vale. Benny pulled his cell phone from his front pocket and Google searched "news Kauffmann's Vale" and waited. Benny had wifi installed in the hotel. It wasn't fast but it worked and he waited some more.

The first headline to pop up made his jaw hang open. He clicked on it and read it and when he was done he decided he wanted nothing to do with those men. Not anymore. A double murder and a missing girl? One thing Benny learned from his experience with the government was when they turned their eye on you, there was no escape. They were like that goodamn eye in that movie, what was it again? The Lord of the Rings. That big red eye. He imagined the pressure the government applied would be one thousand times worse when it came to murder. He didn't want Ray or any of those men calling him ever again. Were the cops listening in on Ray's phone right now? Tracing it or whatever it is that they do? Did they know Ray called him?

Benny wiped a hand across his mouth, stuffed his cell phone back in his pocket and said to Darryl, "I'm going out. I'll be back soon."

"Where you going?"

Benny didn't answer. He got into his truck and drove a few short blocks to the pharmacy. Outside the pharmacy, they had an honest-to-God phone booth. The last one left in town. Benny parked a few spaces away from the phone and turned off the truck. He checked his mirrors, spun his head around, not knowing what he was looking for, spies in the bushes or something and when he didn't see anything of interest, he stepped out of the truck. He stretched, lit a cigar and did his best to appear casual as he approached the phone.

Ray answered the phone, "Hello?"

"Hey, it's the proprietor of a northern establishment."

"What?"

"People called, really interested in you and your friends. My associate answered the phone. He let them know that although you guys paid for the rooms, you didn't show up."

"Shit."

"Yes. It couldn't be helped. Don't ever call me again. And you guys are no longer welcome at my hotel."

"Well...yeah."

Benny hung up the phone and walked back to his truck. Once inside he saw a patrol car driving towards his hotel. The cops wanted the statement from Darryl pretty bad. Benny knew they would want to talk to him too, but he wasn't ready for that. He decided to go out of town, catch a matinee and think over what he was going to say to the police. He couldn't avoid them. They weren't investigating a theft from Wal-Mart here. This was a double murder and a missing girl. He'd have to talk to them soon. He just needed some breathing room first.

18

Ray had fed Lynda and closed the door on her, tired of her sullen stare and caustic remarks. She enjoyed telling him he had a small penis because that's how girls insulted boys or men and even though he knew she'd never seen his penis, the comment still struck home. He never thought he'd been big but he didn't think he was small either. There was that one girl, taken from London, who laughed at him when he pulled his underwear down when he was ready to go at her. His penis wilted under her mockery and when she saw that, she laughed even more. He made her pay for that. He'd taken her arm with a bowie knife for that. Waved the disembodied limb in front of her as her shoulder wound pumped dark, almost black blood onto the floor. She wasn't laughing then. Now Lynda was opening the old wound with sneers, comments and disdainful laughter. He wanted to twist her fucking head around. That would take the smile off her face. The bitch knew she was untouchable and used the knowledge to pick and pick and pick at him. Just today she had levelled a fresh insult at him, "Hey Ray, you know the difference between your dick and your jokes?"

He never answered her. He never did. It only provoked her. He handed her the plate of food and a can of soda with a frown.

Smiling sweetly she said, "Nobody laughs at your jokes."

His face flushed red, she laughed and he closed the door on her laughter.

Walking away from the door, wondering why the teenager was getting to him, the phone rang and he looked at the screen. Ray didn't recognize the number but this was a throw-away phone so that didn't mean anything. If anyone was calling him, it was because he gave them the number or a telemarketer was calling.

He answered. Benny gave him the bad news. Ray clicked end on the call. Holding it up to his ear, the hairs on his arms stiff as wire and his brain buzzing with static inactivity, he stood frozen. White noise filled his ears.

He blinked. A trail of drool slid down his chin. When he came to, his body shook like a dog coming out of the pool. And when he recovered from it, he found himself staring at Lynda's door. The only tangible evidence sat eating lunch behind that door. And he kind of hated her.

19

Officer Kelly clicked end on his phone after the conversation with Darryl of the Woodborough Hotel and tipped his hat further back on his head. He scrunched his nose and locked eyes with Jodie.

"They never went up north?"

Kelly shook his head and said, "Nope."

"Why would they lie?"

"To be fair, only Neil and Greg ever said they went up there. We haven't talked with Ray. Yet."

"Huh. Where is Ray?"

Kelly shrugged.

"What do you mean? This is goddamned weird."

They were sitting amidst the refuse of a Wendy's lunch. Jodie liked their cheeseburgers and Kelly liked their salads. They went through the drive-thru and then drove to the recreation centre and parked to eat. Kelly didn't mind sitting inside Wendy's to eat but Jodie did. Messed with her appetite trying to eat while people were staring at them. Kelly in his police uniform and her with a gun on her hip were a stare-worthy combination. When Jodie unwrapped her cheeseburger with bacon, Kelly groaned and said, "That smells so good."

Jodie turned a shoulder to him, protecting her burger and said, "No one forced you to get a salad."

Once they finished eating, Kelly called the hotel. Jodie expected the clerk to say, yup, they were here, they left Monday, blah-blah-blah and that would be a checkmark on her to-do list and nothing more. But it didn't work out that way. Things just got more interesting.

Jodie said, "We can't find Lynda and no one has spoken to Ray. I need to get the spin guys up here. I need them watching Neil, Greg and I need them to find Ray." She turned to Kelly, "Do we have a number or address for Ray?"

"Yeah. Only Neil and Greg said Ray decided to stay up north and finish out the week fishing since it was already paid for."

"Wait. Neil's daughter goes missing and his good friend Ray decides to stay on his vacation? Didn't that sound strange to anyone?"

"Well, maybe. You've seen our resources though. Two dead bodies and a missing girl, well, we were stretched paper thin. Hell, that's why you're here isn't it? To help us out?"

"I'm not trying to be critical. I know how short you guys are. All police services are feeling the crunch. Doesn't matter now. I'm going to get the surveillance team up here and after that, we'll go visit Greg and then strategize how best to interview Neil without, you know, accusing him of anything."

Kelly said, "It still could be they are covering for each other. Maybe Greg's having the affair or Neil and it gives them a reason to get out of the house once a year."

"Why wouldn't Ray be having an affair?"

"He's single. And he lives with his mother."

Jodie said, "He lives with his mother?"

Kelly frowned, nodded and said, "We really should have looked for him more."

"You think? It hasn't been close to a week yet and there was a lot to organize, but yeah. Let's just concentrate on finding him now. You said we have his phone number and address?"

"Yeah. It should be on file."

"Okay. You call him. I'll call surveillance and tell them what I need. If he doesn't answer, drive to his house. If he does answer, arrange an interview today, within the next hour if you can."

"Got it."

•   •   •   •   •

Jodie called her boss, the one at O.P.P. headquarters in Orilla and gave her a status report and requested surveillance. Her boss called her back and said the one team available was the one headed up by Bryce, the one they had used to spy on Graham. She didn't like Bryce too much because of their last interaction, but she didn't have a choice in the matter. She called Staff Sergeant Gary, let him know she was bringing in surveillance and told him why. He said, "Shit." And Jodie agreed. She asked him to have one of his people prepare backgrounds and photos of the targets and asked him to forward the information to her email and Bryce's email. That done, she turned to Kelly and said, "Ray?"

"No answer."

"Okay. Send a patrol officer to his house and if he's there, have the patrol officer call you and we'll head right over."

"I thought we were going over."

"I thought we'd visit Greg first. See what he has to say about all this."

"You going to ask him about the hotel?"

"Not yet. There's no reason to think he knows that we know he never went up there. Let's see what he has to say about the whole thing. Make it a routine interview."

"You want to see if he lies to you, don't you?"

"Yes. Yes, I do."

Greg was eating lunch in the break room surrounded by his coworkers when his secret phone buzzed in his pocket. He suffered a sharp pain in his heart, making his face tighten up with a bite of bologna sandwich bulging his cheek.

Barry, a heavyset man shaped like a potato noticed the wince and having gone through a mild heart attack, (that's what the doctor called it although to Barry, there was nothing mild about it) asked Greg, "You alright, man? Is it your heart? I can call an ambulance, you don't want to mess around with your heart, man."

Greg waved him off, stood, pulled the phone from his pocket and fled the break room and went outside to where all the smokers enjoyed their little sticks of slow death. The phone continued to buzz and he dragged it out of his pocket and put it to his ear, "Yeah."

Ray said, "Took you fucking long enough."

"I'm at work, man. What's the problem?"

"The cops know."

Greg's heart lurched again and his eyes roved the street looking for flashing police lights and straining to hear the high pitched whine of sirens. He eyed people walking through the lot, potential cops watching him, waiting to pounce on him and toss him in a little cell for the remainder of his life.

He said, "They coming for us?"

Ray said, "What? No. They know about the hotel. They know we never went to the hotel."

Greg exhaled, rubbed a hand along the back of his neck and offered a weak laugh, "Is that it? I thought they were coming to get us. I thought they found the cave or something."

"Shut up about that. These phones aren't registered to us but they are cell phones and people could be listening."

"So what? Even if they were, they wouldn't know what the hell we are talking about. Relax."

"Relax? How many stupid sandwiches did you eat today? Relax, he says. Tell me smart guy, when the cops ask you why, in the middle of a double murder and a missing girl, the missing girl being your niece by the way, why you decided to lie about going to a hotel, what are you going to tell them? Eh, smart guy? What are you going to tell them then?"

"I don't kno-"

Behind him, "Greg?"

He spun, the phone at his ear, to see Officer Kelly and a black woman with a badge on her belt and a gun on her hip.

She said, "I'm detective Reyes. May I ask you a few questions?"

Through his ear, before he hung up, he heard Ray say, "Fuck."

•   •   •   •   •

Greg wasn't the smartest out of the group. He took direction well, was a good little soldier and was appreciated for it. He did do all the grunt work and he knew with a rare sort of intelligent awareness that planning wasn't his strength, but he didn't mind the grunt work because the rewards were so good. Drugs, sex, rock and roll with a little murder thrown in now and again. Not a bad way to spend a week. And it let him explore different sexual avenues. He didn't think of himself as gay. What got him off was the degradation of another person, a man more often than not. To take from a man that which he didn't want to give gave him a hard on, the type of hard-on he had to stuff under his belt so it didn't tent his pants. To him, it was different with a woman. A big guy, athletic, Greg was a bull of a man and he didn't think there was a woman out there he couldn't physically force to do what he wanted. So going after a man produced the intense arousal that he didn't get from a woman. In the end though, he didn't think of himself as gay because he didn't want to. It would tarnish the self image he had of himself as being a man's man, the type of guy who smoked cigars, hunted deer and cleaned his own kill by hanging the animal upside down and skinning it while Johnny Cash sang from his radio and taking breaks to swig from a can of beer. His ignorance prevented him from knowing that gay men, other than sexual preference, do everything heterosexual men do. And that was fine with Greg. He didn't want to know such things. He dismissed the fact that in order to have sex with his wife he needed a couple of shots of whiskey and he had to close his eyes and pretend his wife was a man going down on him. He convinced her to stop shaving her legs in the winter because he liked the feel of the hair under his fingers. But no, he wasn't gay. His brother Neil brought it up once, why he only wanted to pick up dudes and they ended up breaking a coffee table and a few bottles of beer with their fighting. Ray broke up the fight and it was understood by all that the topic of Greg's sexuality wasn't up for discussion.

The simple fact of the matter was that without Neil or Ray around to tell him what to do or what to say, Greg was a mess. Now he was sitting in the back of a patrol car, with the door open because he wasn't under arrest and this was simply a friendly discussion according to the detective, with sweat running down his face as though there was a hose hidden in his hair and being asked questions he had no idea how to answer. The detective asked him how he got the injuries to his face. He paused, opened and closed his mouth, not prepared for the question but remembering what he told his wife and the people at work and so he repeated it to them. He told them he fixes up old motorbikes and sells them. He was removing a stubborn bolt and it popped off unexpectedly and he smacked himself in the face with a wrench. Jodie said, "A wrench? That line is pretty straight. Almost like a door or something."

Greg issued a high-pitched laugh and said, "No, no. It was a wrench."

The back divider window in the patrol car was open. On this shelf sat an audio recorder. Over the top of the recorder was the detective's eyes. Dark, intelligent and judging, always judging. Greg knew fear under that gaze and he didn't have the tools to hide it from his own expression.

She said, "You alright, Greg? Is it alright if I call you Greg?"

"What? Yeah, sure. I'm fine."

In the rearview mirror, Greg caught Kelly's eyes. Flat as a still pond.

Jodie said, "You're sweating quite a bit."

"It's hot back here."

"You could close the door. That way the AC would reach you."

Looking at the door, knowing that if it closed he'd be locked in here, Greg swallowed and shook his head. Sweat droplets sprinkled like jewels. He said, "No, no. I'm fine. Listen, is this going to take long? I have to get back into work."

With a smile that didn't reach her eyes, Jodie said, "We shouldn't be long."

•   •   •   •   •

They weren't long. When the interview finished and Greg eased out of the cramped backseat, his watch told him he'd been interviewed for close to twenty minutes. His eyes bulged looking at the time and he wanted to rub the watch face, to make sure the time was right because to Greg, they had been the longest twenty minutes of his life. Even now, walking into the air-conditioned building, he didn't remember most of what they had spoken about. He nodded a lot, laughed at times that didn't merit it and sweated through his shirt until it clung to him and became a part of his skin. Certain he was about to be arrested, his mind froze and all he could do was retreat into the story they had concocted before they left the burning SUV and Lynda in the basement. Yup, they were at the hotel. Neil got the call and rushed home. Greg wasn't far behind him. Concerned for Lynda, he paid his bill and left. Ray stayed at the hotel, wanting to make the most of the week. The fishing was so good you could let your boat float on a current and reel them in one after the other. Ray bragged he could have his freezer full and eat fish all through the winter if he had a mind to. He spun this story and in his gut knew it was wrong. Ray had just called him and told him the cops knew they all never went to the hotel so what in the holy-hell was he doing telling the cops in front of him that they were all there? He felt trapped. He had nothing else to tell them except the story they agreed on, the one they practiced for the last twenty years. He thought if he refused to talk to them, they'd be suspicious or if he made up a lie without the guiding hands of Neil or Ray, he'd fuck them all. Forced into a corner where any outcome resulted in Greg getting fucked, the unimaginative Greg stuck to what he knew even though it was a big fat old lie and the cops knew it was a lie. The detective asked him, more than once, was he sure he was at the hotel? Grinning and nodding like an idiot, he said sure he was, they all had been. Damnit! What were they going to do? Wiping an arm across his forehead, the sweat matting down the hairs on his forearm, Greg's heart pinched inside his chest and he stopped walking with a grimace marring his face.

He stood in the alcove, sweating in the machine cooled air with his left hand over his heart, frozen into immobility. The secretary, an old man with wisps of white hair over his pink scalp asked, "Are you alright young man?"

Greg turned to him, mouth open, surprised someone was there. He shouldn't have been surprised. He had passed by this man five times a week for the past ten years.

Greg shook his head and said, "No. I'm not alright. Can you tell the boss I'm going home sick?"

"Will do. You get on home and take it easy."

"Thanks, Pat."

Greg turned around and walked outside. In the same spot as he left them sat the cop car and the two officers inside. They were staring at him. Greg froze for two seconds and then squinting at the ground, he moved back and forth as though he'd lost something and was looking for it. Not seeing what he was looking for, he walked back into the building with the two cops' eyes burning a hole in the middle of his back.

Without looking at Pat or stopping his forward momentum, Greg said, "Feeling better. Going back to work."

Pat put down the phone.

Kelly said, "What in the hell was that?"

Jodie, frowning said, "I don't know. That is one weird dude."

Kelly said, "Did he forget we were sitting here? I mean, he just left us!"

Jodie didn't answer. The interview with Greg had been one of the weirdest experiences she ever had in a career littered with weirdness. He shook, laughed at strange times, winked at her for no reason she could fathom and sweated more than a fat man in a sauna doing pushups. And he lied about the hotel. She had given him multiple opportunities to change his story. She couldn't remember how many times she asked him if he was sure they were all at the hotel. Could he have gotten the week wrong? Was it possible they went to a different hotel? Yes, no and no. All lies. And she could tell looking at him that he knew she knew he was lying. Had someone tipped him off? Ray? Neil? But how would they know? Who had he been on the phone with when they surprised him? None of this made sense. She had never seen a more guilty witness. This wasn't a guy who was afraid his wife would find out he's been fooling around. This was a guy who saw in his future a small cell with bars. He knew something or he had done something. They needed surveillance up here immediately. She called Bryce. She told him she had two more targets to be watched. He swore, said he'd call her back and hung up. He phoned back five minutes later and said the team wouldn't be up there until tomorrow morning at the earliest because, with three targets, he'd need three teams to manage the job. She thanked him and hung up the phone. She rubbed her eyes with her palms.

Jodie said, "Okay. Can you call your boss and have someone pull everything they can on Neil, Ray, and Greg? I want to know everything they can find out? Do they own other property? Do their wives, or in Ray's case, his mother own any other property? Do they have vehicles we don't know about? I want a complete work-up going back to their elementary school days. Maybe we can get enough to get a warrant to listen in on their phones. Cancel the interview with Neil and Jamie. I want more information before I talk to them again. Especially Neil. I want to know where he is at in all this."

Kelly said, "Because if he is a suspect in your mind, you have to caution him and all that, right? With a witness, you don't have to."

"Right. Also, see if the uniform officer has gotten a hold of Ray. I really don't like that no one has talked to him yet. I mean, he's sure as shit not at the hotel is he?"

Kelly said, "You think they have something to do with all this?"

Jodie said, "Don't you?"

Looking at the door that Greg had disappeared back inside to, he said, "Maybe. That was some strange shit Greg just did. Only, I can't see Neil or Greg doing anything to Lynda. I really can't. You should see the way Neil doted on her. That shit wasn't fake. And since Greg uses Neil's brain to think, he couldn't hurt Lynda either. It could be Greg is protecting some other secret. Maybe they all are."

Jodie stared out of the window. The lie about the hotel, the interview with Greg, his walking out the door and the frozen deer expression on his face when he noticed them still sitting there, remembering all that, Jodie said, "Fuck that. They know something. And one way or another, they are going to tell me."

-22-

Greg stopped answering the throw-way phone. It rang all afternoon, well, buzzed in his pocket all afternoon. It would be Ray or Neil and he didn't want to talk to either one. He had messed everything up. He knew it and he didn't want them to tell he ruined it because he didn't want it to be confirmed. Now that the blind panic that the interview had induced faded to a dull-throbbing panic, he ran over his talk with the police in his mind. Over and over and over again. He had truly dug himself a hole here and then not satisfied with it, he went and took a crap in it.

Working on the assembly line, his hands moved without the aid of his brain. He could do his job with his eyes closed. While his fingers flew over the objects, assembling the acceptable pieces and discarded the warped ones, he worried over what to do and cursed under his breath whenever he remembered some part of the interview. Like when he winked at the detective. Why did he do that? What the hell had she asked him that he thought a wink would be a good response? Idiot. It was done now. He had done it and whatever happened after this was his fault. What could he do about it?

The phone buzzed in his pocket again. He tensed, waiting for it to end and when the vibration stopped, his shoulders lowered from the height of his ears. He couldn't tell Neil what he had done. Ray either. He loved his brother and didn't want to disappoint him. Ray simply scared the shit out of him. He felt like he was in the back of the cruiser again: trapped. What should he do? What could he do? How could he stop them looking into them? A distraction of some sort? Greg struggled to form a plan. After reviewing all the limited information he had, he decided two things. One: none of this shit started going south until that damn detective arrived and started poking her nose around. Two: the interview he had done was on an audio recorder. The detective and Kelly had the audio recorder. If he killed them, he could get the audio recorder back and it would prove a distraction from the case. A huge distraction. This plan of his, it was a big risk. He'd never done anything before without at least talking to Neil about it. What if he made everything worse? Again? Could he though? Right now, things were pretty damn bad. And what if the detective like, dumped the audio recorder off at the station, put it in an evidence locker like they do on TV? Then what?

Too many variables slipped through Greg's mind. Keep it simple. Kill the cops. Get the recording. Don't tell Neil. And definitely don't tell Ray. He could do it. He could do something on his own and maybe, just maybe, it would save them all. With the plan in mind, the energy of his fear went to the conceptualization of how to kill them both tonight. It had to be tonight because to Greg, it would give him the best possibility of recovering the recording before anyone else heard it or it was secured out of his reach. He understood how much of a gamble he was taking but still, thinking of killing Kelly made his loins fill with blood. Greg shifted and with one hand, surreptitiously pushed his erection down the side of his leg. The sensation resonated in his balls. He hummed under his breath as he worked on the line and planned through how to do it. He did know it would have to be at night and he'd have to have an actual alibi. Not like the fake hotel stay one. He exhaled. Too many problems. He hoped he was smart enough to pull it off. And lucky. A little luck couldn't hurt.

23

Kelly was a social animal. So when he dropped Jodie back at the hotel after a briefing with the Staff, he changed out of his uniform and instead of going home to an empty house, he went to the only bar in town, Jenny's Blarney. Jenny had styled it after an Irish pub. Jenny, not at all Irish, had visited the lovely green island and fell in love. She changed the theme of her honky-tonk bar and got rid of the horseshoe above the door and any decoration that was cowboy related. Dark wood, low lighting, good pub food and kegs of Irish ale transformed the place from a cowboy bar breaking even to an Irish pub making a marginal profit.

Kelly liked the place and he liked Jenny. An older woman who didn't take any crap, she routinely tossed out men who had too much to drink and by consequence, loose tongues. In her youth, she had almost made the woman's Olympic powerlifting team and still had the natural strength to pick a man up by the back of his neck and toss him outside. Kelly had to deal with complaints from men who had been tossed out. Jenny had every right to toss out an unruly or rude customer and most times, the reason the man was so upset was that he got thrown out by a woman and he knew he'd be berated and harassed by fellow ignorant men. That wasn't Kelly's problem and the men usually left with a pouty, protruding lip and a grave injury to their pride. What pissed them off was that Jenny wouldn't allow them back in until they apologized for their behaviour. They'd have to stand in front of her, explain why they were sorry and promise to never do it again. Kelly had seen it once. The man resembled a child standing in front of a disappointed parent. Chin tucked into his chest and hands clasped at the waist. Most men did apologize but only because Jenny ran the one bar in town. Kelly visited the bar often and everyone in town knew it, including Greg.

By the time he walked in through the front doors, it was after 9:00 o'clock at night. He would have to get up early tomorrow to get to the station, change into his uniform and pick up Jodie to do whatever it was she had planned, so he decided to have a quick meal with a Guinness before turning in for the night. He stopped at the entrance and enjoyed the smell of baked, greasy food before making his way to a bar stool. Families sat in booths, a baby cried and Irish folk music played softly from speakers. Young waiters dressed in white shirts with black ties hustled about. Jenny stood behind the bar staring at a screen. The glow lit her scowling features. She noticed him, smiled and said, "Hey Kelly. How are we tonight?"

"Hey, Jenny. Fine."

"Any luck finding Lynda yet?"

"Not so far."

Frowning she said, "That's a bad business."

"Yes, it is."

"What can I start you with?"

"A Guinness. Sirloin steak, medium with garlic mash."

"You bet."

Kelly drank his beer, ate his dinner and spoke to people passing by, everyone curious about Lynda and what, if any, leads they had. With his social quota filled, Kelly paid his bill, left a tip for Jenny and left.

•   •   •   •   •   •

In the parking lot, he passed people walking in, said hi to those he knew and nodded to those he didn't. He took the keys out of his pocket, jangled them and approached his pick-up truck sandwiched between a minivan and another truck. He was considering watching the new episodes of *Brooklyn Nine-Nine* recently added to Netflix and since each show was twenty-one minutes long he thought it wouldn't keep him up too late. He didn't want to be dragging his ass tomorrow. Detective Reyes moved fast and he needed to be fresh to keep up.

He clicked the unlock button and reached for the door handle on his truck. A shadow popped up in front of the minivan and rushed him. He put a hand up, said, "Hey!" The knife slid under his outstretched arm and sunk into his stomach. His knees shook and he locked a hand onto the wrist holding the knife. A fist crashed into his jaw, he let go of the wrist, saw bright stars wavering before his eyes and he felt the sharp blade leave his guts.

Kelly said, "Don't!" The knife rammed into his chest and was yanked out. Blood ran out of him. His clothes soaked some of it up. The rest ran down his skin. With his back to the truck, his legs weakened and he slid down the door. Another flash of silver and the knife went into his chest again. He heard the other man grunt. Kelly dropped to the pavement, his breath in shallow gasps as the shadowed man stuck the knife in him once more. The man knelt down beside him and patted him down, went through his pockets. All this for a robbery? Stab a man for the change in his pocket? The man put his hands on Kelly's midsection and grunted as he pushed him under the truck. With every grunt, Kelly slid further under until he could see the undercarriage. There was beer on the man's breath and maybe some marihuana, something strong and earthy. Kelly raised his hands to hit the man, or did he? He wanted to, oh god, he wanted to except his body wasn't listening to him anymore. Kelly was freezing. Strange, because the blood leaving him was so warm. His teeth chattered.

"Hey! What are you doing? Get away from that truck!"

The man with the bad breath said, "Shit," and ran away from the voices.

Kelly heard boots on the pavement and the clicking of heels.

"Think that fucker took anything from the truck?"

A woman replied, "No. I think you scared him off."

Kelly gurgled, trying to say, 'hey' or something, anything to get their attention. So cold. All he could see were jeans, boots and pale legs in red heels.

"Good. Some asshole took my wallet from my car one time. You know how hard it is to get all your ID back?"

The woman said, "What is that?"

"What?"

"That. Is that...a person?"

The man said, "Holy shit!"

The boots rushed over.

Eyes peered at Kelly. Kelly smiled. He thought he did. Didn't matter once the darkness came.

24

Greg ran from the parking lot to the dark area behind Jenny's Blarney wearing a dark ski mask and a backpack on a hot summer night. Definitely suspicious looking and he needed to get out of sight. He hopped a fence and sped through a green space where, during the day, people used their lunch hour to walk their dogs. He had parked his truck 1.74 miles away, according to Google maps. Hurrying along, he slipped off his backpack, took off his ski mask and stuffed it inside. He pulled off his gloves, turning them inside-out and put the knife in the bag as well. Concentrating on what he was doing, he had to make a real effort to stay on the trail. The lights from the plaza dimly lit the path and made the shadows darker, almost black. Out of the glow, the forested area was dark as pitch. He zipped up the bag and using his phone's GPS map, he ran-jogged the trail, waiting for the wail of sirens to start heading towards him. Squinting at the bright screen, he kept losing his night vision whenever he looked at it but it was his guide and he needed the damn thing to find the fence surrounding the quarry. Looking down at his phone, he walked into the fence meant to keep people out of the area and from falling a few hundred feet at the sudden drop-off onto sharp rocks. He grunted, dropped the phone into the brush and the light went out.

"Damnit!"

He knelt and swiped his hand across the ground to where he thought the phone landed.

"Where is it?" He said through clenched teeth. He tensed, his shoulders climbing up to his ears. He heard it then. The sirens. He moaned and turned back to the ground, the tension pulling at his bowels and he thought he just might have to take a crap out here. He realized the saying wasn't just a saying, was it? Scare the crap out of you? That could actually happen. He was touching cotton here and he needed to go and he couldn't take a crap on the forest floor after committing a murder and he couldn't leave his fucking phone. It was the burner phone. He needed it, but the ambulance was coming and behind them? That's right. The cops. They might even have a dog with them. Follow his stink right here, where he had shit himself looking for his stupid phone in a dark forest and his hand closed over the hard plastic and he was so relieved, tears blurred his vision. He stood and stuffed the phone in his pocket. Holding the handle of the backpack tight in one hand he waited for his night vision to return. He saw the fence line and didn't think he'd be able to throw it far enough from here. He moved along the fence watching where the earth ended and the drop into the quarry began while the screeching sirens announced their impending arrival. There. He found a spot. He gripped the handles, aimed for a gap in the trees and tossed the bag over the fence and into the quarry below. He made his way back to the path and hustled to his truck. One cop down. If he wanted to get both of them, he had to move. If only those two people hadn't stumbled upon him shoving Kelly under the truck. He had wanted to go through the truck and see if the recording was in there. Too late now. Goddamnit. Still, he knew that could happen so no reason to bitch about it now. Besides, the detective probably had it. She was the detective after all. And who knows? It might work out for him. If he could get to the hotel before the detective hears of this, he could ambush her. Not in the lot, there were too many cameras there. Too many cameras everywhere. But he could get her leaving the lot when she gets to the road. He scouted it before and he could roll up on her, fire a couple of slugs from his Mossberg pump into her and be done with her. Wait. How would he get the recording then?

He stepped out of the bush, scanning the road to make sure all was clear, and then he ran to his truck and climbed in. He had another ski mask and gloves in the passenger footwell. They were under the top rack in his toolbox. He turned on the truck and mulled over the problem. He'd need time to search the hotel room and the detective. How could he do that? He'd have to be bold. He'd have to be fast. It'd be ideal to kill her in her room. He grinned in the darkness. He loved this shit. He loved killing and remembering the way Kelly had dropped under his knife, like he had cut off his legs instead of just stabbing him, thinking about it made Greg grow erect. A painful pleasantness in the confines of his black jeans. It'd be fun doing the detective too. But Kelly? He'd remember that forever. He had to get a move on though if he wanted this to work. Time for the detective. No reward without risk. He put the car in drive and peeled out.

-25-

Jodie was reading in bed when she got the phone call. She was wearing comfy jogging shorts, a tank top with no bra because it was that glorious time at the end of the day when she could unstrap the tight undergarment and just...relax. She was listening to the audio recording of Greg and typing it out on a word document to be added to the case file later on. She wanted to finish it and send it to the file coordinator so it would be done and she could start the day without having to worry about it. The TV was on, playing a cooking show where the contestants had to cook with set ingredients to have their self-esteem shredded by the master chef judging their dishes. Jodie saved the file of Greg's interview, emailed it to the file coordinator and frowned. She thought again how strange he had acted and wondered what she was going to do about it. She turned on her iPad and settled on reading a Joe Lansdale novel about Happ and Leonard through the Kindle app. The TV muttered in the background and everything was fading away as the book pulled her into the story. She was disrupted by her ringing phone. She had plugged it in and left it on her nightstand. She jumped when it rang and thought she should turn the volume down on the ringer because right now, it was obnoxious.

"Hello?"

"Detective Reyes?"

"Yes."

"It's Irene? Down at the station?" She spoke like that, statements as questions and it irritated Jodie.

"What is it, Irene?"

"Kelly's been stabbed? They're rushing him to the hospital?"

She tossed the iPad onto the pillow beside her and flicked the blanket off her legs and put her bare feet on the floor. Although it was quiet in her room, the TV a low murmur, she pressed the phone to her ear.

"What? When? Is he ok?"

"We don't know?"

"Is there someone that does know? Is Staff Barnes around? Can I talk to him?"

"He got called at home too? He's on his way to the hospital? The big one in Sarnia? He's the one who said I should call you?"

Jodie nodded. She'll have to thank him later.

"Alright, Irene. Thanks for calling."

Before Irene could answer with a statement-question Jodie ended the call and held the phone in her lap, staring at her reflection in the glass and marvelling at how bright the white tank top was against her dark skin, with her thoughts on pause. When she came out of it, she gasped and stood. She needed to get dressed. Where were her clothes? Some were in the closet, some were in her carry bag. Should she shower first? No, no, get dressed, get moving. Who was working the scene? Never mind that now. Get fucking dressed and go see how your friend is doing. And that's when she realized she thought of him as such. Not an actual good friend but there were the makings of one there. He was definitely someone she thought she could count on in so short a time. She scrambled about the room, slipping off her shorts and pulling on a pair of jeans. She pulled a T-shirt on and over her tank top and slipped her badge onto her belt. She removed her pistol from the portable safe the department had given her and after slapping in a full magazine, she put it into her holster and scooped her car keys off the counter by the front door. She slipped her hotel card into her pocket and after looking around the room to make sure she hadn't forgotten anything, she opened the door and stepped into the hallway. A man wearing a ski mask and a long dark coat entered the hallway from a stairwell. Seeing her, he opened the flap on his coat and raised a shotgun.

26

Have to be bold. Have to be fast. Greg had one chance. He had called the hotel earlier before he had dealt with Kelly and was mulling through the possibilities. He asked to be connected to her room, the clerk said sure and Greg stated like he knew, she's in room 210 right? And the clerk said no, she was in 341 and once the clerk connected the call Greg hung up. He didn't want her picking up the phone. On their website, they had the floor plans listed so Greg even knew where the room was in the hotel. Almost too easy. Like fate was telling him to do it. He thought if he could get to the detective before she left the hotel, before she even got out of her room, he could keep her in the room and have time to talk to her. Time to persuade her to give him the recording or to tell him what she had done with it. Then he'd kill her because asking about the recording, she would know whose face it was under the ski mask and wielding a shotgun. Greg would use the shotgun if he had to though. Pretty damn loud, blasting one off in a hotel. He had another knife on him. Hell, he had plenty of knives and they were so much better to use than guns any day. They were...personal. He thought of Kelly's eyes, the total fucking surprise man, the like *what the hell* expression on his face and then the blood pouring out and coating his glove. He could feel the warmth of it through the leather. Damn. No other feeling like it. He had to get to the detective quick, though. If she was already gone...huh, he could search her room at least. Make it look like a break and enter or something. He shook his head. No one would buy that shit. Kelly getting stabbed and the detective he had been driving around town had her room broken into? Still, what could they do about it? Provided Greg got back before midnight, he'd have an alibi and everyone could go and fuck themselves as far as he was concerned. Including his brother and that tool, Ray.

Greg was steaming along, thinking his angry thoughts as he navigated through the town on autopilot. He didn't need to think of where he was going. He grew up here. He knew every little place. He knew the hotel was right by the main road into town and behind it was the failed paper plant. It was abandoned and about to be torn down to make way for more businesses, more hotels, more everything. Greg knew there were no cameras there. He pulled into the lot and turned off his headlights. If he'd pull this off he'd be a fucking hero. Neil and Ray would beg to kiss his ass. And he might even let them.

He crammed a dark ball cap on his head and stepped out of the truck. He threw on a long, dark coat to hide his shotgun. He could tuck the butt under his armpit and hold the barrel through the fabric of the coat. Anyone looking at him would see a man walking weird but no one would think *gun*. He stuffed the other set of gloves into the mask and put them in his pocket. He opened a little paper packet and poured a bit of powder on the webbing between his thumb and index finger. He'd taken some before leaving the cabin because fuck those guys. He snorted the cocaine and felt the lightning in his blood as the drug shot energetic tendrils to his brain and he said, "Goddamn!"

He picked up his shotgun and tucked it under his coat. Staring at the lights of the hotel, the cocaine made him feel invincible, he smiled, locked his truck, and jogged through the construction churned dirt to the detective.

The lights drew him on. The cocaine buzzed under his skin. His heart bumped his ribs and his breath expelled in a hard rasp. Even with the cocaine to aid him, he thought he should try to get into better shape. The drugs conjured up the idea that, once all of these loose ends were tightened, he could start running, maybe even compete in a marathon or something. The good thought brought more good feelings fuelled further by the synthetic happiness coursing through him. He stopped at the hotel lot and breathing hard. Standing on a curb outside the radiance of the adjacent gas station lights, frowning at the sign and sweating from jogging in the heavy coat trying to calm his hammering heart, he considered his options. He couldn't walk in like this, could he? Especially not through the main lobby. Bound to be cameras in there. What the fuck was he thinking? Cocaine had many side effects but the most common one happened to be paranoia and Greg wasn't immune. He straightened with fear. What if the cops were here now, waiting for him, wanting to ambush him? What if they knew he had stabbed Kelly and hoped he'd come here so they could justify shooting him down? He swallowed a hard lump and he checked his surroundings without looking like he was trying to check his surroundings. Anyone watching him would be suspicious of a man wearing a hat pulled low, long heavy coat on a hot summer night with his head on a swivel. He would give off all sorts of 'uh-oh' vibes and thinking this made him step off the curb and continue walking with as much cool as he could. A lucid part of him convinced himself the cocaine was making him paranoid and that his plan was still a good plan. He just needed the balls to pull it off. He decided not to go through the lobby and hope the good detective hadn't heard what had happened to Kelly yet.

He walked around the side of the hotel careful to stay out of the light. Cars dotted the pavement and bright circles of light from overhead posts shined off paint and chrome. No one wandered through the lot. He knew you needed a card to get in the back way and he didn't have one. It wasn't like he could just go in and register for a room now. With his free hand, he started biting his nails, wandering back and forth along the wooden fence line in the shadows. What was he going to do? Fucking recorder. Fucking stupid lying in the back of the cop car while they sat there and let him keep lying about it like they didn't know! They were cops! Weren't they supposed to call people on their bullshit?

A car pulled in the lot and Greg slid behind a bush and ducked. The headlights swept over him and he waited, his hand cramping from holding the shotgun tight to his side for so long. He heard the car park and peered around the bush. A middle-aged woman exited, tight jeans, with her hair done up in nice glossy black ringlets. Going on a date? Coming back from one? Didn't matter. Greg could do this. He had to time it right, but it could be done.

The woman rummaged in her purse, looking for who-knew-what, and then satisfied, began walking towards the door. Greg picked up his pace while trying to stay silent. Someone running up behind you is liable to startle you and he didn't want that. He wanted to be a nice hotel customer, reaching the door the same time she did so that she wouldn't think to ask him for a card or even care. And that's what he did. He heard the beep of the card reader and she yanked open the door and he was behind her to hold it wider while she walked inside. She glanced at him, offered a corner cheek smile and went through the fire exit door into the first-floor hallway and Greg was left alone. He stood still, listening for steps on the stairs above and hearing nothing he took his hat off and removed his mask and gloves. He stepped away from the door because he had to put the shotgun down to get on his gloves and mask and didn't want anyone walking in on that. He wanted to see into the lot before anyone could see him. Hurrying, he put on the gloves, pulled down the mask and put his ball cap into the pocket he removed his mask from. Tucking the shotgun under his coat again, he paused, listened for footsteps or a banging stairwell door and hearing nothing he inhaled a few quick breaths through the cotton mask and ran up the stairs. This was the tricky part. Running up all exposed like this. There was no explaining away this weirdness.

He opened the door on the third floor, listened at the open door, heard nothing and then pulled it open and stepped into the hallway. And there she was, maybe fifteen feet away with her eyes all big in her face looking at him, like the dummy he was, standing in a hallway with a ski mask on. He pulled out the shotgun, wanting to scare her, get her hands up and hopefully talk her back into her room. He was raising the barrel to bring the sights up to his eyes and the detective's hand dropped and like magic, a gun appeared in her hand. His eyes widened, feeling like they were going to pop from his skull concentrating on the detective's gun rising to point at him and then the sights of his shotgun were level with his eyes and he thought, too fast, she's going to fucking shoot me and so he pulled the trigger first but as he did it, he knew he was way off and he was. He cringed from the deafening boom of the shotgun and managed to keep his eyes open to see the shot tear into the roof above the detective, tearing drywall and shattering the plastic glass over the ceiling lights. She dropped to one knee, the gun aimed right at him and he backed up hoping to pop open the door with his butt and her gun fired. The glass plinked behind his right ear and he jerked and following her example he dropped to one knee and the glass behind where he'd just been was rapidly being shot out. He was going to fucking die in this damn hallway! He had the drop on her and everything and she was kicking his ass out here and he was going to fucking die and his brother would be pissed and the shame of that, the bitterness of a lifetime of disappointing his older brother made him gather himself for one more push and he dove onto his stomach with the shotgun held out before him, bringing it to his shoulder to take aim except he had his finger on the trigger when he hit the ground and it boomed before he could properly aim it. The shot skimmed along the ground and this time he closed his eyes because his chin hit the floor and made his teeth clack together painfully. He heard a scream, thought, *got her*, and considered finishing her off or making sure it had been a kill shot when he heard sirens in the distance. Fear made his sphincter loosen and he clamped it shut. It was hard to run with a load of crap in your pants. He stood, grabbed the handle to the stairwell door, yanked it open and hearing one last yelp of pain he grinned in his mask. Serves her right. Another shot plunked into the metal frame on the door, where his head had just been. He flinched, said, "Fuck!" And fled down the stairs. He ran out the door into the parking lot bothering to hide the shotgun in his coat. He ran all the way to his truck, sticking to the shadows, gasping for air with sweat soaking him under his pits, across his chest and running into the crack of his ass. At the truck, Greg put the shotgun on the floor of the truck behind the seat. He ripped off his mask, took off his coat and gloves and tossed them on the passenger seat. He started up his truck and within twenty minutes, he was in his driveway and sneaking into his house using the walk-in basement door out back. Once inside, he wrapped his shotgun, coat, sweaty clothes and mask in plastic and sealed it with duct tape. He put the package in the sump pump well. He took a shower in the basement and then walked upstairs. His wife was smoking a cigarette in front of the TV, and blowing the smoke out the open window. He barely talked to his wife, a situation that suited them both, but he wanted her to remember him being at home. He made a big deal of telling her he'd be working in the basement garage earlier for that reason. It was a gamble. Because if she had gone down there, he wouldn't have been there but then she never went down there. Too busy smoking cigarettes and watching TV. Not much of gamble, really.

"What you watching?"

Stephanie turned to him, squinted suspiciously and said, "*Scandal.* Why?"

"No reason. I uh, finished rebuilding the Yamaha. Should be able to sell it for a good price. Maybe we could go to dinner and a movie sometime."

He shouldn't have pushed his luck. Asking her to go on a date? What was he thinking? She paused her show to look at him, to see him and exhaling a plume of smoke, she stared at him and said with a searching look, "Okay. That'd be nice."

Greg said, "Goodnight."

Stephanie said, "You wanna fool around? Maybe?"

Thinking, *fuck*, he forced a smile and said, "Sure. Finish watching your show though and I'll see you up there." He waggled his eyebrows and she laughed before turning back to the TV.

Greg went into the kitchen and took out a bottle of Jack Daniel's. He threw back three shots, paused, and poured one more. Thinking of having sex with his wife, he shivered, drank the shot and walked upstairs like a man on death row approaching the electric chair. The things a man has to do to build an alibi.

27

Graham had been busy. His goal was to be completely independent at his home in the woods. He wanted to generate his own power, have access to his own water and grow most of his food. There were some barriers to being self-sufficient. He liked milk in his coffee and in his oatmeal but he didn't want a cow. He'd have to make a pen, buy feed, and then wouldn't he have to get the cow a friend? Another cow to socialize with in cow-speak? A good first step was to make his own power and have a source for water. He was growing oats but the processing part of turning it into edible oatmeal also didn't seem to be worth it. He'd been having the extras delivered to him once a week, same time (9:00am), same place (the road into town) and this was his day for pick up. He ordered the same items every time and paid the account yearly in advance by sending a cheque through the mail. He didn't like the outside world but not because he hated people, only because of what being around too many of them did to him.

Sitting at his table, coffee by his hand and an empty bowl of what had been oatmeal in front of him, Graham planned his day. He always had music on in the background and while he planned, he tapped the pencil against the table. The music helped to calm his brain. In this peace, he considered what he needed to do. He wanted to expand the solar array because he wanted to increase the size of his hydroponic garden and for that, he needed more energy. He would need to clear away more land and he was looking forward to the hard work. Nothing made him sleep better at night than pure, physical exhaustion. And, Graham had to admit, there was satisfaction in accomplishing something tangible, something real. Considering the areas on the map of his land he had surveyed, he heard the radio change from music to news but he wasn't hearing it, it was more of an awareness to the change in sound. A fraction of his concentration on the task list wavered when he heard the name Kaufmann's Vale. It didn't draw him out but it did draw him closer to the now, to the present. When he heard the name Detective Jodie Reyes, his one eye turned to the radio, his list forgotten. Listening, his pulse rate increased when the announcer in a grave, serious voice, the same voice Graham had heard him use when talking about anything, like inflation, said Detective Jodie Reyes had been shot and another officer had been stabbed and they didn't know either officer's status at this time. The pencil dropped from Graham's hand with a *clink* to the table.

•   •   •   •   •

Graham used his satellite phone to call Jodie. It rang and rang and his heart tugged on the arteries and veins inside his chest. He'd been clenching his teeth together and one of his teeth bit into his gums. His mouth had been badly damaged after the shooting and because they didn't line up, in times of stress, like right now, grinding his teeth ended up shredding his gums and filling his mouth with salty blood. He tasted it now and it pissed him off that he'd forgotten that he could no longer clench his teeth. Like in so many ways, he was different, a freak now, and normal no longer applied to him. And why wasn't she answering? How hurt was she? They didn't know on the radio? Really? A cop getting shot was big news. Either they knew and weren't saying, or they didn't know because no one was telling them. Graham knew why, sometimes, the police didn't share all their information. When someone was killed, it was in poor taste to broadcast it on the news before the family had been notified. Is that what they were doing? Trying to get a hold of Jodie's parents first? He clenched his jaw again. Pain lanced through his jaw up to his eye. He spat the blood from his mouth into the sink. A red octopus shape on the stainless steel. Why wasn't she answering? A headache was growing behind his eye. He knew the feeling. If it grew it could put him down for the rest of the day and leave him whimpering in a dark room with a cool cloth on his head. No. That can't happen. He needed to get control of his anger. Right now, it burned hungrily, taking all of Graham's worry and compressing it tighter and tighter and waiting for enough fuel to explode. And all the time, the damn phone rang in his ear. Click. Jodie's voice greeted him cheerfully and encouraged him to leave a message. He disconnected and white-knuckled the phone in his fist. He inhaled until his lungs filled and he expelled the air for a count of five. He repeated the action until his head cleared and the rage waves stopped rippling and Graham was left with a clear, placid mind. It had taken some time for the anger to fade, but it did and now he could think. What to do now? He had to go to her. But how to get there? There was no way he was hanging around here, waiting, not knowing. What would he do? Go back to working on the solar panels? Even that wouldn't still the fears swimming along the surface.

He paced in the kitchen, considered calling his mom, see if she would drive him but being in a car with her for that long, well, that would be a challenge to his patience. She was great in small doses. A long car ride was not a small dose.

Graham lifted the phone and with his thumb ready to depress the redial button, it buzzed and rang in his hand.

"Hello?"

"Hey, Graham."

"Jodie? Ah, man." His voice trembled, "It's good to hear from you. The radio said they didn't know how bad you were injured and I didn't know who else to call."

"Graham."

"Yes?"

"They killed him, they stabbed him and left him in a parking lot to die and..." her crying filled his ear. He ground his jaw. More blood filled his mouth. His hand was so tight on the phone, he could feel the muscles beginning to cramp.

She rambled in between cries, "There was no reason to do it...not that I could see, we weren't close to anyone, he was a good guy...Kelly, really funny and nice and he liked people, wanted to help them. So different from the other cops who want the good pay and pension and could give a shit if they help anyone...I don't know what to do, I don't know where to start-"

"Jodie?"

"Thank God I don't have to talk to his parents or do you think I should? I don't-"

"Jodie?"

"Graham, I'm so glad you called, I was going to call you, they have me on painkillers here and I thought I was going to pass out, and maybe I did, what time is it? Doesn't matter. I got off easy. Couple of stitches in my left hand and along my rib cage, not like Kelly, stabbed in the chest and goddamnit! We must have been close or else why would they do this? I'm not thinking straight. Greg. He's something. I don't know what, but he's something. Would he-"

"Jodie. I'm coming. I'll be on my way soon. We'll get them."

"When do you think the funeral will be? Wait-what? You're coming?"

"Yes."

Graham heard Jodie's voice sober immediately. This was detective Jodie on the phone now.

"Graham. I don't know what it is that you do or how you do it, but can you stop this? Like you did with Francine?"

"Yes. I think I can."

"But it will hurt you, won't it? A lot? I know you never told me, how you do it, but I get that it hurts, right?"

"Yes."

"Will, whatever it is that you do, will it, could it, kill you?"

"I don't know. Maybe."

She said, "I don't want you to be in pain, Graham." She didn't tell him not to come. She wanted him there but she also didn't want him there. She was worried about Graham but a girl was still missing. There were three people dead, including a cop, and Jodie could have been killed too. He had to go. They both knew it and because of the knowledge, they also knew how much their friendship meant to each other. Looked like Graham would be calling his mom after all.

"I know."

"See you soon."

"Yeah."

After talking to Graham, Jodie phoned her parents and assured them she was alright. She didn't call them right away. She needed time to pull herself together. If she fell apart speaking to her parents, her parents would make the long drive to see her and she didn't want to worry them. They worried enough as it was. She surprised herself with how calm she had been when talking to her mom and dad on speakerphone. An officer she had been working with had been killed after all, and presumably, the same person had tried to kill her too. What if they came back for her? Who was protecting her? Bombarded by all these rational questions in her dad's musical island lilt, she told him she was fine, she was going to be discharged soon and she would have to return to work right away. If they came to see her, it would be maybe a five-minute visit before they would have to turn around again and go home. So, they shouldn't bother. She was fine. They needed to trust her. She needed to get back to work. After many assurances, placating promises of taking time off right after this investigation, Jodie hung up the phone, almost certain her parents wouldn't be driving up here to see her. Once she finished with that, the effects of the painkillers had cleared from her mind. From her hospital bed, she started making phone calls. The first thing she wanted done was for Greg to be interviewed again, then Neil and someone had better find out where this Ray guy was. While that was being taken care of, she would begin her campaign of annoying the hell out of the hospital staff to expedite her release.

The shotgun blast had never touched her. The two shots fired at her had tore into the ceiling and the floor. Pieces of glass left scratches on her face and the doctor spent some time plucking out the shards all the time remarking how lucky she had been that none of the glass had gotten into her eyes. A piece of wood from the floor, a three-inch splinter, ripped into her left hand between the index and middle fingers. More wood from the same shot shredded her shirt along with the skin on her ribs. Small pieces of wood and debris gouged her ribcage and bits were embedded in her skin. They had been worried some of the shrapnel had pierced her internal organs and they rushed her into x-ray to assess the damage. Nothing had penetrated deep enough to cause further concern. A few stitches and dressings and she was good as new. The splinter in the hand was the worst. They made her sleep for that part of the surgery to repair what they could. She may never have full use of her left hand again. She was right-handed and as long as she could hold her gun, it wasn't a huge concern of hers. Considering everything, the doctor was right: she had been lucky. Kelly's smiling face floated in her mind. With her phone in hand, crying overtook her and when she sucked in some air to push her sadness aside, she drew from her anger to give her strength. Her eyes cleared and her nostrils flared. Jodie was pissed.

•   •   •   •   •

A few hours after talking with her parents, Jodie left the hospital and returned to her hotel. The manager wasn't happy to see her but after much grumbling, he gave Jodie a new room on a different floor because when Jodie arrived, police were still processing the hallway outside of her room. Once in her new room she cleaned up, put on new clothes and wearing a bulletproof vest this time, she drove to Greg's work. Bryce and his team had set up on him in the parking lot. They didn't get him leaving his house in the early morning because they arrived in town too late for that. Another team attended to Neil's work and had positioned themselves to wait and watch. As for Ray, no one had seen him yet.

Jodie spoke with Staff Sergeant Gary Barnes prior to leaving the hotel. He offered to send her another officer to drive her around. She declined. Kelly's smiling face and his stupid hat haunted her. She knew she shouldn't be speaking to suspects alone, and that is what Greg was now, a suspect, so she requested a uniform officer to meet her at Greg's work for safety reasons. The surveillance team was also in the lot. It bothered her that no one had found Ray yet. A lot about this investigation bothered her. She turned into the lot and seeing the cruiser idling near the employee door, she thought of Kelly and blinked moist eyes. Goddamn Kelly. Why did they kill him? Huh. Why was she thinking they? Because she believed Greg and Ray to be involved? Even Neil, though considering it was his daughter missing, that was a stretch at this point. Not impossible, but not likely either.

She parked the car, scowling, her sadness morphing into anger. She turned off the car, opened the door and sucked in air and winced. She opened the door with her left hand and the stitched hole between her fingers didn't like the movement. Waiting for the waves of pain to recede, she blinked and breathed deep. When the pain became bearable, she stood and cringed and hung onto the top of the door frame with her good hand. Her ribs didn't much like that movement either and she gritted her teeth, hating this helpless feeling, hating it more than anything.

"You alright?"

The uniform officer, seeing her struggling, approached to help. An older woman with deep laugh lines goal-posting her mouth, her eyebrows were drawn down with concern.

"Yeah. I think so."

"Okay."

The woman stood behind Jodie, scanning over the top of cars and taking the lay of the land as uniform officers tended to do. Jodie closed the door and patting the gun on her hip, she nodded at the officer and walked to the employee door. She was irritated and she knew it. Never a good idea to interview anyone when in such a mood. Anger would ruin her objectivity. She couldn't help it though. With the officer on her heels, she yanked open the door and in a tone that had the secretary leaning away from her, she demanded to see Greg. Jodie was told he'd be out to see her in a minute.

•   •   •   •   •

The air conditioner in the lobby made the whole area cold. Cold enough that Jodie expected plumes of her breath to escape her mouth. At first, walking into the lobby was refreshing but it didn't take long for the cold air to become uncomfortable. The air raised nodules on Jodie's arm. Despite the cold, when Greg walked into the greet them with his awkward smile, he was sweating. His T-shirt sported dark circles at his armpits and a jagged sweat line ran from the collar to the middle of his chest. Jodie took to rubbing her arms because they were so cold and here was Greg, inside of a minute talking to her, sweating as though he had finished running a marathon, smiling an obsequious smile, saying he was more than happy to cooperate but after she issued him the caution, refusing to attend to the station with her to talk on video and even refusing to conduct another audio statement. He'd talk to her in the lobby just fine, but not for long, he had to get back to work and her showing up every day was beginning to make him look like a bad guy or something. Jodie's flat eyes examined the sweating liar because that is what she saw in front of her, a big, sweating liar.

But she knew that already didn't she? Lying about the hotel. What did that prove exactly? There was no direct evidence linking him to anything and if she was going to arrest everyone that lied to her, they'd have to build more jails. She felt it in her gut though. This was the guy. Greg was involved. So she asked him, concentrating on his whole being for when he answered. She said, "Where were you last night?"

"At home. I re-build old bikes. Just finished an old Yamaha."

"Witnesses?"

"My wife."

"She at home?"

"She's probably at work."

"She'll verify you were home last night?"

"She should. I was."

Jodie stared at him. Greg smiled back. She'd wipe that stupid smile off his face.

Jodie said, "Did you kill officer Kelly?"

The smile slid. He swallowed and peered over Jodie's shoulder at the other officer and when he answered, Jodie saw the lie in his face. "No, no. Of course not. I was at home all night."

Putting the smile back in place, Greg said, "Can I go back to work now?"

"Yeah."

He turned away, a fast swing of the shoulders.

"Greg?"

His shoulders climbed up to his ears before he turned, "Yes?"

"I'll see you around."

•   •   •   •   •

Outside, the uniform officer said, "Motherfucker." To Jodie, "You think he killed Kelly?"

"Yeah."

"Why the hell isn't he in cuffs then?"

"A little thing called evidence. Maybe you've heard of that before?"

Frowning, the officer said, "He needs to get done."

Nodding, Jodie said, "Yes. He does."

They stared at the employee door, anger a rod in their postures.

Jodie said, "Would you happen to know where his wife works?"

"Sure do. I'll meet you there."

29

Stephanie, Greg's wife, agreed to follow them to the station. She told Jodie, "It would mean I at least get a couple of hours away from this place," and winked at her. She didn't even ask what it was all about which meant that either Greg had called her or she wasn't very bright. Jodie soon found out that it was the latter.

Before going into the interview room, Jodie removed her vest and her gun-belt and it wasn't until they were at least five minutes into the interview before Stephanie said, "My goodness, what happened to your hand?"

"Actually, that's why I wanted to talk to you."

"To me? Whatever for?"

"Was your husband home last night?"

"Yes."

"All night?"

"Yes."

"How do you know?"

"I saw him."

"Can you tell what you did when you got home from work until the time you went to bed?"

"Yesterday?"

"Yes. Yesterday."

"Well, I got home around four o'clock, same time I do most days, got myself a drink and parked it in front of the TV. Greg got home ten minutes after me, like he does most days, and then he made Shepherd's pie for dinner. We ate in front of the TV and then he said he was going to work in the basement. He rebuilds old bikes in his spare time. He said he was almost finished with this one, something about all it needing was a new starter. He went on about it for some time, I don't remember all that he said, usually he doesn't say more than a few words to me before he disappears somewhere. Then at around ten o'clock, maybe a little after, he came upstairs and said he had finished the bike and it'd be good to sell for a few bucks. And then he said maybe we could go out for dinner with the extra money, which is strange and then we went to bed. Together." She blushed, shrugged and said, "That's about it."

"You said something was strange. What did you mean by that?"

"Whenever Greg has extra money, from the sale of one of his bikes, he spends it on himself. New hunting gear, new fishing gear, some upgrade to the truck. He tells me he gives me enough damn money and the little extra he makes is for him. Makes a big deal out of telling me that, like I might forget or something. Wanting to spend the extra money on dinner, together, was damn weird. Greg is not into spending time together. I thought he was hitting on me, which is something he never does, not since we've been married. I almost always have to get it going." She paused, looked away from Jodie and said, "Huh."

"Yes?"

"Come to think of it, I got it started last night, too. I thought the dinner thing was his way of saying he wanted some action. He didn't make a move, so I did." She giggled and said, "It was very romantic."

Jodie said, "Is there an exit from the basement or would he have to walk past you to leave the house?"

"Oh, there's a sliding glass door but to get around to the front he'd have to pass by the window I sit beside when watching TV. I'd see him. That's for sure. And I didn't. He was home all night."

Jodie ended the interview. Stephanie left the station and returned to work and Jodie fumed, thinking what in the hell was she going to do now? It wasn't the best alibi but it was an alibi, wasn't it? Stephanie saw him go down to the basement early in the evening and saw him again later on. By using the TV show Stephanie had been watching, Jodie figured Stephanie saw him between 10:30 pm and 11:00 pm. After the time she had been shot at but pretty damn close. But he did live in town. And the town wasn't that big. Was it possible he snuck out the back after he made sure Stephanie saw him? You bet. And he made a point of talking to her when he returned, something, according to Stephanie anyways, she said he rarely did. Why would he do that? To strengthen his alibi, of course. It was entirely possible his brother Neil or even Ray had been the ones running around last night stabbing and shooting at cops. The surveillance team hadn't arrived yet and the bad guys could have been out and about and up to all sorts of mischief. Hmm. Maybe Jodie should call Jamie, see if Neil had been home last night.

Jodie, deep into her thoughts and drumming the nails of her good hand on someone's desk, knew all of this had to be connected. The killings, the abduction or more probable, the murder of Lynda, and the three men who said they went out of town to a hotel but never actually went. She had to get her nails under some layer of their story and pull it back to expose the underneath. Greg, who she thought from the initial interview would be the one to give her something now had a fairly solid alibi. But she goddamn knew he was involved. She saw it in his face. She needed to pull the three apart and go at them one at a time. She needed to find Ray.

"Detective Reyes?"

She spun to see the officer who accompanied her earlier.

"Yes?"

"There's a Ray Bolton here to see you."

"Oh."

A smile curved her lips. But it wouldn't last long.

30

"I can tell you why the boys lied to you only, I need your assurance we won't get into any trouble over it," he smiled, pausing and holding up his thumb and index finger an inch apart he said, "because it's a little illegal."

They sat in an interview room together. Before Jodie entered the room, she called Bryce, the surveillance team leader and told him where he could find Ray. They could be on him after he left. Jodie sat on a padded chair with wheels and Ray was seated on a hard plastic chair. The chair didn't allow anyone to lean back in it. Ray either had to slouch forward or sit uncomfortably erect in his seat. He choose to slouch. Ray agreed to speak to her on video and after the required cautions, he nodded, smiled and Jodie got the weird feeling he was trying to flirt with her. It made her like him less than she already did.

"I can't promise anything like that without knowing what it is. Actually, I can't promise you anything. It's what the courts call an inducement."

"That's not any fun."

Jodie shrugged, "The courts aren't known for being fun. Anyway, it is up to you. You can tell me and if there is evidence and a reason to charge, I'm obligated to do so."

"Yup, yup. I thought you'd say that. Only I think you need to know, to help you out and get you looking elsewhere for poor Lynda. Neil and Greg are all torn up about it."

"Not you?"

"Not me what?"

"Neil's one of your best friends right?"

Ray nodded.

"And Greg?"

"Yeah."

"Well, if my best friend's little girl was missing, I'd be worried sick. I don't even know Lynda and I'm worried. But you said Neil and Greg are torn up about it. Not you. Neil and Greg."

"I didn't think I'd have to say it. I'm here, aren't I? About to tell you something that could get us all in some trouble just so you guys can focus more on finding Lynda than investigating the people close to her. I'm only trying to help here." He smiled again and Jodie thought, *bullshit.*

"Okay. So what do you have to say."

He rubbed a hand over his mouth and said, "Alright, here we go. I got a little backwoods grow operation going."

"What?"

"I'm growing pot. Out in the woods. Every year I harvest it and the boys help me. Tell the wives they are going fishing, charge the room to their cards and then we harvest the weed, dry it, package it and sell it."

"Where do you do this?"

"I'm not telling you that."

"What?"

"I'm not telling you that. If I told you that, you might be able to get that evidence you were talking about earlier, you know? I read about it, before coming here. You need the pot to send off to be tested to prove it's pot in order to you know, convict me. If I told you where I grow it at, you'd be able to find something and then I'd be fucked. That's why I asked if you could assure me we wouldn't get in any more trouble. You said you couldn't, that it'd be an inducement. Since you can't promise me anything, I'm not giving you the evidence to throw me in jail little lady."

"Jodie."

"What?"

"My name is Jodie. Not little lady. Or if you prefer, detective Reyes. Not little lady. My name is never little lady."

Ray held up his hands, "No offence intended."

"Fine. But let me get this straight. You come in here, tell me a story as to why you and your friends lied about going to a hotel around the time two murders and an abduction happen but when it comes to proving the story, you're saying no? You don't want to give me the part that I could check and not just rely on your word alone? That isn't helpful to anyone. Actually, it's a steaming pile of crap."

"What would it take for you to believe me?"

"The obvious. The drugs, the place where you grow it, the vehicle you transport it in and where you offload it. That's just off the top of my head. I'm sure given time I'd think of more."

"You want me to make the noose and give it to you to hang me with?"

"I want something tangible. Something that I can touch or take a photograph of. You know, evidence!"

He frowned. "I need to talk to a lawyer first."

Jodie stood and said, "Maybe you should have done that before coming in here and wasting my time. The other officer will see you out."

•   •   •   •

Jodie walked out of the station and took a deep breath and winced when the stitches in her side flexed with her breathing. These group of assholes were clever, she had to give that to them. Greg has his wife covering for him and all he had to do was be nice to her for one evening and act like she existed. Then Ray came into the station, told a story he couldn't prove and the clever part, the part that had Jodie ready to scream at him in the interview room was that she couldn't disprove it either. It was reasonable for him not to tell her the location of the grow operation, how they transported it and who they sold it to. Who in their right mind would tell all that to the police? And it wasn't like they had them against the wall where they were looking at getting arrested and charged with murder if they didn't give up the drugs. No, these were voluntary statements. Cautioned ones, but voluntary nonetheless because if at any time Ray, Greg, or Neil told her they didn't want to speak any more than that was that: interview over. There was no pressure. She had no leverage to use on them and everything was spiralling out of control. And the worst part, through all of this, there wasn't even a hint of Lynda. Normally, Jodie would bet on her being dead and she would be bringing out the cadaver dogs the minute they had an area to start the search from. Except this case was unique. She was positive Neil, Greg and Ray were involved in this. And from what she heard about Neil, she didn't think he would allow anything to happen to his daughter and if something had happened, and she was dead, he wouldn't have hidden the body. He would want her buried. He would want the closure for himself and maybe even his wife, even if he was responsible for her death. The best course for them would have been to kill her. If they killed all the witnesses who would care if they lied about the hotel then? Without any physical evidence to tie them to anything, Jodie couldn't arrest or charge any of them. None of that would matter if she could find Lynda. Find her alive. That was what she was really out here for. For a missing teen. The search teams had turned up nothing and the longer it went on, the more volunteers they lost. They had a life to return to. Families and jobs to look after. They couldn't be expected to keep searching indefinitely.

"Damnit. Think. What can I do here? How can I push this forward?"

She heard a car enter the lot and she glanced at it, didn't focus on it, and continued to pace. A car door closed and steps kicked pebbles across the pavement. Jodie looked up, saw Graham, frowned and said, "How'd you get here so fast?"

She expected him sometime tomorrow or maybe even the day after. He didn't have a car. He didn't even have a valid driver's license so it wasn't like he could rent a car. Strange that she didn't ask him how he would get to where she was and even stranger that she hadn't thought about it. He said he was coming and she trusted him to do that. Now here he was.

He gestured behind him with his arm, "My mom. Would you like to meet her?"

Although it wasn't the ideal time or circumstances, Jodie was curious about who raised Graham and with a tired smile, she said, "Yeah. I'd love to."

31

Jodie found herself answering more questions than she asked. It seemed Graham's mom was curious about Jodie too since she was the only person in a long time who could draw Graham out of his self-enforced isolation. Graham's mom ended the meeting with a quick hug, kiss on the cheek and a "Look after my boy," whisper in her ear.

"I will."

Graham said, "You will what?"

"Never you mind dear. I'll be going now. Maybe one time you'll visit your father and me again instead of just using me for a long, long ride. And you being such a conversationalist and all, the time really flew by, didn't it?"

"Mom..."

"It's fine. Take care of each other." She winked at Jodie and said, "I trust I'll see you both later?"

"Yes."

"Good luck. Find that young girl."

Graham nodded and said, "We will."

•　　•　　•　　•　　•

Jodie tossed Graham's bag in the trunk of her car and asked him to wait for her inside the car. Jodie went back into the station and spoke to Staff Sergeant Barnes so she could update him on her progress so far. She also wanted to know the areas the search teams had been in and if there were any new developments. There had been none. She didn't mention Graham. Carting a civilian around during an investigation like this wasn't exactly by the book. In fact, if her bosses find out about Graham being along for the ride, she may find herself pushing a cruiser in a small town, at the northern tip of Ontario where summer sun and green grass didn't exist. Only barren trees, grey skies and snow...lots and lots of snow. That was one of the reasons why Jodie didn't ask Graham to come with her at the start. She didn't know how he did whatever it was he did and she couldn't figure out a way to explain any of it to her bosses even if she did understand. What would she say? He was good at finding people? How did she know that? What were his skills? She didn't even know. To bring him in without answers, without qualifications could taint the investigation. Imagine Graham on a witness stand? Jodie would never want to put him through that. At this point though, Jodie was getting desperate. Too many people were dead and the longer it took to find Lynda the less the likelihood there was of her ever being found at all. In Jodie's mind, her primary job, her primary responsibility, was to find this girl and bring her home alive. Everything else was secondary. And Graham knew it too and was willing to maybe risk his health. Maybe his sanity. To help Jodie achieve her end he was potentially subjecting himself to great pain. Walking back out to the car, she patted her gun and slung her vest over her shoulder. It was too hot to wear right now and the people she thought were involved in trying to kill her were being monitored by surveillance so her vest would be fine in the back seat.

Graham, wearing a wide-brimmed fisherman's hat, peered at her with his one eye. She got in the car and started it.

She said, "I'll get the AC going."

"No problem."

She turned the fan on high. The hot air hit her face and she waited for it to cool before driving to the exit of the lot. She paused at the exit and said, "You know where we're going?"

Graham, his eye fixed on a spot in the distance said, "Yes. I've known since I got here. Turn left."

Jodie turned left and keeping an eye on Graham, noticed a line of sweat navigating the runnels of his shattered face. His fingers drummed a steady beat on his knees. She reached over and held his hand. She said, "I'm glad you're here, Graham. And not just because you're helping."

"I know."

"Can you tell me how this works? What is it that you're seeing?"

"Right now I see a black tornado, spinning in the sky. It's big. Real big. Bigger than I've ever seen before. It scares me, Jodie. Something is there and I can tell we're not going to like what we find."

Jodie scanned the sky ahead of her. Clear blue with sparse cotton drifts of clouds. The flat yellow sun burned the asphalt. Although she couldn't see anything, she didn't doubt that Graham saw it. But she was curious about it and said, "How are you seeing that? Do you know?"

"No. I don't understand any of it. Only that it is. And the fucked up part, the part that made me doubt my sanity was the fact that I'm not seeing any of it with my one remaining eye. I see it out of this hole in my face, where my old eye used to be, overlaid onto the real world. I don't know what it is I'm seeing. It's like residual fear, or residual horror. The stain left by people who have either committed terrible things or have had terrible things done to them. Sometimes, I see it over people thinking about doing a terrible thing. I can't explain it so for the most part, I don't even try. I do know it hurts me. Whatever it is. It's like my brain is baking in my skull or its swelling in there, pushing against the bone protecting it and it feels like my eyeballs are going to pop out of my skull from the pressure. Yeah, I said eyeballs because I can feel what used to be when the dead eye-hole sees what no one else sees. And I can't even close my eye against the visions. There is nothing to close."

"That's why you live the way you live."

"Yeah. That's part of it. After the hospital, my parents were driving me home, well, to their home and I saw this blackness at this intersection. It moved and swirled as though it were alive and I knew it was bad. I could feel it in my stomach. I could smell it on the air, a rancid smell that was thick on my tongue. It looked bad, it felt bad, it smelled bad and I didn't want to go anywhere near it. I started screaming in the back seat." Graham smiling, one of bitterness and not of pleasure continued, "My dad almost drove off the road and my mom, she clamped her hands to her ears while my dad pulled the car to the curb. I was yelling 'Get away!' And my parents thought I was yelling at them but my dad stopped right in the thick of the blackness. It swirled around the car and I thought it would creep right in through the window and it would get in my mouth. I didn't want that inside me, I didn't want to taste that...filth. They didn't know what to do and I didn't know what I was seeing, not yet and my brain felt on fire, like someone funnelled gasoline in my skull and lit it and I remember my mom shaking my shoulders and my dad leaning over the back of the front seat holding onto my wrists, so I wouldn't hit anyone I guess and the pain building in my head was unreal. I thought my brain would burst and ooze out my ears and all the time, that black smoke swirled around us and then I passed out. I woke up in the hospital, again. It was two days later. My mom told me I had a terrible fever and the doctors couldn't explain the reason for it. They thought it was viral. Couldn't figure out why they couldn't lower my temperature to normal levels. I was released a week later and for some reason, one I couldn't tell you, I googled the intersection. Two days before we passed through, there had been an accident. A car versus a delivery truck. The car caught fire and a family of four was trapped inside. They were burned alive. The car was too hot for anyone to get near to even attempt a rescue. They screamed for a long time. Even then I didn't figure out what I had seen. It wasn't until later that I realized I was seeing the residue of their pain. Their terror, their agony left an otherworldly stain of sorts. No one else could see it. If someone could, we would know about it by now, wouldn't we? Then I thought maybe some people could see it and learned early on to keep it to themselves or else end up in a hospital somewhere with a bunch of doctors telling them that what they could see wasn't real, just a hallucination brought on by repressed guilt or unresolved daddy issues. Who knew? I didn't and I couldn't talk to anyone about it. I also thought that maybe getting shot in the face may have scrambled my brain and I wasn't seeing anything real. That the images I could see through a non-existent eye were synapses not firing or firing differently than they had before. I didn't know what was going on. I was scared. I was angry. Angry all the time. Not only that though, I was seeing little clouds of darkness over people's heads and sometimes in their eyes. All the white gone, only blackness. The denser the cloud, the more dangerous the person was. You remember a couple of years back, when for no reason, some guy on the subway platform pushed that woman in front of an oncoming train? Remember that?"

"Yeah. I do."

"I saw that guy before he did it. I was leaving physiotherapy from downtown. I couldn't drive anymore. The headaches, the anger, I just couldn't do it. I'd take the bus from my parent's house to the Yorkdale station to get to my appointment downtown. I hated those appointments. Even on the hottest of days, I'd wear my hood up to cover my face and people would stare at me anyway. Keep my hood down, get stared at, put it up, get stared at. I couldn't win. Anyway, I hopped off the train at Yorkdale and I saw this darkness hovering over a man's head. He was seated on a bench, leaning over his knees, his hands clasped in his lap staring at the ground. The cloud was black, thick and swirling like a mini tornado. I stopped, mouth hanging open because of how thick it seemed. He must have sensed me looking at him because his head popped up and he stared at me. His eyes were black pits in his head. I felt a cold breeze passing through me, right at the navel. Sweat collected on my brow and my head began pounding, throbbing like an, I don't know, an aching tooth. I ran out of there and just made it to my bus. The further away from him, the better I felt. When the bus pulled away from the station, I was relieved to be moving away, to be leaving. I could still see the cloud in the air. I bet it was right above where the man was sitting. The next day, they had his picture in the paper. After I left, he pushed that woman in front of the train. She was pregnant. I knew something was wrong with him and I left. I just left."

Jodie said, "I remember that. They ran the story for a few days. The woman he killed looked a lot like his wife. He found out she had been cheating on him. She was leaving him. So he killed this stranger because he couldn't kill his wife, I guess."

"Whatever it is, it drains me. It hurts. After I found Francine, I was sick in my bed for four days straight. My head hurt so bad. I didn't move. I laid in the darkness, sweating, wondering, because of what I can see, if there really was an afterlife and would I see my family again? I don't know. All I do know is that I don't control it, it's weird, whatever it is, and the longer I use it, or it uses me, it hurts."

He didn't tell her the time when he had an argument with his father. He had an idea of what it meant but to say it out loud would make it real and that, ability or curse, scared him the most. Especially because his anger seemed to be a separate entity from him. A malignant growth sprouting unwanted and once released, uncontrollable.

"Do you see it now? This cloud?"

"Yes."

"Have you tried looking at a map? Would you see it on Google Earth or something?"

"I never tried. I don't have a tablet. Honestly, that never occurred to me."

"You might be able to pinpoint the location better."

"You believe me then?"

She glanced at him with a frown, the look reserved for idiots and she said, "Of course I do. You're my friend Graham and even if you weren't, I now understand how you found Francine. You went for a walk and saw the cloud. Right?"

"Pretty much."

She smiled, "Jesus. I never would have figured that out. I mean, who would, right?"

"Because it's crazy."

"It's not crazy if it's real."

"Sometimes, the real is crazy."

"Yeah. But I still never would have figured that out."

"What did you think I did?"

"I don't know. Something. But not that. Still, grab my tablet from behind my seat, pull up the maps app and type in Kaufmann's Vale. See what you see."

"Alright."

Graham, aware of the approaching cloud, did as instructed. He switched the view to satellite and the incorporeal eye burned in his misshaped socket.

"Jesus. What's going on in this town?"

"What do you mean?"

"I see three clouds. Three different sizes and three different shades of darkness."

"Let's go to the biggest and the darkest. Could be Lynda right? The darkest one?"

"I don't know. This isn't something I've ever seen before. And I read up on all this paranormal stuff. God, I hate saying that word."

"Paranormal?"

"Yeah. Like I'm some cliche from the X-files show."

"The what files?"

"You're killing me here."

He zoomed in on the biggest cloud and saw that in order to get to it, they'd have to pass the lightest shade of cloud. He told her this and Jodie said, "Point the way, oh mystical one."

Even though a headache was beginning to form, he smiled. Even after all this time his face still felt weird. Muscles pulling, bones moving to create an expression that had once been so natural now felt disconnected from him. As though someone was using their fingers to push his cheeks one way and his jaw the other. His parts didn't respond to his wishes and because of that, they felt alien to him. He sighed. There was nothing he could do about that.

"Slow down. You're going to want to turn off soon. There's an old road running behind some trees."

Jodie, easing on the brake said, "This is where Bruce and that unknown girl were found. At the end of this road. If it's the same one."

"Turn here."

"This is the road."

She drove through the low hanging screen of foliage onto the rutted dirt road. Branches assaulted the paint on all sides. Small golden breaks in the overhead leaves dotted the road. At the end of the road, where the burned out truck held the murdered corpses, small piles of ash spotted the ground. Jodie parked outside of the death zone and turned off the car. She stepped out of the car and touched her side. Her bandaged ribs throbbed from the movement. She grabbed her portable radio and patted another pocket to make sure her phone was there. Three areas of darkness. She wanted to call them in but what would she say? My friend can see things others can't. I believe him because I've kind of seen him in action so yeah, if you could just go and check these areas, I'm pretty sure you'll find Lynda. All this worried Jodie. If they did find Lynda, how could she explain it without sounding crazy? She couldn't tell the truth and she certainly felt gross having to lie. Made her feel almost physically ill. There were no secrets in her investigations. It was wrong to do the job that way. But what was more important here? Her integrity, or the life of a young girl? Frowning, Jodie didn't hear the other door open. She turned back and saw Graham sitting in the truck, his one eye glowing like a searchlight.

She opened the door. "You okay?"

"No."

He removed a plastic pill container from his pocket, cracked the top and shook two pills into his palm. He tossed them into his mouth. She heard him dry crunching them as he replaced the top. He sighed, cast a glance at Jodie and then opened the door and stepped out. He turned his face up to the sun. He shivered.

"Let's go."

The sun felt wonderful on his face. It combatted the cold growing in his bones. The warm rays didn't penetrate as deep yet they warmed him and helped him to remember there was pleasure in life. Even in moments of great pain, great fear.

Darkness swirled around where a burnt hulk used to be. It gave form to what wasn't there anymore. An outline of the truck, an outline of the bodies. He could smell the lingering fear of the killers, their indecision and worry, as pungent as crushed garlic. He told Jodie a lot of what he could do and he felt better for it only he kept some of it back. He didn't know why. She believed him and he had no idea how important that had been to him until he saw her belief, her trust, etched on her face. In that moment, he recognized he loved her, as he would a best friend. Jodie, the nosey detective whose curiosity made her befriend the gremlin in the woods. Even still, that wasn't enough for him to share everything with her. Years of secret keeping instilled in him a phobia of revealing too much. Or maybe some things were a little too crazy, a little too much for even a best friend to take. Was there a tipping point? Where she would say, *ok now, let's not get crazy here, Graham. I can only accept so much.* He didn't think so. Why was he keeping some if it back? Didn't matter. Not now. A larger, darker cloud spun in the distance. It's where Lynda had to be, right? It smelled of fear. It smelled of pain.

"This way."

Graham walked past the boulder, tracing a finger over a carving etched into it, onto a trail he knew was there. He pushed the branches aside. Jodie's footsteps trailed his.

-32-

All in all, Ray was happy with the way the interview turned out. After Greg's colossal fuck-up last night, they had to scramble to come up with something. He remembered the phone call from Neil, trying to downplay what his brother did. The call came in at 3:18am. Ray had been sleeping and had been dreaming about cutting Lynda's nose off and feeding it to the dog in front of her. A great dream as far as dreams go because Lynda was getting on his goddamn nerves. She wasn't afraid of him and she let him know it at every opportunity. She called him her daddy's whipping boy and he wouldn't dare touch her and did he know why? Because when it came to being tough, he didn't have it. That's why he needed her dad and her uncle. Without them, he was nothing more than a pervert jerking off to bondage porn in his mommy's basement. God, how he was getting to hate her. Those inventive insults pulled the scabs off of his insecurities and laid them bare to the cold air. She stole his power from him. She made him feel weak. She made him feel useless. He wanted to gut her and pull her intestines out and strangle her with them. What was stopping him? Neil. So in that at least, she was right. But there would come a time when they would have to kill her and that time was fast approaching. Ray believed he could take out Neil alone if he had to but Neil *and* Greg? He wasn't so sure about that. And since Greg was Neil's puppet, he would end up facing both of them. What made the whole situation worse was that he liked Neil. They'd been great friends since, well, since first grade. He guessed the dream was the only way that he could attack Lynda without repercussions. He was enjoying that dream. Seeing the hole in her face where her nose used to be and feeling the dog licking his fingers after he had fed it the tasty morsel. Yeah, it was one hell of a dream. Until the burner phone interrupted it.

"Hello?"

Neil said, "We got a problem."

Understatement of the year. Greg messed things up and they had to deal with it. They came up with a plan. According to Neil, Greg was certain his wife would be his alibi and after Neil explained why, Ray had to admit that

Greg had handled that part well. And surprisingly, with some intelligence. The totality of what he had done was a dumb-fuck thing to do but since it was done, and not too poorly, they had to deal with the fall-out. How Greg thought killing two cops would be helpful was beyond Ray. Didn't he know killing or attempting to kill a cop would bring a whole slew of cops to their little town? You won't be able to move without bumping into one from now on. Ray told Neil to expect undercover cops to be tailing him from now on. They believed one major question running throughout the investigation had been, where's Ray? The cops asked Neil, they asked Neil's wife, they asked Greg and his wife and no one had an answer that satisfied them. Hell, they even pestered his old mother about where he was. She called him up (he gave her the burner phone number in case of emergencies) and spat the usual vindictive words that had caused him to start cutting himself off from her when he was twelve. He still cringed under her barrage of insults. No one could hurt you more than your mom. One of his many fantasies involved cutting her head off with a rusty hacksaw while staring into her eyes. Would she fear him then? Respect him? It didn't matter. At the end of their discussion, they decided Ray needed to make an appearance to quell their suspicions. But then once he exposed himself, the surveillance team would pick him up and trail him back to Lynda so that was a problem since once they found her all of them would be going to jail. So how to deal with that? They wrestled with that one for a bit. What it came down to was Ray would have to slip away from the surveillance team. Easier said than done right? Get away from cops who were trained in that shit? Probably wore disguises and all that crap you see on TV. The plan they eventually came up with was rather simple. Before he walked into the police station that morning, Ray parked his mother's old beater, a Toyota Camry, outside of a house two blocks away from the police station. Taking side streets, he ended up on a trail that ran parallel to the fence line at the back of the police station. The scary part was creeping up to the fence while seeing the police station through the trees and the little cameras on the corners of the building. He was sweating like crazy when he started cutting a line through the chain link vertically beside the steel post. He didn't want to walk through the neighbourhoods with bolt cutters sticking out of his back pocket so he had to use a small pair of wire cutters. It took time getting through the fence and at the end of it, his hand and wrist ached. Every time a car drove into the lot, he slunk back into the trees and waited for it to park or leave his sight. After that, using the trails to stay out of sight, he jogged to his mom's place to pick up his own car. He then drove to the police station and parked at the back of the lot, along the fence line near where he had cut the hole. The spot he wanted was taken. He reverse-parked two spots over, the last available space near the cut fence and turned the engine off in annoyance. He muttered, "Nothing is ever easy." After making himself mentally ready, as ready as he could be, he walked into the station and introduced himself to the detective.

After the interview, he sat in his car and took out his phone and pretended to fiddle around on it for the benefit of whoever might be watching. He didn't turn on the car and he kept the windows up. Sweat dotted his forehead and lined his collar. What must the surveillance guys think he is up to? Ray smiled and waited. Jodie stepped out of the station. A man exited a car and Ray frowned. The man walked with his head down, wearing a big hat. He walked like a man who didn't want to be seen. Curious. An older woman got out of the same car as the man and they all talked at the car for a bit and Ray wished he had one of those parabolic mikes you see the FBI guys use in the movies when they are trying to listen in on the mafia. The man hopped into a different car beside Jodie while she went back into the station. The car the man arrived in, turned around and left the lot. Still, Ray waited. Two cars passed by his nose. Smaller sedans. Not helpful. Jodie exited the station, got in the car with the hat-man and they too left the lot. Sweating in the hot car, getting irritated, Ray saw what he was waiting for. A middle-aged man hopped into a pick-up truck. He carried a police uniform shirt and pants under one arm. An officer leaving work. Ray didn't care about that. He cared about the big truck the man got into.

Ray placed his hand on the door handle of his car and waited. He would have to be quick. He figured the one place someone could watch him from was in the same lot he was in or at the exit. If they were in the lot, they weren't close to him. Ray had scanned all the cars walking to his own and didn't see anyone. He might have missed someone sitting in the back of their car but he didn't think so. They wouldn't want to be too close would they?

The large truck rumbled past the nose of Ray's car and at the same time, Ray opened his door, rolled to the ground while closing the door behind him. He scrambled on all fours to the back of his car and gathered his breath. Someone might have seen him. He wasn't as fast as he thought he would be. Getting older.

Ray crab-walked to the fence line, slipped through the hole he had cut and in seconds was screened by the branches of thick summer trees. He fast-walked towards his mom's car, shooting a look over his shoulder, certain they hadn't seen what he had done with every step but still glancing back to make sure. If they were in the lot, they would notice that he wasn't sitting in his car any longer. If they were watching the exit, he'd have some time before they got curious enough to send someone into the lot to check. Either way, he had some time and now he could slink back to his hidey-hole and consider what exactly was the benefit of keeping Lynda alive. He'd either have to convince Neil they had to kill her to avoid jail or kill her, and tell Neil from a distance and hope the guy would eventually see it as the right thing to do. Either way sucked. But the longer this dragged on, the longer the spotlight would be on them for.

Ray made it back to his mother's Camry in good time and wanting to get out of the populated area of town before he was seen, he sped towards their cabin. He caught up to a red sports car with the top down, an older man at the wheel with his white hair slapping at his bald spot and he had to slow down. Trying to peer around the car to see if was safe to pass, Ray saw a car turn off and disappear into some trees. What the hell? Ray tapped the brake as he neared the turnoff and saw branches swaying back and forth and red tail lights flash amidst drifting dust. Could that have been Jodie and the stranger? It looked like the car Jodie was driving. Why would they go back there? The scene had been cleared as far as Ray knew. And who was that dude she was with? He chewed on a nail. For some reason, he didn't like it. He continued to the cabin, wondering what it meant.

•   •   •   •   •

At the cabin, Ray went downstairs and knocked on the secret door.

"Fuck you, Ray! Eat a bowl of dicks while you're at it, loser!"

Ray nodded and satisfied, but annoyed, that Lynda was okay, Ray made himself a cup of instant coffee and entered his study. He turned on a monitor and reading a Louis L'Amour western, waited. Jodie and the stranger heading to the rock worried him. It was strange because he couldn't see any reason for them to be visiting a cleared crime scene but he wasn't a cop and what he knew of how they did their job was from TV. And that was almost always a poor representation of real life. It didn't hurt to sit here and wait and see if the motion sensor cameras at the cave were activated. Neil had them installed years ago just in case some errant hiker or hunter stumbled on it. They recorded when activated and could be checked remotely using a website. The footage could be wiped remotely as well. One of them in the group was supposed to check it nightly when they could. Since Ray was single, the task usually fell to him.

Ray read two chapters, folded down the corner of a page and put it on the desk. Ray had been gone from the cabin for a time and Lynda might need to use the washroom soon. She could do with a shower too. He hated that part. She had a mouth on her, that's for sure. And the longer she stayed here, the more bold and angry she got. He'd catch her staring at him, measuring him up. A part of him wanted her to attack him. He thought of letting her get in a few good licks on him, injure him, so when he killed her, he could tell Neil it had been in self-defence. He wrinkled his nose. He didn't want to deal with her. Not yet. Then the monitor turned on. He leaned forward in his chair, mouth slightly open, thinking everything had officially gone to shit. The stranger appeared on the screen first. The detective followed behind, the white bandage on her hand catching a stray beam of sunlight making her hand glow. The stranger moved ahead, chin pointing straight, moving with confidence. The stranger reached out and moved aside a screen of leaves. The same screen Ray and Neil had made by threading fake leaves on branches through a web of fishing line.

"Fuck me..."

They had found the cave. Now the police would never stop looking for them. They'd be around forever, hunting and haunting them. Goddamnit. Ray's eyes misted, thinking about the unfairness of it all. He slammed a fist on the desk. The monitor jumped.

He called Neil.

"They found it."

"What?"

"They fucking found it!"

"How?"

"What am I? A mind reader? I don't know. I'm watching them walk into the cave right now."

"How many?"

"Just two. That detective and some dude I've never seen before."

"That it?"

"Yeah. What does that matter? They found it!"

"Okay. But have they told anyone yet? That's the real question."

A faint glimmer of hope. How fast could Ray get there? Could he ambush them? And then what? This was no better than what Greg had done. Like trying to plug a hole in a dam. Cover one hole and two more leaks spring in another place. If they didn't plug all of them, pretty soon they would drown.

"You gotta take them out, Ray."

"Yeah."

Birds chirped. Leaves rustled as unseen animals manoeuvred in the woods around Graham and Jodie. The foot-trail faded in parts as the forest reclaimed less used sections over time. Not a well traveled trail but evidence of fading red Coca-Cola cans lining the path showed signs of use. The sun peeked prying golden eyes through gaps overhead. The heat was stifling. Graham's breath came in short measured gasps. He was used to walking in the woods and knew how to breathe properly. Jodie, sweating and cursing trailed further and further behind. In the back of his mind, Graham knew he should wait for her but something else was pulling at him, drawing him forward as though he had a rope tied around his waist. Whatever was ahead wanted him to proceed with haste. He lifted the hat off his head and flicked the sweat off the rim. The droplets caught the sun before disappearing, winking white. Jodie crashed through the brush behind him. He blinked sweat from his eye and pushed the hat down firmly on his head, never once slowing his stride. At the clearing, where the two young people were found burned in the car, a distant drone had gathered in his brain. The kind of drone that sometimes precluded a debilitating migraine. Pushing on, getting closer to whatever the dark clouds in the sky directed him to, the drone buzzed more insistently. It reminded him of the time he and his wife had seen Pearl Jam in concert and after leaving they had a hard time hearing each other. It was like that, yet not. The buzz was similar but he could still hear Jodie complaining behind him.

"Graham! Wait up!"

He stopped on the trail. He wanted to move forward, keep going because the buzzing demanded it and it was taking a supreme effort of will to wait for her.

She stopped behind him, breathing hard and said, "How much farther?"

"We're close."

"Wish I wasn't wearing this damn vest. It's hot out here."

Graham walked ahead.

Jodie said, "Nice talking to you."

Graham parted branches with his hands, ducked under another and stood before a wall. Jodie stopped behind him and said, "Is this it?"

"Yes."

Inhaling a deep breath she said, "What are we looking at? It's just a wall."

"No, it's not."

Graham stepped forward. The dark clouds were dense here. The droning inside his skull became frantic. It was here. Whatever it was the buzzing was making him move toward, it was here. His guts squirmed. His sphincter tightened. Oh yeah, this was the place.

Graham reached out and touched the leaves cascading down the wall in a tight pattern. Too tight of a pattern. An unnatural pattern. The leaves felt waxy to his fingers and underneath them, what was that, a fishing line? Graham hooked the fishing line with his fingers and moved the green curtain to the side. A dark hole greeted them.

Jodie said, "Holy shit."

Graham said, "Do you have a light?"

"Like a lighter?"

"What? No. A flashlight."

"Oh yeah, right."

Jodie removed a small flashlight from her vest and shone it into the hole. She said, "It's big."

"You're going to have to go first. With the light."

"Yeah."

Jodie stepped in front of him and entered the crevasse. Graham followed. His head ached. It felt as though his brain was jiggling inside his skull. The dark clouds twisted and swirled about, coalescing and thinning with violent speed. Strange. With his real eye, he saw the real world. With the eye that was no longer there, he saw another world. To him, they were both real. Moving deeper into the rock hill, Graham knew Lynda wasn't here. They were about to stumble upon something worse. The tunnel they were in was wide and tall enough for them to walk comfortably. Not side by side, only in single file, but they didn't have to duck or turn their shoulders to move into the area. The cave smelled musty, old and earthy, like the scent of worms after a storm. A cool breeze caused the sweaty Graham to shiver. With the breeze came another smell. A scent compelled Graham to cover his nose with one hand. Jodie said, "Goddamn. I know that smell."

Jodie turned a corner and her flashlight exposed the interior of a cave. Jagged walls, cracked soil and bodies. A lot of human bodies.

"Shit!"

The light shone on bones in a pile. Tattered decaying rags partially covered their frames. An arm bone, a leg bone, and other miscellaneous pieces littered the floor from when scavengers tore at the rotting meat left for them. The smell of death would be strongest when a fresh corpse had been deposited. The dark enclosure held the remnants of the scent of putrefaction. The bone pile stood three feet wide and covered eight feet of the ground. The bodies had been pushed into a corner the way a teenager would toss their dirty clothes.

Jodie said, "Look at this! A mass grave. Mass murder." Looking at Graham, the light catching her wide eyes she said, "You shouldn't be in here. This is a crime scene. The biggest crime scene I ever worked on. You're not a cop. You shouldn't be here." Her light flashed on the ossifying pile. She said, more to herself than Graham, "How many do you think? These poor people."

"Thirty-two. Young boys, young girls. Not all their bones are here. Some bodies were taken out by the animals." Graham's voice shook. The inside of his head felt on fire.

"Thirty-two? How do you know?"

"I just do." He couldn't explain it but when she asked how many, the number popped into his head and he knew it was right.

"Of course you do. Yeah. Well, we need to leave. I have to call this in. Get a crew up here. Process this. God, what a mess."

"They left some here. While they were alive. Left them in the cold, in the dark, laughing at their whimpers, at their cries for help. I can see the pain, the fear. It's dark and ugly. So ugly."

"C'mon Graham. Let's get you out of here."

She took him by the arm and he let himself be lead. Directing his own feet and his own body was too much. His hands shook. A sharp pain grew behind his ghost-eye. It wasn't until they were outside did he feel better. Not great, but better than when inside the cave. He inhaled a deep breath and lifted the hat off his head as though that would help him breath better. All it did was release the collection of sweat from under the hat brim. The sweat ran down his face.

Jodie lifted her chin up to the sun and closed her eyes. She turned to Graham and said, "Are you ok?"

"Maybe."

"I bet you could go for a coffee right about now."

"Yeah."

"Me? I'd like a box of wine."

"A box?"

"Yes. A box of wine and a funnel."

She reached into her pocket and retrieved her phone. She said, "I don't know how I'm going to explain finding this." She exhaled, opened the phone screen, frowned and said, "No reception here. We'll have to walk down."

"Try your portable."

"Oh yeah."

She clicked it and spoke with a dispatcher. She requested a crime scene crew and some uniform officers to meet her at the scene of the SUV fire.

They started their trek back to the car. Jodie wasn't worried too much about the scene. She didn't think anyone else would find it to mess with it and she wouldn't leave the area until the crime scene crew showed up so there would be some continuity. Not ideal but you had to work with what you're given. Graham breathed easier the further from the cave they traveled. The stench no longer filled his nostrils and the swirling, inky darkness no longer clung to him, no longer made him hear echoes of pain and loneliness. Following behind Jodie, his head filled with a dull throb, Graham couldn't wait to leave this place. They still had to find Lynda and his stomach twisted at the thought. The doubts about coming here returned. Jodie was in good health and she didn't need him to protect her. Jodie needed no one to protect her but was that why he came here? No. It was so they could end this and she would come home. So she would be safe. This was the exact type of thing he had been trying to avoid by living out in the wilderness with minimal contact with other people. He didn't want to see the clouds and he didn't want to invest his emotions in anyone. Because of what it cost him. Nothing he could do about it now. Jodie was his friend. He had to help her because in doing so, he was helping himself. Besides, shouldn't he try to help Lynda if he could? But where would that stop? Would he never be free from this?

Jodie stopped before him, breathing hard. She looked at her phone and said, "Still no reception up here. You'd think being this close to town there'd be more cell towers."

Graham shrugged and then something caught his eye. Not his physical eye. Downhill, off the path, darkness hung suspended amongst the trees. Graham could feel the fear, the anger and most importantly, the ill intent. He said, "Jodie. Someone is close by and they mean us harm."

She ducked down and seeing him standing there in the sunshine, pulled him down by his arm. She stuffed her phone into a pocket in her vest and removed her sidearm. She whispered, "Where?"

"Waiting for us. Down there off of the path."

"Can you tell who it is?"

"No. But they want to hurt us. They want to kill us."

"I shouldn't have brought you. What was I thinking? Here, take this..." She started to peel the straps securing her vest. The strong velcro tore breaking the silence of the forest.

"I'm not taking your vest. You-" The boom of a gun cut him off.

34

After Neil hung up the phone with Ray, he chewed on a fingernail, tasted blood and grimaced. If he was going to do something, now would be the time. Ray would be out of the cabin and he could grab Lynda and...what? If he released her she would tell the police and then they would all go to jail for a very long time. Neil shook his head as though the motion would dislodge the thought. The walls were closing in on them. Once word about the cave got out, there would be nowhere to hide. The cops would dig and dig and dig until they found the persons responsible. They would never let it go. Especially that cop that had shown up at his house with Kelly. That damn detective. She knew they were involved and she would push on them all. She would poke and prod and find the evidence and trot them all to jail. If they did get rid of Lynda...no, no, no. Don't think like that. Get rid of her? Like some street trash? He could do better than that. Neil would go get her, talk to her, get her to keep her mouth shut and keep her daddy out of jail. If he left her there in the cabin while Ray was out, he might never have the chance to get her out again. Everything was getting out of control and the only eyewitness to their crimes lived and breathed in the basement of their cabin. And even though that witness was Neil's daughter, Ray wouldn't stand that for much longer. If Neil didn't go and get her...eventually she'd be dead. Neil knew he wouldn't be able to live with himself if he let that happen when he could have stopped it. He would get her. He would talk to her, convince her to stay quiet. They could think up a cover story together. But then he remembered how she looked at him the last time he saw her and he knew she hated him. There would be no cooperating on a story. She would tell as soon as she finds out Bruce is dead, she'll tell. Knowing Lynda, he already suspected she knew Bruce was dead but no one had told her that yet. Once that was confirmed, whatever deal they might have been able to work out would be over. But what choice did he have? He was her father. He couldn't let Ray kill her. Not his little girl. He had to go now and get her and hope she would listen to him.

Decided, Neil left his work. The bright sun stunned him at the door and he waited for his eyes to adjust.He fast-walked to his car. Once inside with the engine started and the AC blowing hot air into his face, he thought of what Ray had said to him, about how the cops might be following him. Nothing he could do about that now. He had to get Lynda. This would be his one chance. That didn't mean he had to be stupid about it. As he put the car into drive, he remembered two things. He had his fishing gear in the trunk and Ray's mother's car was at the cabin. Would Ray have taken the car to the cave? Probably not. Ray would probably have taken the dirt bike from the cabin. That way he could sneak up pretty close to the cave without being seen or heard. Be almost stupid to take the car. Not when you're running an errand of murder.

35

Neil had guessed right. Before he left the cabin, Ray loaded up his shotgun, a Mossberg pump and walked outside and stopped, staring at his mom's little Camry. Would it be smart to take the Camry? What if someone saw the car? Saw him in it? What if some butthead decided to park by the rock carving, like those hunters, and see his car? If he took the dirt bike he could approach unseen. Leave the bike in the trees and get in close on foot. Go up the path and either ambush them inside the cave (making clean up real easy) or on the pathway as they were walking down. Why take the chance of being spotted in the car?

He slung the shotgun over his shoulder, rolled the dirt bike out of the shed. Their dog had been gnawing on the thigh-bone of Mickey in the yard as Ray passed. The dog barked at Ray, guarding his bone and Ray told the dog to shut it. Seconds later, Ray was on a trail with the wind pushing his hair out of his face. He kind of felt like a badass. He smiled into the wind and a bug slammed against his teeth. He slowed down, spit the remnants out and continued on his way with his mouth closed. He should have worn a helmet.

• • • • • •

He heard them before he saw them. Footsteps crunching through dry leaves, branches brushing against fabric and then their voices. He hunkered down behind a tree, cursing his luck. It would have been so much easier if they had still been in the cave. Shaking his head he thought, *nothing was ever easy.* Peering around the tree, insects buzzing around his sweaty head, Ray waited. He saw the detective first. He glimpsed the bright white of her bandaged hand through drooping branches. He gripped the shotgun tight and held his breath. This was big time, what he was about to do. There was nothing bigger than killing a cop. But she was the one who was bringing their long ride to an end. She was the one closing in on them. Stupid to have left the SUV near the cave with a body in it. At the time, it seemed like the best solution to the problem. They'd been using that trail for years and they had never seen anyone else in all that time. Just bad luck to have a couple of asshole hunters stumble on it. Even still, the cave had been well hidden. No one should have been able to find that. Hell, Ray even had trouble finding the entrance and he knew where it was! He had no idea how she did it, but she found the cave. Never in a million years did he think anyone would find their corpse hidey-hole, but she had. She was the reason he was sitting in the woods clutching a shotgun contemplating the very dangerous action of murdering a cop. How the hell had she found the cave?

They stopped on the path. He exhaled a deep breath. The man in the hat, the stranger was staring at him. It was hard to tell with the shadows of the trees and the wide-brimmed hat on his head as if the stranger was looking at him, but it felt to Ray that he was, that there were eyes on him. It wouldn't have surprised Ray if the man raised a finger and pointed it at him. What the hell was going on? He shouldn't be able to see him. Hell, Ray could see only parts of the man in the hat through the trees. Then the detective turned her head towards him too.

He whispered, "Fuck."

Ray, ever so slowly, turned the barrel and aimed down the sight. He'd go for the detective first. He knew she had a gun so she was the most dangerous. He had the sight on her and worked out what to do. The shell was a slug, a large bullet and at this point he wished he had loaded it with birdshot. The spread from this distance could hit both of them with one shot. It'd at least knock them down and give him a chance to rush them and pump more rounds into them. He didn't think of that though. He wanted a powerful slug, a solid bullet to tear into them from close up. Too late for that now.

He brought the sight up onto the detective's torso, saw she was wearing a bulletproof vest and raised the barrel higher, for a head shot. A difficult shot in the best of conditions. Ray was confident of hitting her from here though. He was a good shot and even though shooting uphill was more difficult because people misjudged the angle, Ray thought he could pull it off. At this point, he had no choice.

He pulled the trigger. The gun boomed and rocked back into his shoulder. At the moment he fired, the detective leaned back, reaching for the straps on her vest. This put her head and part of her torso behind a tree. The slug skimmed past the tree as Ray had adjusted his aim when he saw her move. Bark and wood shrapnel exploded from the tree. Ray fired again but both of them had dropped to the ground. He fired a third time and then there were bullets were flying at him. They buzzed and ripped through the branches around him. He dropped down, slid backward on his knees and elbows and when the bullets stopped, he stood and ran down the incline towards his bike thinking he fucked up, he missed them both! His heart ba-boomed and his mouth was dry as a hill of sand as he continued to glance back to see if they were following him. They weren't. He made it to his bike, jumped on it and sped away. The only consolation to the whole sad, sorry business was at least they didn't know who he was. They could guess, but they couldn't know.

Halfway back to the cabin he had to stop. His bowels loosened and the urge to empty them was overwhelming. Crouching behind a tree, spilling his guts out through his butt, he thought this is where the expression, 'so scared I shit my pants' came from. Experiences like this. In a rare moment of empathy, he thought this is how some of their victims must have felt before they killed them. Ray wasn't used to introspection so the thought was dismissed as quickly as it formed. He wiped himself with a leaf, making sure it wasn't poison ivy, grimaced and stood. His stomach gurgled and on shaky legs, he mounted the dirt bike and slinging the shotgun over his shoulder continued the drive back to the cabin, taking it slow because of his sensitive guts.

The whole thing was falling apart. Nothing was going right. The only good thing was Ray knew that if the cops had enough to arrest him and his partners, they would be in jail already. That meant they had a chance to avoid jail provided they got rid of all the evidence. They'd have to burn the cabin for sure. Sooner rather than later. They'd have to dump their burner phones and of course, kill Lynda. Sorry Neil, but it's going to have to be done and done right now. Thinking about killing her brought a smile to his face. She was such a bitch! He could use this shotgun one last time. He imagined the shell ripping through her skull. It made him happy. Then he'd have to get rid of the shotgun. In his haste to be away from all the bullets flying around him, he left the shells behind for them to gather and do all those tests they do. They might find the shells and they might not. Better to get rid of the gun and not even have to worry about it at all. He'd get to the cabin, open the little door in the wall and boom! Slug right in her face! He wondered what it would do to her head. Would it explode like a watermelon? Would it pop out her eyes? Interesting to find out. He'd never done that before. Should he wear a raincoat?

His mood lightened, Ray manoeuvred down the trail and out of the woods onto the back of the cleared property at the cabin. He stopped the bike, stunned. The rear taillights of his mom's Camry lit up as it drove away from him down the dirt driveway. Ray muttered, "Motherfucker!"

Gritting his teeth, he sped after the receding red lights.

36

Betty Farqa was the surveillance officer tasked with following Neil into the woods. Neil had stunned the team when he sped out of the parking lot after leaving his work. He wasn't expected to leave until four in the afternoon when his dayshift was over. The team had settled in, with one member covering the lot, another two covering east and west of the employee parking lot and the last officer covering the exit to call out to the team which way Neil went when he did leave work. Which was supposed to be after four. When he was scheduled to be done work.

They were teasing each other over the radio on their own encrypted frequency, exaggerating each other's shortcomings and generally entertaining each other knowing much of surveillance was actually sitting there, doing nothing for hours, waiting and being ready for when something did happen. Betty was covering the east side, reading a book about ultra-marathons thinking how crazy those people were while at the same time wondering if she could do it when she heard Ayed say, "He's out. He's moving. He's getting in his car." Ayed was in the lot, keeping an eye on the door and Neil's car. He was the junior guy so he got the most uncomfortable assignment. Sprawled out in the back seat of his car, he had his eyes just high enough to see Neil's car and the door without creating a shadow through the tinted windows of his car.

Betty tossed the book on the seat beside her and listened to the call-outs.

"He's moving, he's driving out fast and I've lost sight."

The member at the entrance, Terry, said, "I got him. He's waiting for the traffic. It looks like, yeah, he's heading west. He's moving now, picking up speed. I'm gonna lose sight soon."

On the west side, Cheryl said, "I got him."

They all moved out, following, switching off being the lead car, so every time Neil looked back (if he did), it would be a different car behind him.

Betty was behind Neil when he slowed and pulled off the road to park in an area meant for trail riders and hikers to get ready for whatever activity they were doing that day. She called it out and kept going, driving past Neil.

She scooted onto a side road and making sure to be out of sight of the main road, she pulled over and listened.

It was Terry again. "He's out of the car. He's going to the trunk. I'm going to lose him soon, I can't just pull over here."

Cheryl said, "I'm behind you a bit."

Terry said, "Okay. I'm past him, looking in the rearview here. He's closed the trunk. I don't know what he grabbed or if he grabbed anything."

Cheryl said, "He's got a fishing pole and a tackle box. He's on the trail. He's out of sight. He's gone."

Ayed said, "So he rushed out of work, drove like a maniac to what? Go fishing? Is there even a river here?"

Cheryl said, "Yes. I can see it on Google Maps here. Hey Betty, there is no place here to watch his car without sticking out. You have your hiking gear with you? Maybe you could go on a walk and if you can't find him, stay close to the car?"

Betty sighed. This was a junior guy assignment but Cheryl was right. She did have her gear here. It was in the backseat because when the assignment was done, she wanted to hike the trails around here and Cheryl knew that because she had mentioned it to her, hoping she'd want to come along.

"Yup. I'll put some of it on and get over there."

"Perfect. Thanks."

•   •   •   •   •

Betty parked her ride a car space away from Neil's. She tossed her portable radio into her backpack and making sure her firearm was secured in the lockbox under her seat, she stepped out of the car and shrugged on her backpack. She opened the back door and kicked off her boots and put on her Hoka One trail runners. She put on a ball cap and shades. She closed and locked her car and after moving hanging branches aside, found herself on a well-worn trail. Tree roots, thicker than her forearm, were like wooden snakes along the trail. Sunlight filtering through the trees wasn't as bright and she noticed a temperature change once underneath the canopy of trees. It was much cooler. Nice. Moving forward on the trail, she saw no sign of Neil. Not that she was a tracker of any kind. She was a city girl who liked long hikes or runs through nature. She wouldn't want to live in or near nature though. She didn't think she'd ever be able to sleep without hearing cars honking and people chatting outside her window late at night. No Neil though and, no hope of finding him out here. Not in a place he was familiar with and grew up in. She called Cheryl, the team leader. Bryce, the other team leader, was busy trying to find Ray. He hadn't advertised he had lost Ray from when he had left the police station after his interview so no one knew that Ray was out there and on the loose.

Cheryl answered her phone, "Yeah."

"No sign of him. And if I go too far in here, I'll probably get lost."

"No you wouldn't. Your phone has GPS."

"Yeah. True. So, what's the plan then?"

"I don't know. Wait in your car? Let us know when he gets back and we'll go from there."

"If he gets back."

"Why wouldn't he come back? His car is there."

"You want me to hang in my car?" Which meant she'd have to hunker in the back seat, with the car off, in the stifling heat.

"Yeah. I do."

She sighed, "Alright."

•   •   •   •   •

So she waited. In the car. In the heat. Like a damn rookie. She heard from the team on her radio that shots had been fired at the detective who had been shot at last night.

Stunned, she blurted, "Again?" Most cops went their whole careers without being shot at or having to shoot at anyone. Getting shot at twice in less than twenty-four hours was a big deal. They were discussing the incredibility of it when Betty heard the distant whine of a motorcycle. It wasn't the deep rumbling of a Harley or a Honda large engine cruising bike. She thought she heard the high pitched whine of a racing bike. It wasn't so unusual to hear but it did draw her attention to the roadway. She saw a Toyota Camry zip by with two occupants in the front. The windows were open and a flash of blonde hair fluttered around the window frame. Behind it came a motorbike. A dirt bike actually. It was making that high pitched whine, making Betty think it was going faster than it should be going. An older man rode it, with no helmet, looking really, really pissed. What surprised the shit out of Betty, because it wasn't something anyone would normally see any day, was the shotgun strapped across the back of the angry, dirt-bike driving man.

Betty depressed the button on her portable and said, "Uh guys? There is a guy on a dirt bike following a Camry with a shotgun strapped to his back. He's heading into town."

37

Jodie was speaking with uniform officers and the crime scene crew when she heard the call about the shotgun man. They were standing in the shade of a tree. Sweat collected under her vest and was aggravating the cuts along her ribs. Her head throbbed and her hand ached. She was amazed at her own resiliency. Getting shot at twice in a twenty-four hour period was nerve-wracking, of course it was, but here she was giving instructions to the officers who arrived to help after and chugging a bottle of water from a case of them the crime scene crew seemed to carry with them everywhere. Graham sucked a water bottle back as well and retreated behind her, keeping the brim of his hat low after drawing the curious stares of the arriving police.

The shotgun slug had turned the bark into dust. The sharp wood pieces surprisingly didn't cut or scratch Jodie or Graham. It scared the hell out of them, that's for sure, but no new injuries. Jodie had dropped and dragged Graham down with her. Another two shots buzzed over them and then Jodie, more than pissed off at all the shots flying at her recently, emptied a magazine of her rounds into the area where the shots had come from. She slammed in a new magazine and waited. Her ears were ringing and the smell of cordite hung heavy in the still air. After a time, she heard the sound of an engine starting. The noise receded and she knew the bad guy had gotten away...again.

Talking to the crime scene tech, she told them where the gunfight was, how to get to the cave and what to expect. One uniform officer was tasked to go the entrance of the cave and guard it until the crime scene people could get there. They had to process where the gunfight took place and see if the shooter had left any evidence behind. They were discussing all this and they were teasing Jodie about all the paperwork she would have to do for all the crap she had gone through and although Jodie played along and smiled and laughed, she was pretty damned annoyed by the whole situation and was having a real hard time finding anything funny about it. One crime scene tech asked who Graham was and Jodie said, "A witness." She hoped they would leave it at that but it looked like they wouldn't. Before she had to answer their follow-up questions, the dispatcher called her on her portable radio.

Jodie said, "Reyes here. Go ahead."

"Surveillance team said an angry man riding a motorcycle and carrying a shotgun on his back was headed into town."

Jodie turned to Graham and said, "That's our guy. The one who shot at us." Into the portable, Jodie said, "Send every officer you can spare. I think he might be the guy who shot at me. Tell everyone to be very, very careful. I'm on my way."

The two uniform officers moved close to Jodie. The one officer, a young woman whose name tag read Grover, said, "We're going. We can't sit here and guard a scene with that going on."

Jodie nodded and said, "Okay. Get going then."

Grover smiled and said to her partner, "C'mon then! You heard the boss!"

•   •   •   •   •

Jodie rushed to her car with Graham behind her. She turned on the car, blasted the AC while Graham picked up the iPad and opened Google Earth.

"That other one, the dark cloud, it's not where it used to be. It's uh, it's moving."

Jodie said, "Where's it headed? Can you tell?"

"It's stopped."

"Where?"

He zoomed in on the screen using his thumb and index finger. "The mall. The cloud is at the mall. And it's getting bigger."

-38-

Lynda didn't know what was going on. She had spent so much time in the hole in the wall with no one but the butthole Ray to talk to a smile had lit her face when the door opened and her dad peered in. For one reason, it wasn't Ray and for the second reason, it was her dad. Then she remembered what her dad had done. And she remembered her dad had left her here, with Ray. She did realize a major reason why she still lived and breathed was because of her father but he had hurt her in a way she didn't know she could be hurt. In a way she didn't think it was possible to be hurt. He had hurt her soul.

She had thought that her dad was a kind man. A patient man. The man who braided her hair better than her mother. The guy who made her lunch and knew she liked her jam sandwich toasted with butter put on it first before spreading the thick strawberry jam on top. She told him how she liked it and he remembered and he made a point of delivering it to her. He did that for every aspect of her life. He was safe. He was dependable and as far as she knew, he was a good and caring person. To see him unmasked committing and being a part of a brutal murder, it tore at her. It shredded and ripped a belief system she relied and believed she could rely on for a long, long time. He was her dad and she loved him, but now she hated him too. Hated who he was and what he had wrecked within her. Her face broke into a smile when she saw him open the little door and he paused, surprised at his reception and a cheek creased as he reached a hand in for her.

Seeing him about to smile after what he had done, was doing, brought the hate back, burning a hatred-hole in her chest. She slapped his hand and with a scowl and a shine to her eyes, she said, "Don't you fucking touch me! Don't you ever fucking touch me again! I'll come out on my own."

He jerked back, as though stung. He said, "We're getting out of here. You need to move."

Crawling out she said, "Where's Ray?"

"Gone for now but he'll be back. Better if we weren't here when he returns."

They were in the car and had made it to the main road before her dad, looking in the review mirror said, "Fuck."

Lynda turned in her seat and behind them was Ray on a motorbike, his crazed eyes seeming to find her own.

Lynda said, "Damnit. Now what?"

"I don't know."

Ray stayed behind them and her dad drove them into town. She saw that Ray was in a dangerous situation. He couldn't drive them off the road because he was on a bike and they were in a car. All he could do was follow them until they stopped and then what? What did he think he could do?

Getting closer to town they approached an intersection. The light was red.

Lynda said, "Uh, dad?"

"I see it. I know."

"You can't stop."

"I have to."

"Why?"

"Because someone will call it in. The cops will be on us."

"For a red light? I think they have better things to do. Like trying to catch you assholes."

"Hey. Language."

"Really?"

Years of conditioning caused Neil to slow the car for the light. He scanned left and right for traffic thinking if there was a break in it, he'd just go through, just like Lynda said except he could see cars moving fast through the intersection. From one direction, he saw a large orange tractor and trailer. He pressed the brake and came to a stop at the light keeping an eye on the rearview mirror.

He said, "Uh-oh."

Ray pulled up beside them. Lynda saw him lean forward and reach around to his back. The bottom half of his face was visible. A teeth grinding grin decorated it. When his hands came back again, they were holding a shotgun.

Neil said, "Shit!"

Neil slammed his foot on the accelerator, the car shot ahead, the shotgun boomed, glass shattered and warm liquid sprayed Lynda's face and she closed her eyes against it. An air horn blared, surprisingly close and when she turned her head and opened her eyes, a large silver grill, filling her vision, was boring down on her.

She screamed, "Daddy!"

He yelled, "Shit!"

They cleared the intersection without getting struck and in the chaos, she heard her dad whimper. He said, "Honey. I'm hurt. I'm hurt bad."

Blood covered the far shoulder of Neil. The interior driver side door was red and shiny.

Behind them, the motorcycle's engine roared.

Neil shook his head and exhaled out through his mouth. His eyes narrowed. He blinked away sweat. The sign for Kauffmann's Mall with an arrow pointing to the left hung above an oncoming streetlight. Neil yanked the wheel to the left, his eyes closing and jerking open when the wheels bumped against the curb. He drove towards the main entrance, between the Pizza Pizza and the Starbucks.

Neil said, "You're going to have to run for it." His words were slurred, weakened. "I didn't think he'd go this far. You have to run, find help."

"Daddy?"

He said, "Hold on."

The car jumped the curb and Lynda's head hit the roof. Neil's blood sprayed the inside of the car. The steering wheel and the windshield was spattered with a fine red mist. The seatbelt tightened across her chest as her dad stomped on the brake.

His eyes were fuddled, confused as they tried to focus on her. He couldn't get out any words. His hands still gripped the steering wheel and he swiped the fingers of his right hand towards the doors of the mall. He was telling her to run. She could hear the motorcycle getting closer. Taking one last look at her father, a murderer who loved her, she opened the door and ran inside the mall.

•　　•　　•　　•　　•

Neil heard the engine of the bike shut off. Footsteps approached. A shadow fell on him. He tried turning his head but couldn't. His body wouldn't obey his commands. He wanted to see Ray. He didn't know why. He just did. Darkness encroached on his vision. The Toyota symbol on the steering wheel blurred and defined with each breath.

Ray said, "You ruined us. You ruined me."

Neil wanted to say they were ruined a long time ago. They had been cruising on luck for years and when it broke, boy did it ever break. He couldn't tell him though. Couldn't even move. Everything slowed right down. Even when the impression of the shotgun barrel pressed against the side of his head was felt, all he could manage was a small smile. He didn't hear the boom of the shotgun.

On her portable, Jodie heard, *All officers, shots fired at Kauffmann's Mall. All units respond. Report of an active shooter.*

Jodie said, "Shit."

She put the car in drive and shot down the dirt rutted road. They bounced in their seats, the iPad flew from Graham's hands and coffee cups jumped from the cup holders and rolled along the floor of the car. In the middle of navigating the road, she flicked on the emergency lights and the sirens. The marked police cruiser, curtained by the rising dust, followed close behind and broke through the cloud, the back end of the car swinging into the road before straightening. It seemed like forever before they hit the paved road and Jodie increased her speed once her tires bit into the asphalt.

Graham said, "How far out are we?"

"Maybe five minutes."

From the portable, *he's shooting people! He's heading to the food court!*

Graham said, "That's a long time."

Gritting her teeth, Jodie said, "I know." She pressed down on the accelerator.

Lynda ran into the mall, sweeping her eyes around the entrance. She saw a group of people at a table inside the Pizza Pizza. Their eyes bulged. A teen with shaggy hair had part of a slice in his mouth, not chewing. Blood dotted Lynda's face and painted part of her clothes. She saw a cell phone on the table in front of the shaggy teen. She moved towards it, eyes fastened on it like a person in a desert, dying of thirst, spotting an oasis and the promise of cool water. A boom sounded right outside the doors behind her. Her shoulders jumped to her ears and she spun to see what caused it. The inside windshield of the Toyota was a solid, dark red. Ray, carrying a shotgun, saw her and smiled. He started running towards her.

To the teens, Lynda said, "Call the police!"

She ran from Ray. She didn't have a plan other than to get away. She saw murder in his smile. And the smile was for her alone. She turned a corner and behind her, she heard Ray yell, "I'm gonna shut you up now, Lynda! You better fucking believe it!"

Jodie squealed to a stop outside of the mall's entrance behind the Toyota. Other police cars were there, lights rotating on their roofs. Sirens blared.

Jodie turned to Graham and said, "Stay here."

She hopped out of the car, patted her vest, took out her firearm and ran into the mall through the sensor operated doors. The cops following them ran past Graham's door.

Graham shook in his seat. He was back at the outlet mall with his family. He saw the barrel come over the counter again. He saw it pointed at his face. He flinched as though it had gone off again. His brain burned. He stared at the iPad screen to reconnect to the now. The cloud he could see on the screen above the mall grew denser. A black blanket of ill happenings. A stain of murder only he could see. His brain burned in his skull. His breath rattled in his throat. He opened the door and stepped out. He glanced up into the sun. His live eye took in the flat white disc. His non-eye saw an inky sky. He inhaled the day's air as though it might be his last.

He stepped away from the car. His feet were taking him into the mall.

People fleeing ran past him. Jellied faces covered in tears. Some bumped into him, some circled wide around him.

Graham stepped inside the mall into the cool manufactured air. The smell of pizza reached him. His stomach awoke to the scent. He continued past the storefront. He heard gunshots but even without them, he would know where to go. The dark clouds provided a trail.

His feet moved faster. He went from a stiff-legged walk to a jog and to a run. When he arrived at the food court, he stopped, mouth open. He felt as though he'd been transported back in time.

In the Starbucks line, a man sat on the floor, under the Order Here sign. His hands were holding his guts. Intestines bulged between his fingers. His brow was creased as though he was not understanding what he was seeing under his hands. In the middle of an aisle, a woman was sprawled over the top of a screaming child. A large red hole in the back of her shoulder pulsed the last of the woman's life. Two cops were huddled behind a ceramic tree box. Their guns were pointed at the sky. Sweat dotted their skin and slid into their mouths frozen in a rictus of fear. At their feet was a body missing the top half of their head. More cops converged on the Orange Julius stand. Jodie crept along, bent low at the waist, making her way there as well.

A man popped up from behind the Orange Julius counter. In his right hand was a shotgun. A young girl's head was trapped in his left elbow. He was choking her with that arm. Her eyes bulged red and blood spilled from her lips. The man pushed the girl down on top of the stainless steel counter and using her as a shield and a prop, he shot at the approaching officers. BOOM! A police officer screamed and rolled on the ground.

The man laughed and yelled, "Woo-eeeee! We're having some fun now aren't we?"

Using the end of the shotgun, he hit the girl in her back. She yelped and he said, "I fucking told ya didn't I? Told ya I'd shut you up! You have nothing smart to say now do ya?"

Graham whispered, "Not again. Why is this happening again?"

Without realizing it, focused on the gunman behind the counter, Graham walked towards him. The little girl trapped under her mother's body cried and sobbed. As Graham passed her, he heard her say, "Mommy? Let's go, mommy. I want to go home. Please, mommy."

Tears blurred Graham's vision. He said, "Not again."

He walked past the two police officers behind the ceramic tree box. One of them saw Graham, made to stand and his partner hauled him down. To Graham, she said, "Sir! Sir! Get down!"

Graham moved forward, eye on the man yelling at his hostage, a length of saliva falling from the man's mouth onto the girl's blonde hair.

•   •   •   •   •

Jodie saw the officer go down not more than ten feet from her. He had been behind a garbage receptacle and trying to creep closer to Ray when Ray fired off a shot at him. The plastic receptacle shredded. Bits of the plastic tore into the officer's face and he dropped to the ground, dropping his gun and putting his hands to his face screaming, "I can't see! I can't fucking see!"

She yelled at him, "Get back behind cover!"

The officer continued to roll on the ground and scream.

Jodie exhaled. Sweat stung her eyes and she blinked. The bulletproof vest felt constrictive against her ribs. She couldn't seem to get enough air.

She put her back on the half wall. She was tucked under an overhang where people could sit by themselves and eat and people-watch. A trail of blood was making its way towards her. The person it was coming from, a middle-aged woman in yoga pants and Lycra top wasn't moving. She was breathing. Jodie could see the rise and fall of her stomach but she was losing a lot of blood. How much longer would she have? Jodie needed to end this and fast. How to do that? His shotgun against her handgun? The shotgun would win every time. She closed her eyes. People were crying all around her. Her portable chirped continuously. Jodie opened her eyes and getting low to the ground, she peeked around the corner.

Ray was resting the shotgun on Lynda's back. He was leaning on her making any shot at him difficult. His eyes were scanning the food court and they swept towards her. She pulled back just before (she hoped) they reached her. How was she going to do this?

She leaned out again and noticed Ray standing upright using an elbow on Lynda's back to keep her still. He was focused on something and whatever it was seemed to be confusing him. His brows were scrunched, his mouth hung open and the barrel of the shotgun was pointed away from Jodie. Now. Now was the time.

She steeled herself to be ready. She brought her feet underneath her so she could pop up and still use the half-wall as cover. She exhaled and popped up, bringing her gun up and putting the sight on Ray, going for the biggest part of his body; his chest. Off to her right, she heard, "Not again!" She knew that voice. The barrel of her gun dipped. She turned to look at Graham, wondering what the hell was he doing here and was that really him walking towards to a man with a shotgun unarmed?

In her peripheral vision she noticed the shotgun barrel swinging to her. She snapped back on Ray but the barrel was already there, the dark eye staring at her, about to deliver her death. She raised her gun anyways, thinking she might get out of this, but knowing in her heart she was a goner.

•   •   •   •   •

Graham didn't have a plan. He didn't know what he would do. He wasn't armed. The noise, the screaming, the heavy, familiar scent of gunpowder and the splayed and bleeding bodies removed all common sense from him. He walked ahead, eye focused on the man with the shotgun and the dark clouds circling him and emanating from him were so violent and erratic, it reminded Graham of a flock of disturbed crows. All his concentration was on the man. Graham felt pulled by him, a swirling vortex around the man intent on consuming him. As he walked forward, for some reason, the image of his dad at the table, clutching his chest came to him. He shook it off and continued on with a burning ember of anger igniting and growing within his chest at what he was witnessing. The frightened girl pressed against the counter, face bloody and contorted with pain while the man above her gloated and laughed, actually laughed at her pain and at the mayhem he was causing. All the mourners he was creating with every trigger pull of his shotgun and for what? Why do people do such things? Why the compulsion for cruel destruction? In this moment, Graham truly understood hate because he hated this man in front of him. Hated all the people like him. His stomach roiled with it, his brain heated by it, he continued to walk forward and even when the man stopped scanning the food court, smiling his devil's smile, to focus his attention on Graham, it did not slow his step. Graham's fear was replaced with hate. The only thing he knew to do was to keep going forward. The man stopped smiling. He squinted his eyes at Graham and moved the barrel of the shotgun so it was aimed at him. This did not slow Graham's step. Instead, Graham yelled, "Not again!"

The barrel swung away from him and he followed the arc. Not twenty feet from him stood Jodie. The barrel stopped at her.

Graham yelled, "No!"

And he felt it again, the same sensation that dropped his father except this time it was stronger, a hundred times stronger. It flew from his non-eye, a wave of energy, a wave of heat shooting out of his body towards the gun-toting man and leaving Graham weak and cold. His legs trembled, his arms palsied, a string of drool spilled from Graham's mouth and the floor rushed up to meet him.

●   ●   ●   ●   ●

Jodie, focusing on the front sight of her gun saw it pass the steel counter and trying to get it aimed at Ray and she thought, *I'm too late,* and then Graham yelled, "No!"

Jodie, expecting a shotgun slug to take her in the face, felt a front of heat pass her, so hot it took the breath from her lungs. In the wake of the heat wave passing, Ray's head exploded. Blood painted the inside of the stand. Lynda's piercing scream filled the court. At the same time, Jodie noticed

Graham drop to the floor out of the corner of her eye.

Jodie yelled at one of the cops behind the ceramic tree box, "Check on the girl!"

She could hear her screaming. A hysterical, ear-hurting pitch.

Jodie ran to Graham. Blood marred the white tile under his head. He had fallen straight onto his face. She turned him over. His one eye remained open and she smiled, thinking he's okay until she noticed that he wasn't breathing. Starting compressions, she yelled, "I need some help here!"

Graham had died in the mall. He was dead before Jodie could turn him over. He was clinically dead for close to three minutes. They were the longest three minutes of Jodie's life. Jodie's compressions and the fact the ambulance personnel were close had saved his life. They had been waiting outside for it to be safe before they came in to help. When he woke up, it was three days later and he was surrounded by the bip-beep of hospital machines. Confused, his heart lurched as he was transported back to that time in the past when he woke to find his family dead and his face a mangled mess. A slanting beam of artificial light lit upon Jodie sleeping in a chair beside his bed. His heartbeat slowed, his breath felt hot in his mouth. His brain throbbed. He was so tired. His body burned with exhaustion. He closed his eye and woke up after another two days. Jodie was still there like he knew she would be. He smiled, it hurt to do so and so he stopped. Still, on the inside, he was smiling. Graham went home a week later.

Another wonderful summer day. Jodie and Graham sat in his backyard. He had a coffee and she had a glass of wine. Birds chirped, leaves drifted to the ground foretelling the coming fall. Jodie had been suspended for involving a civilian in a homicide case. She knew it could happen so when it did it wasn't a complete surprise. But still, after saving so many lives, it hurt to be penalized for it, well, investigated for it at least. Professional standards, the people trying to stick it to Jodie, had been trying to get a statement from Graham. Living off the grid like he did, they had to tramp through the woods to see him in their suits and shiny shoes. Well, the shoes started off shiny but by the time they reached the cabin, they were a muddy mess. Still, they smiled at Graham with their collars sweat-dampened and their expressions hopeful. He told them to leave. He told them he had nothing to say to them. They left with their fake smiles melting from their faces with the promise from Graham that if they showed up again, they would be considered trespassing and he might have to call the local police to have them removed. Jodie had been here when they showed up. She watched the confrontations from the cabin, peering out of the window. She had been spending most of her suspension time with Graham. He seemed tired and moved slower after the incident in the mall, like someone recovering from a stroke. She worried about him. Her best friend. The professional standards people didn't like her being there and Jodie knew they would be reporting her presence with Graham to her bosses, but at this point, after all she had gone through and what she had done, she couldn't care less. And that is what bothered the higher-ups the most. That and the media backlash they had suffered for suspending the hero cop.

Graham took a sip of his coffee and said, "So Greg? Lynda's uncle? He got arrested I take it."

"Oh yeah. Lynda spilled the beans and after being confronted with her statement and some of the evidence in the bone cave, he gave a full, tear-filled confession."

"Really?"

"Yeah. But, and this is a big but, he's saying Ray and Neil forced him to help. Forced him to keep his mouth shut or they'd kill him. He'd been living in terror for years. He had no choice but to do what they said."

"Will that work?"

"No, no. Lynda is going to be a great witness. That's the best part of all this. No matter what they say I did to screw up this investigation, Lynda saw Greg, Neil and Ray kill a girl and beat on Bruce. Not only that, they abducted her and held her captive. Greg had plenty of opportunities to go to the police and he didn't. So...he's not getting out of anything. Which is good, because I hate that guy. I'm sure he's the one who killed Kelly." She put her glass of wine down and pulled her legs underneath her in her chair. It was a position Graham had only seen women do. She looked comfortable. He thought he might try it after she left. He'd rather not give her a reason to laugh at him. Not on purpose anyway.

She said, "So yeah. Greg's going to jail for a long time. The most his pity-me story will do is possibly keep him from getting on the Dangerous Offender Designation."

"What's that?"

"That's where the court says, after mountains of evidence and years of deliberation, that this person, Greg, is too dangerous to be released. Ever. Paul Bernardo is considered a Dangerous Offender and hopefully, he's never getting out of jail. It's the only real life sentence possible in Canada."

"Huh."

"Yeah."

A blue jay alighted on a branch. The branch dipped a little and the bird sang a note before flying off.

"Graham?"

"Yeah?"

"The thing that happened to Ray. Did you do that?"

"Yeah." He sipped his coffee and said, "I don't know how. I didn't try to do it. It just happened. But it was me. I...killed him. I hope you're okay with that."

She reached out, grasped his hand, squeezed it and let go.

She said, "You saved my life. It is driving the investigators crazy, though."

"What is?"

"Trying to find whatever it was that blew his head apart."

Graham smiled and said, "Yeah. I suppose it would. But that's not my problem."

Jodie laughed and said, "No. It isn't."

NOTE FROM THE AUTHOR

Word-of-mouth is crucial for any author to succeed. If you enjoyed the book, please leave a review online—anywhere you are able. Even if it's just a sentence or two. It would make all the difference and would be very much appreciated.

Thanks!
John

About the Author

A busy father of four with a dog and cat, John Hunt lives and works in Guelph, Ontario, Canada. He has had nine short stories published in various anthologies and is a member of the *Horror Writers Association*. He is the award-winning author of *Doll House*, *The Tracker*, and the apocalyptic novella, *Balance*. He is also a co-host on the Movies of the Damned!! Podcast.

Thank you so much for reading one of our **Crime Fiction** novels.
If you enjoyed the experience, please check out our recommended
title for your next great read!

Caught in a Web by Joseph Lewis

"This important, nail-biting crime thriller about MS-13 sets the
bar very high. One of the year's best thrillers."
–*BEST THRILLERS*

View other Black Rose Writing titles at
www.blackrosewriting.com/books and use promo code
PRINT to receive a **20% discount** when purchasing.